AN IMPERFECT DEATH

THE UNLIKELY HEROINE

LIZ GRAHAM

ONEEAR PRESS

CHAPTER ONE

The first time her husband died, Diana was celebrating their twenty-fifth wedding anniversary in Paris. Champagne breakfasts, long sensual mornings in bed, and fine dining in hidden romantic nooks in old Mont-Martre; even her companion was a man most women could only fantasize about with his swarthy Euro looks, smooth body and that damn sexy accent. It was picture perfect, but not in a family portrait kind of way.

Her husband Mark was somewhere off the coast of Mexico at the time, presumably celebrating the occasion in his own fashion.

Money was a wonderful thing; perhaps it couldn't buy true happiness, but it could certainly create a near perfect illusion of it. Especially when there was lots of it floating around. Mark Quenton was an investment banker in Baserville, and he was the closest thing to a guru that this well-heeled society had. He took their money and spun it into gold, and for this they loved him dearly. Over the years, their money and their love for him grew exponentially, like a carousel that turned faster and faster, the music growing more frenzied and loud, casting a spell of glamor that was hard to resist.

Until he died and it all fell apart.

·❥·❥·❥·❥·❥·

As she stood below the east transept window of Notre Dame, she smiled as she relived the reaction to the announcement of her celebration plans. What a novel idea to choose Paris in the fall of the year, everyone agreed, trust Di to think of that.

'The fall colors, my dears, nothing like it, and the weather is perfect, the foliage and light like a watercolor painting.' Spring in Paris with its rain and cranky French people was rather over-rated, she had confided regretfully to the Baserville Women's League members over which she reigned.

A shiver brought her back to the present, standing in the middle of this gloomy old cathedral freezing her ass off despite the cashmere cardigan drawn close around her generous figure. Really, Notre Dame was no different from any other medieval structure, so why the big deal? But she needed to get a selfie of herself here for FaceBook, to show her followers back home what a great time 'they' were having.

And it was a miserable place to spend a fall morning, she could almost see the mist rising from the cold stones while her breath froze in front of her. Yet even at this time of year there were still crowds milling around, couples and groups all chattering together as if this was the first cathedral they'd ever seen in their lives. God, they bored her.

Tourists with their sneakers and saggy sweatpants built for comfort, not caring a whit about how they looked. And the fanny-packs! Those were the worst. Fanny-packs symbolized all that was cheap and classless of these voyeuristic travellers, those herds of sheep all clustered around their guides, vying for the best spot and constantly baaing out the regurgitations of the guide-books as if each was a new and brilliant thought. The god-damned fanny-packs circled every large belly as if the paltry sums of money inside were worth protecting and the passports of interest to anyone. What self-respecting thief would want to steal *their* identities?

She flicked her shoulder length blond hair over her shoulder as she caught the lens of her phone's camera in delighted surprise. It was a well-rehearsed manoeuvre and worked every time. Di inspected the result with a critical eye, and she was pleased. The blues and reds in the stained glass glowed through the morning sun, the perfect background for the expensively coiffed confection that was Diana Quenton.

This mission accomplished, she tossed the phone back into her Hermes bag and turned to barrel her way through the crowds toward the exit, but it suddenly came to life in the depths of her purse with the tones of Wagner's *Ride of the Valkyries* erupting through the ancient church. Someone wanted her. She allowed it to play a moment longer so as not to seem too available.

The music of her cell phone had been carefully selected, as Di considered herself an equal to the Valkyries - tall, blond, well-built and a force to be reckoned with, the born leader of her social circle. And who better to command the ladies of their home town? She was, after all, the richest of them.

She accepted the call with a smile in her voice, despite the glares from the tourists, the priests, and even the snooty cleaning lady who had no business being so rude. She raised her voice to compensate for the lousy cell reception within the ancient stone walls.

Keith's strangled voice rose through the static. 'Mark is dead,' she thought she heard him squeak, then a string of incoherent words.

Mark dead? Nonsense. 'Keith, you're not making sense,' her voice echoed forcefully off the high rafters. 'What are you saying? Calm down.'

Presumed dead at any rate, Keith told her after taking a deep breath. His rented yacht had been found wrecked floating off the coast of Mexico. Pirates, he told her, the police suspected pirates, and didn't hold out much hope on the culprits being brought to justice.

'Presumed dead is not the same as proven dead,' she proclaimed, focusing on the word presumed and ignoring the bit about the boat wreck. She didn't believe the news for a minute, but she was touched by the grief she thought she heard in his voice. Keith, just like Chicken Little, forever claiming the sky was falling and they were doomed. Totally useless in an emergency. She could almost hear him flapping his arms in distress, and pictured his comb-over flapping in sympathy, thick glasses askew. He was the business's lawyer, but he would have made a much better accountant. He was lucky he had Mark to prop him up. 'Not to worry, I'm sure he'll surface. Mark's a great swimmer, you know.'

Keith paused before continuing in his reedy, irritating voice. 'True, they haven't found his body, but...'

'Don't you worry about a thing,' Di cut in calmly. He couldn't see the rolling of her eyes. Why was she the one doing the comforting? Mark was her husband for God's sake, she might be a widow. But then again, people like Diana were just born leaders. 'You'll see,' she continued in her most soothing voice. 'All will be well.'

'It's just... There's something going on with the accounts...' The panic was rising in his voice and he was starting to flap again.

'This is hardly the moment to be concerning yourself with business matters. Mark will have everything in hand. We need to get organized. I'll start back ASAP.' Diana would get to the bottom of this. She didn't have the money-brains that Mark did, but she was a pretty smart cookie herself and would hold the fort till Mark surfaced. 'And Keith – whatever's going on here, I don't want a word of this getting out. Do you hear? *Not one whisper.*'

Diana didn't believe for a moment that Mark was dead. The one thing they had in common, besides the twins, the large mansion, the cottage on the lake, extreme libidos and their absolute control over the social life of Baserville, was that they were both omnipotent in their self-belief. This, along with the sex of course, had sparked the attraction all those years ago and despite the difficulties in the years since then, it was the pillar of their enduring marriage. Together they'd hauled themselves out of non-descript backgrounds, from poverty misplaced and out of line with their ambitions. Despite how much they had grown to hate each other, they had always made a formidable team.

She was as good as her word, and set back to her hotel with a pause only to browse through the boutiques on Rue Fauberg. A black silk pantsuit found in the House of Dior was perfect for the travelling widow, for she might as well act the part, just in case.

Diana strode into her suite, placing the classy paper bag on the table under the mirror, where she automatically paused for assessment. Forty-five years old, and she looked great. Money helped, although that personal trainer wasn't doing his job for he couldn't shake the last few pounds or twenty off her middle. But hell, the men in her life would never complain about her generous curves.

'Jean-Luc, wake up!'

There was no reply.

In the bedroom, she stripped the duvet off the king size bed to expose the well-bronzed body of her lover.

'*Tabernacle*, Diana,' he groaned, rubbing his hand over his bristly face. 'Let me sleep.'

'I have to leave Paris, pronto. You need to go home.'

Finally some movement. His hurt brown eyes gazed up at her. '*Cherie*? What is wrong? Why do you send me away?'

'It's not all about you,' she said as she removed the suitcase from the closet and placed it onto the table provided for that purpose. She stripped off the sweater and jeans she was wearing and stuffed it all into the luggage along with the contents of the drawers. 'Something's happened to Mark, I have to go back to straighten it out.'

Now he sat up, petulance still on his face. 'What is it? Is he in jail?'

'Don't be silly! He's gone missing somewhere off the coast of Mexico.' She turned to her jewellery box and tossed it on top of the clothes. It wasn't till after the suitcase was squished in and zipped up that she spotted the diamond necklace still sitting on the bureau, Mark's anniversary present to her which she'd chosen, and which had so delighted Jean-Luc last night in their after-dinner games. Diana tucked it into the hidden side pocket of the carry-on.

Jean-Luc was by her side in a moment, cradling her from behind with his bed-warm arms. He stared over her head at the mirror, admiring what he saw. So did she; he looked damn good on her, she liked her lovers buff and tall. The French-man was an underwear model, they'd met in Monaco three years ago. It was an on again/ off again relationship, whenever she could get away from Baserville. Jean-Luc always made room in his schedule for her.

'Is he dead?' His breath was hot on her neck. God, he knew what she liked. She leaned against him, just for a moment, luxuriating in the feel of his bare skin against hers. The waxed chest smoothed slowly against her back, a light sheen of sweat already forming as she felt the movement down below.

'No such luck,' she murmured, then forced her-self away. 'None of that right now, I don't have time.'

Jean-Luc did not let her go and squeezed his arms closer, enveloping her in his warmth. '*Non, cherie*, there is always time for love.'

Even his cheesiness was sexy when accompanied by that hard body pressed up against her. She tried to turn away but he had a firm hold on her and was caressing her neck with his lips. The smell of last night's sex hovered all around him, threatening to draw her back to his lazy, sleepy bed.

'No, Jean-Luc, no.' She ignored the tingle starting deep within as she attempted to twist away. 'I'm serious. I need to pack.'

He swivelled his hips against her, firm and persuasive in his movements.

'You don't say no to me.' He ran his hands over her front and gave a slight, subtle twist on her breasts, the almost pain of which travelled right down her body. 'Hmmm? My Didi cannot refuse me.'

'No, I need... there's a flight this afternoon...' She groaned and leaned back into him. He was right, she could rarely refuse him. Adrenalin still coursed through her body from Keith's call, for it wasn't just Jean-Luc who was excited by the idea of Mark's disappearance. She shouldn't get her hopes up but... in that moment of time, she'd caught a glimpse of the life she could have without her husband on the scene, and she sure wouldn't be stuck in Baserville anymore. She would be free to be whoever, whatever, she wanted to be. She could be a big fish in a bigger pond. Maybe a lake. Maybe the Mediterranean.

One more for the road wouldn't hurt, and it might be a long time before Jean-Luc had the pleasure of her company again. She glanced at the clock on the television out of the corner of her eye even as she relaxed against her lover's warmth. Yes, there could be time.

Sometime later, Diana rolled off him, sweat drying on her now and laughter bubbled up as she lay on her back.

He turned on his side with his head in his hand to look at her, a petulant expression growing on his face again. 'Why do you never let me be on top? I am the man,' he pointed out in his charming French accent. 'You should be more... more feminine.'

'It's never bothered you before,' she pointed out as she struggled to bring her underwear back over her hips. 'You saying this is not womanly?' She held her arms over her head so her breasts pushed against the bra, and indicated her fleshy curves.

'You are my goddess,' he said in all seriousness. 'But...' He turned his back on her with a humph.

'But what?'

'You are leaving me,' he said into the duvet.

'I have to go,' she reminded him. 'And fix up whatever it is that Mark has done.' She slapped him lightly on the butt.

He complained into the 400-count Egyptian cotton duvet cover.

'What? Don't mumble, I can't hear you.' Her mind was already planning her flight home as she re-pinned her hair, loving the added height it gave to her figure. And she was needed at home. Though she might never admit it, it had been a long time since anyone had needed her, and she was impatient to get started.

'My birthday,' Jean-Luc said, lifting his head a little. 'You are leaving without giving me my present.'

'Ohhh, is that it?' she teased. 'Look in the drawer of the bedside table, I think you might find a little something there.'

He scrabbled over the huge bed and yanked open the drawer. There lay a rectangular box, wrapped in plain white paper with a thin red ribbon.

'Oh *ma cherie*, you remembered,' he said, ripping off the paper. He sighed with pleasure and held the Cartier watch to the window to see the light gleam off the gold. She left him crooning to the trinket while she took a quick shower and got ready for the flight.

'Alright then,' she said. 'Kiss, kiss.' She held her lips out expectantly. He jumped up and embraced her, lingering as if reluctant to let her go. Just as she was beginning to lose patience and about to shake him off, he spoke.

'So Mark,' he said. All play had left his voice. 'If he's dead, what then?'

'If he's really dead, then I get all the money.' A small smile formed on her face as she thought about it again. 'Then I sell the business and get more money.'

'And me?'

'What about you, Jean-Luc?'

'You will marry me, and we will live happily ever after. Okay, *ma cherie*?'

'We'll talk,' she said, breaking the embrace. 'I'll be in touch.'

·♥·♥·♥·♥·♥·

As expected, the Departures board indicated a direct flight to New York City to leave within three hours and even though it was such short notice, Di had no doubt she would be on that plane.

She sailed past the snaking throng for economy and on to the first class desk where she tapped her long nails on the counter for what seemed an inordinate amount of time until she received attention of the reluctant clerk. *That's the French for you*, she thought. *Customer service was not a priority here.*

'I need to fly today,' she informed the woman, efficiently thrusting the printout and her passport across the counter.

The petite French woman at the desk glanced at the paper, looking down her nose despite her disadvantaged height. 'You are not registered for today's flight.'

'Which is why I need to *change* my flight,' Di said, her voice sharpening, ready to nip any attitude in the bud. The resentment of the French lower classes knew no bounds – their revolution had failed and they needed to get over it. The wealthy were here to stay. 'It is imperative that I change my date.' She thumped her finger on the printout between them.

'There are no seats available on this flight,' the French clerk said, looking past her to see if there was anyone else in line. 'I am so sorry.'

'Nonsense,' Di said, shifting her body into the woman's line of sight. 'I am a Platinum member, there's always room for me. That's why we pay these exorbitant prices.' She trilled a light, self-deprecating laugh.

An abrupt shake of the head was the reply. 'Not today. Tomorrow, we may fit you in. Or there is the midnight flight...'

Being nice was getting nowhere with this clerk, Diana could see, and wondered yet again why the less fortunate hated the rich and beautiful. It was time to switch tactics and play the grief-stricken newly-widowed. 'My husband just died,' Diana raised her voice, placing her hand on her forehead. 'I have to get back to the States immediately. The children need me...' She glanced around between her fingers – good, that had people's attention. She heard murmurs coming from the other line, full of nice fellow Americans. Di gave a loud hiccup of grief for effect.

The woman stared at her with icy respect, acknowledging this would be a losing battle and perhaps not worth her effort for a Saturday. She sniffed and looked back at her screen. 'Ah. Perhaps there is one seat.' She looked up at Diana triumphantly, for there was always more than one way to win the passive-aggressive war. 'It is in Economy,' she spit as she leaned over the counter, daring her to accept.

Their eyes locked as Diana's mind raced. She hated to give points to this upstart but damn, the woman was good. She could always upgrade once she got on board, she knew there would be some sucker to shame into changing seats if necessary, but to publicly acknowledge this unknown woman's win... Still, if it must be done, it must be done with grace and the pretence she was unaware of the game, and done quickly before she was requested to go back and stand in the Economy lineup.

'Thank you, so much,' she said with an almost grateful smile pasted on her face. It only hurt a little. 'You have been so helpful. I will let your *superiors* know how much your kindness has meant to me in my time of need.'

The boarding card was flicked across the counter with another sniff. Diana smiled triumphantly as she heaved the suitcases and hatbox up on the weigh scale. 'Just put the extra charges on the credit card,' she said generously, leaving the clerk to lug and sort the items.

It was the little victories which sometimes made life worthwhile. And funnily enough, there *was* a seat available in first class, she pointed out to the stewardess as she explained her situation. Di settled in for the long flight in her private pod with a complimentary glass of champagne for her troubles, admiring yet again the design of these seats. With the high walls surrounding her on three sides, it was like no-one else on the plane existed. This arrangement suited Diana Quenton very well.

She closed her eyes, thinking about Jean-Luc. He was a gigolo, but a very good one, as well as being very selective with his clientele. As long as she paid the bills, he was hers when she needed him; it didn't bother her one bit to pay a man to be her on-call lover. This was the twenty-first century, and besides, men did it all the time, having floozies and prostitutes and harems. Look at Mark and the string of mistresses he'd had over the years. So what did that make Jean-Luc? Her mister? Certainly not her master. She never allowed any man on top.

Although, she was uncomfortably aware that her husband hadn't been playing the field so much lately, and seemed to be spending most of his time with Amaryllis, his personal assistant. What a pretentious name.

'A-ma-*ril*-liss,' Diana hissed aloud. A willowy, smelly big flower that bloomed quickly, and aged even faster, just like the woman herself. No worries, Mark would never dare to divorce Diana, she told herself, before remembering that he might be dead.

CHAPTER TWO

The overhead announcements broke her reverie, and refreshed after her tussles with Jean-Luc and the French clerk, it was now time to assess the situation. Of course Mark wasn't dead – it was just a language mix-up with the foreign police in Mexico. Why couldn't they all speak proper American English? He was more likely off having a dirty week-end with that slut and ignoring the phone.

However, the whole incident called for damage control. Mark's disappearance rather put a spanner into the works, for it was bound to get out that he wasn't in Paris during their anniversary, you know how people talked. And Keith would talk, he'd flap to his wife, who would spread the word. While Diana had few illusions about her life (not counting of course, those about herself) she fully intended to keep up the facade of their perfect life. She found herself rehearsing what she would say to her friends when she got back home.

'He was called away on a business emergency, looking after *your* money,' she would say firmly to the inquiring minds to explain his absence from Paris. That would stop the tongues from wagging for they liked how he grew their bank accounts. There was even room for her to play the aggrieved, long-suffering wife, a role she thought she might enjoy.

Once upon a time, Diana had dreamed of being an actress. Modelling, the easier route to money and fame, hadn't worked out despite her height and looks, for her athletic build and large bust could never carry off the waif look that was so popular at the time. But on her way to the bright lights, Mark had happened, then the twins came, and he insisted she stay at home and be kept in the manner she quickly became accustomed to. She had channelled her acting abilities very successfully in other ways.

Mark.

But his supposed death – until there was a body, she refused to believe. And no body, so no funeral yet, which was a relief for she had far too much on her plate right now. That being said, she would have to mark the occasion somehow, just in case it turned out to be true.

'A subdued tea for our closest friends and clients,' she said aloud. 'We can open up the two drawing rooms to fit everyone in.' This would be the most appropriate, she felt.

Time to get the plans in action.

First, contact Mrs. Hastings, the longsuffering Scottish housekeeper.

Will be arriving at La Guardia at 4pm. Have the driver meet me.

The driver's name was Samuel, and he'd worked for the Quentons for the past five years. He had aspirations of being a novelist, and his wife had given birth last year, but Diana knew nothing about this. Samuel had no sex appeal for her so she'd never bothered to seduce him, which might be why he'd lasted so long in her employ.

The stewardess hovered over her shoulder like a bloody school marm.

'Excuse me, ma'am, I must ask you to put away your device during take-off.'

'Of course,' Diana said. 'Silly me.' She made a show of placing the phone in her purse until the stewardess had moved on. Then out it came again.

The next text was to Susie.

Returning early. Come round at 9am tomorrow.

After a moment's consideration, she added:
All is well. Don't panic.

Because she would get her knickers in a knot, the silly cow. Diana wished she could have a second-in-command with more backbone and guts, but Susie was the only one in the group who really listened to her, who she could trust to carry out her demands without slacking off or showing attitude. It was just too bad that the woman couldn't be more of an independent thinker.

Diana felt the stewardess breathing behind her and shoved the phone away again before she had a chance to get indignant. She was finished with it anyway so she lay back in the chair and feigned to sleep to avoid the lecture.

If Mark were dead... There would be an upside to his death of course. She looked fabulous in black (everyone told her how well she carried it off) and there would be the comfort of all that lovely money. And best of all, she would no longer have to pretend to be happily married.

However, until they had a body as proof, she would go ahead with the plans for the Animal Gala. Diana Quenton had been called many things over the years, and many people strongly disliked her forceful personality but no-one could ever fault her generosity for four-legged furry creatures.

The thought of a single animal cold and hungry, lost or lonely, was more than her otherwise egotistic heart could bear. Diana knew what it was like to feel lost and unloved, and no animal would experience this if she could help it. Growing up, she'd never been allowed to have a pet as her single mother-of-five had flatly refused to allow another body in the trailer, stating she had more than enough mouths to feed, with the unspoken assumption that her mother didn't really want the mouths she already had. Not that she was an abusive mother aside from the drinking and the boyfriends, for she fed and clothed as she was able, but the arc of her mothering was worn down by poverty and broken dreams, and there was no space to express the tenderness she might otherwise have felt for her offspring.

So Debbie Sears (as Diana was known before she escaped the trailer park and changed her name) grew up starved for affection but found comfort in taming the kittens of the feral cat living in a derelict barn. She fed them and thus wormed her way into their circle. From an early age she cobbled together the funds from her babysitting and other odd jobs enough to care for them and as her fundraising talents grew, the family grew into a colony.

Of course, these days she preferred the company of her dogs because they let her boss them round. You couldn't pull that shit with the cats, but she loved them anyway.

And so the Quentons became the founders and main supporters of the Baserville Animal Hospital and Adoption Sanctuary, and the Gala fundraiser was the finest social occasion of the year. A lot of money was required for the upkeep of the large building and grounds, the full-time veterinarian, three nurses, and receptionist, not to mention the night staff and social worker in charge of the carefully vetted adoptions. Everyone who was anyone was expected to attend the Gala, as they were also expected to adopt a quota of pets. With the Gala looming closely, Diana was far too busy to hold a funeral for her husband.

·♥·♥·♥·♥·♥·

The drive to Baserville occurred without incident, and the dour Scottish housekeeper Mrs. Hastings had all in order back at the mansion. Entering the wrought iron gates after a trip abroad always comforted Diana, the sense that she was returning to safety from the vagaries and small cruelties of the outside world. Here, she was queen, and all was as she needed it to be. She kept her cellphone turned on, but purposefully ignored all calls until she had a chance to regroup.

The dogs were the first to greet her, ecstatic to see their mistress return. Mrs. Hastings the house-keeper, not so much.

'So you came back.'

'Mark is missing.'

'I heard.' An unaccustomed tendril of pity thread-ed through her voice. 'No news then?'

Diana lifted her head from the lashings of doggy kisses being bestowed on her. The two dogs were a mix of Irish wolfhound and other indistinct large varieties. Mrs. Hastings had named them Cerberus and Outhros after the twin dogs of hell from Greek mythology, and no matter Diana's attempts to change the names, this is what they answered to. So Cerberus and Outhros it was.

'Nothing.' She flicked her blonde hair out of her eyes. 'A tempest in a teapot, I dare say. He'll show up. I'm not worrying.'

'Amaryllis is on her way back,' Mrs. Hastings ob-served in a casual voice, as if gauging the effect on her employer. 'Without him.'

Diana's back stiffened. This news was the first real indication that something might truly be amiss. Amaryllis would never leave the comfort of Mark's wallet.

'She said she wants to see you as soon as she lands.'

'I don't want to see her. Don't let her in,' Diana said, shaking her head. 'If something has happened to Mark, *really* happened, then she's out of a job and has no business here. I will *not* have that whore in my house.'

Mrs. Hastings silently waited with a stack of messages in her hand. Dianna dropped her coat and gloves on a chair and flicked through the pink slips. Keith, Susie, Keith, Rev. Pimm (offering condolences no doubt while salivating at the prospect of a bang-up funeral), police (that would be about Mark no doubt), Securities Commission (they really should phone the office), Amaryllis (little tart – ha!), Keith again. She brushed them all aside. They would wait.

Her favorite dinner was served (carb-laden macaroni and cheese) and the soft cotton sheets turned down on her bed. A fire was lit in her sitting room, its warm glow dancing over the golden velvet shadows of the curtains. The dogs lay before the fire, the cats strewn across the sofas. It was good to be Diana Quenton that night.

She would deal with the Mark situation tomorrow. Right now, she drowsed with the animals in the comfort of her domain, and her mind wandered back to a time when they'd been happy. Yes, their honeymoon on that small Caribbean island all those years ago. This was before the wealth, they could barely afford the flights but even then Mark had stressed the importance of the appearance of success. It wasn't a splashy resort with a poolside bar, just a little hut on the beach. But it was all theirs and, being the off-season, no loud tourist voices cutting into their reveries, no nude Germans strutting along the shore.

Mark with his boasting and his dreams – how she'd loved his energy. They lay on the sand, he with his whiskey sours and she happy enough with the local rum. He spoke of his ambitions, firing her up with his passion, and he told her his plans for the future.

'Baserville will be ours.' She had believed him. 'All those snobs who won't give you the time of day? They'll be eating out of your hand. And the Larkhall mansion, the biggest one in town? We'll live there, and buy a cottage on the lake, too. This beach here? We'll own it someday... Ah why stop there? I'll buy that whole island out there!' He gestured with his glass at a tiny islet, away far off on the distant horizon. 'You're going to be a queen, just you wait and see.'

She believed him, and that was the best sex they'd ever had, that night.

CHAPTER THREE

Mrs. Hastings served breakfast in the morning room, that sunny south facing room in the old Larkhall mansion which had been totally refurbished by Diana. It was full of light, a room where one couldn't help but be filled with anticipation for the day to come, and the smell of fresh toast and coffee filled the air. Diana, still dressed in her lacy baby dolls and silk peignoir and hair unbrushed, lingered over her first coffee although Susie was expected in fifteen minutes. But Susie didn't mind waiting.

'There's cars coming up the drive, Mrs. Quenton,' Mrs. Hastings informed her, her gray head bobbing. She poked her long nose between the sheers to better inspect the goings on outside.

'That'll be Susie,' Diana said absently as she flicked through the latest issue of Vogue and sipped her coffee. 'I told her nine o'clock.'

'No,' Mrs. Hastings said decisively. 'That's not Susie. It's men. They don't look happy.'

'Deliveries for the Gala already?'

'Nah, they're not delivery men. They look more like...'

Loud and long bangs at the front door interrupted her. The two women looked in amazement at each other that the peaceful sanctuary of Diana's palace could be so rudely invaded.

'FBI,' Mrs. Hasting faltered.

Di rolled her eyes. The sensible housekeeper had many failings, one of which was a devotion to police dramas which she watched every night. It had quite warped her imagination.

'Go answer the door, for God's sake and find out what they want. They probably have the wrong address. Send them on their way.'

She heard the shouts as the front door opened.

'FBI! Don't move!'

Mrs. Hastings gave a little shriek, and the sounds of heavy booted feet thundered across the parquet hall floor.

'Diana Quenton, where is she?'

The lady in question had already risen and presented herself at the door to the morning room. 'I
am she,' she informed them in her grandest voice.
'Gentlemen, if this is about my husband, I would
think you could have more mannerly ways of ex-
pressing condolences. If that is why you are here,'
she added, just a tad uncertainly. Had they found
his body? Could the unthinkable have happened?
Could Mark really be...

One man who rose head and shoulders over the
others detached himself from the group and stood
firmly before her.

'Mrs. Diana Quenton.' He stated this as a fact,
with recognition and a certain satisfaction in his
tone. His voice resonated from deep within. She
found herself looking up at him and her neck muscles thrilled to this unaccustomed stretch. He
stood at least six foot four, which was five whole
inches taller than herself and a full eight inches
taller than Mark. Dusky skinned of indeterminate
racial background, he wore his hair in an old fash-
ioned brush cut – not the all over shaved look so
popular with men with early balding patterns, but
the full military treatment that told a woman she
would know where she stood with him. His temples
were lightly touched with gray.

Diana felt a strange looseness deep within her, an unaccustomed warmth spreading through her normally well behaved innards. His eyes strayed down to the silk robe wrapped tightly around her not inconsiderable breasts which were threatening to heave like a romance heroine's. She was having a hard time finding her breath.

'What can I do for you, officer?' She was struggling not to sound like Mae West, but it was difficult in the circumstances as her voice had taken on a sudden huskiness. If Mark really were dead, those were arms she could find solace in.

He wrenched his eyes back up to her face and a steeliness grew within them. He flipped an ID badge briefly at her face.

'I am Special Agent Flanagan of Special Operations Branch of the FBI, ma'am,' he barked. 'This house and all the possessions herein are now seized under order of the Chief Magistrate of the United States of America. I have a warrant for the arrest of Mark Aloysius Quenton and Diana Sears Quenton. You are to be detained under suspicion of mass fraud and theft.' He began listing off her rights and her wrongs, relentlessly going on and on in his hard voice.

'But Mark is dead,' she said, unable to wrap her mind around anything else the man was saying. 'You can't arrest him if he's not here.'

He ended his recitation and looked at her with that same satisfaction she'd first noticed. 'Well I guess that leaves you holding the bag.' He reached out and snapped cuffs onto both her wrists. 'Ma'am.'

'Wait... wait,' she said, looking at the handcuffs attaching her hands together, not comprehending what they meant. A slight movement out of the corner of her eye caused her to turn and there was little Susie standing at the open door, right on time as ordered. Her face was blanched white, a horror-filled mask, framed by her blonde bob. She skittered out of the way as Officer Flanagan thrust Diana ahead of him and down the marble steps outside.

'Phone Keith!' Diana shouted her instructions at Susie before turning to the brute who held her helpless as he hustled her to the waiting car. 'I demand to see my lawyer! You can't just take me away. What are you...' Her last words were swallowed up as the car door slammed behind her. Diana twisted her head to make sure Susie understood her orders. Her friend was standing in the entrance, a look of wonder on her face at what she had just witnessed. As Di continued her protest, she watched incredulously as a slow smile spread across her friend's face, then Di was whisked away through the very gates which had spelled security for her all these years.

CHAPTER FOUR

They drove into the city a good half hour away, and not a word was spoken by the two FBI men. Diana tried, oh certainly she made lots of noise, but Agent Flanagan wasn't budging an inch and refused to turn around no matter how much she railed at him and cried. He didn't even offer her a tissue to wipe her nose. Finally she resorted to burning a hole through the back of his head with her eyes, and hoped it was giving him a headache as bad as the one she had.

The car pulled into an underground garage. The steel doors rolled noisily down behind them – there was no hope for escape now.

Agent Flanagan was almost gentlemanly as he removed the cuffs and offered his arm to help her out of the vehicle. She turned her tear-stained face away from him as she struggled to stand, pushing him away roughly as she made her way to the waiting elevator. After her breakdown in the car, she was going to handle the rest of this ordeal as gracefully as possible. There had been a mistake, obviously. She had done nothing wrong and there was no reason for her to be abducted in this manner. When she spoke with his boss, it would all be straightened out in a civilized way. And then she would gleefully sue his butt off.

'Why don't we let you get freshened up?' As the elevator door re-opened he indicated the washroom directly in front of them. She went there only because it was direly necessary, not because he suggested it.

'Oh, God,' Diana whispered, staring at the wreck of herself in the mirror. Her face was naked except for the remnants of yesterday's make-up. She always meant to get into the habit of religiously cleaning her face every night, but rarely remembered. Most of it had been steamed away during her post-travel bubble bath, but that 'everything proof' mascara hung on and could be washed off only by tears, giving a clownish effect that framed her puffy eyes. The bright blue of those eyes she was so proud of only heightened the contrast of the red and her glossy blonde hair was sleep mussed, looking its rattiest. And oh sweet Jesus she was still wearing her silk peignoir with the satin mules. The sleep wear that was so comfortable that it was like wearing nothing at all – and under the harsh fluorescent lights, she might as well have been nude. She re-wrapped and tied the robe but it made little difference, for in the cold utilitarian washroom her nipples were standing at attention. She couldn't go out there looking like this.

Diana washed off the mascara as best she could, scrubbing her face with the rough paper towel till she glowed, then went to the door.

'Agent Flanagan?' She called out tentatively.

'Yes ma'am,' came the reply so close she gave a start. He must be standing right outside the door, not three inches away, on-guard so she didn't make a run for it.

'Agent Flanagan, I have a problem.'

After a pause, he answered in that deep gravelly voice that, under different circumstances, she would find entrancing. 'You have many problems at the moment, ma'am. Which of them is bothering you in particular?'

'Agent Flanagan, I am not decently dressed. I cannot in all conscience go out of this door in my night clothes. I demand...' she stopped herself. Perhaps she wasn't really in a position to demand anything right now. 'I am asking if you can find something for me to wear. I'm cold!'

Another pause, and she heard a rustle. The door swung inwards only enough for a man's black suit jacket to slide through.

'Thank you, I guess,' she said and shrugged it on. It smelled of citrus and soap and an undeterminable spice that went straight to her womanly parts. The suit jacket enveloped her, comforting her, and its oversize made her feel quite... dainty.

·♥·♥·♥·♥·♥·

Special Officer Flanagan believed himself to be a principled man. After all, he was an ex-Marine and son of a Presbyterian minister, and he was passionate in his beliefs. A philosophy major in his university career, he strongly believed in the equality of all men (and women), and he held democracy as the highest indicator of civilization in a society. He embraced the tenets of socialism and believed in sharing the wealth for the good of all, and he knew there should be no hunger or want in a land that advertised itself as the richest nation on earth.

According to his creed, investment bankers were among the scum of the earth and the root cause of the unbalanced distribution he saw in his country, for they didn't contribute, they merely made money off other people's hard won earnings. It didn't help that he himself had lost his entire savings a few years back when he tried to hop on the band-wagon in playing the market and failed miserably, but it was further proof to his mind that invest-ment bankers were a thieving lot and needed to be stopped.

Admirable principles aside, he sometimes dis-liked rich people only because they were wealthier than himself, especially if it was inherited wealth or otherwise ill-gotten. The purposeless pariahs who orbited with them were also despised just as much. Some might dismiss this as jealousy, but he didn't see it that way.

So when the case of Mark Quenton dropped into his lap, he was delighted with the chance to get a small revenge on this class. It was immediately obvious to his finely honed suspicious mind that the banker had faked his death and absconded with the millions. He was also pretty sure in his mind that Diana was party to the scheme and he fully intended to use Mark's partner-in-crime to lead him to the man.

Flanagan had much of it planned out before he even arrested the lady. He was a very clever and creative man and like many of this ilk, continually looked to get the most effect for the least effort expended on his part. He saw this as thriftiness, not laziness.

But after meeting Diana in person, he realized the game would not be as simple as he'd thought. She was not the mindless parasite to be easily broken that he had assumed. No matter. He looked forward to the challenge.

He would set her on a leash to lead him to the prize of Mark, and in doing so would give her the rope with which to hang herself and her husband both. The simplest plans were always the best. If he accidentally stepped over the line of his directives sometimes, it was all in a good cause. Nothing outright illegal, naturally, but he was confident he could gloss over the details in the final report, for a lot could be forgiven in the light of a successful final outcome, and sometimes the end justified the means.

In Flanagan's private movie of his life, he played the lone wolf vigilante, using his position to work under the radar of the law. His record showed that he got real results; it just didn't show how he got those results, not all the time.

Before entering the interview room where she was held, he received a call from a smart young lawyer he knew, one who was looking to establish his name and develop working relationships. In his experience, hungry lawyers were always the best for his purposes.

'So you heard about this one already?' Flanagan asked, holding the phone between his ear and his shoulder. 'Yeah, she's going to need representation and it'll have to be state paid.'

He listened, then spoke again. 'No, sorry, it won't take long, we haven't got enough on her to press charges. But come on in, no one else is volunteering.'

He chuckled as he hung up the phone. He'd found the perfect patsy of a lawyer. Now all Flanagan had to do was harden his heart against the obvious attractions and wiles of Diana and prepare himself for the game of cat and mouse.

CHAPTER FIVE

Diana's life had abruptly changed course in less than twenty-four hours. Previously the well-respected leading socialite of their small town with the freedom and means to travel the world, now she found herself incarcerated in, if not a dungeon, certainly a locked room which reeked of things nasty and unnameable. If she had been of a philosophical bent, she might have reflected on the fragility of the lives humans create and the illusions they build. But she was not a deep thinker, not in that sense, and she only saw a situation that was uncomfortably out of her control.

Where was that idiot Keith? Mark would never have allowed this to happen.

At least she was no longer wearing her night clothes, as someone had provided her with items from her own closet. The thought that they'd been rooting around in her vast closet was perturbing, but her outrage was muted in light of the situation. Whoever had chosen the clothing, they had terrible dress sense and she suspected it was the female officer in the blue shirt and green pants with great clod-hopping black clunkers on her feet. Diana accepted her clothing almost gracefully, even though it was last year's jeans which had shrunk over time and the pilled beige sweater she'd left out to go out to the charity shop. At least they'd had no choice but to bring her sexy underwear, for that was the only kind she owned.

She would rather be armored in Chanel and Jimmy Choo's, but instead, all she had was her formidable self. Diana entered the Interview room with all guns blazing, fully recovered and ready for battle.

'I demand to see my lawyer, I don't care if you're FBI, you are holding me illegally.' Diana proceeded to plead her case in a voice that bordered on hysterical. Flanagan with his calm brown eyes watched her the whole while, but his face remained expressionless and he refused to be engaged. He said nothing for a full two minutes until she paused for a breath.

'Please have a seat Mrs. Quenton,' he said quietly and indicated the hard wooden chair across the table from him. 'You'll be much more comfortable. We may be here for a while.'

With a huff she sat herself down then drew a breath, preparing to continue. A Styrofoam cup appeared before her. The coffee inside smelled acrid as if it had sat on the burner all night, and she wrinkled her nose as she pushed it out of range.

Before she could renew her spate, he held up his hand, palm facing her. 'Let's get something straight before we proceed. I am asking the questions. I will also answer your questions, in as much as I am able, but we will proceed in a civilized manner. And, this conversation is being recorded.'

Diana's nostrils flared as she stifled the abuse that wanted to burst off her tongue. Okay, they both knew he was in control. She would play it his way for now, but she was not conceding, not by a long mile. She could however get in the first shot and perhaps wrest the situation back into her own hands.

'I demand to have my lawyer present,' she stated, knowing her rights even if she didn't understand why she was here. Keith had not answered her call yet, which could only mean he was not aware that she had been abducted and was being held captive in the FBI headquarters. The Quentons' well-being was his livelihood, and she was damned sure he would never allow her to stew in a jail cell. His hefty paycheck was worth more than that.

Keith wasn't a forceful lawyer, they all knew that, but he was well-versed in the law and particular about particularities. His renowned honesty had smoothed Mark's acceptance into the community in the first place. Teaming up with Keith had been a successful tactic on Mark's part, and Diana suspected he was kept on the payroll for just that reason. But where was the man when she needed him?

And what the hell was happening here? She stifled the urge to panic, took a deep breath and forced herself to remain calm.

'Lawyer not returning your calls, eh?' Flanagan said, finally allowing the slightest smile on his face. He drew himself to his full height in the chair. 'Well Mrs. Quenton, there is a good reason for that. You see, Keith is being held next door, and finds himself in much the same situation as you yourself are in.' The unspoken sentiment was that they were two peas in the same dirty pod, but he would never voice such a thought, not when the conversation was being recorded.

'You've arrested Keith?' Now she was gobsmacked. 'Keith? He could never, *would* never, do anything wrong.' This came out of her mouth unrehearsed and with a sincerity which was not missed by Flanagan. She took the hitherto rejected coffee in her hands, drawing on the warmth it still held.

Her shoulders relaxed slightly as her mind quickly worked. Whatever was going on, the FBI were obviously way off course. It had to be a big misunderstanding, because one thing she knew was that Keith, despite being a solid 'yes' man to Mark, would never have the balls to participate in anything illegal. Why, Mark often joked that Keith was his conscience, keeping him on the straight and narrow.

Flanagan tilted his head slightly and narrowed his eyes as if reading the course of her thoughts.

'Do you have any idea why you have been arrested?' he finally asked.

More certain of her footing now, she no longer felt the need to fight. 'I believe the words 'Grand Theft' and 'Fraud' were bandied about as you so rudely burst into my house,' she said as she rolled her eyes. Just a little, she couldn't help it, the situation was ridiculous and would soon be cleared up. She gave a deprecating laugh and turned a warm, genial gaze on the tall man before her. 'Now, let's get to the bottom of this, shall we? I'm feeling generous. If I'm out of here before lunch time, I may even drop the law-suit. Maybe.'

She never knew that brown eyes could frost over so quickly.

'That's what we're here for, Ma'am,' he answered. 'You are aware that tens of millions of dollars are missing from the accounts of Quenton Inc.?'

Tens of millions? No. She was not aware at all and her expression conveyed this, as for once in her life she had no words. Did they have that much money? She'd never had to worry about the financial side of things. But wait...

'All that money is missing from my husband's business? Well, is it not our money? Why would you think I stole it? And how can I steal my own money?' She sat back, satisfied with her solid logic and pretty sure release must be imminent.

His eyes bore into her as if to gauge her level of true ignorance in the matter. 'This money is held in trust,' he informed her slowly in that cold voice of his. 'For the investors. In other words, the money that is missing belongs to your friends and neighbors. Your husband's clients.'

Oh, well, that put a different spin on things. A very bad spin, she realized. Her friends must be quite perturbed by this turn of events.

'Oh my God,' she said. 'What's happened?' Her mind raced back to Keith's phone call while she was in Paris. He'd mentioned pirates, didn't he mention pirates? 'How could they have gotten hold of all that money?'

'Exactly who are you referring to when you say 'they'?'

'The pirates, the bandits, the ones who wrecked his boat. He must be kidnapped! Why aren't you out looking for Mark?'

Disbelief was written on his face. 'Pirates,' he repeated.

'Pirates,' she enunciated slowly, her fists curled on the table. Was the man stupid? 'Keith told me that Mark is presumed dead, and said the Mexican police think it was the action of pirates.'

He continued to stare at her, holding her gaze for a long moment. Flanagan opened his mouth to speak, then shut it again, then drew in another breath.

'Tell me, Mrs. Quenton. Tell me honestly,' he said, leaning forward, his eyes never leaving her face. 'Do you believe that Mark is dead?'

She stared at him with her chin held high. Flanagan obviously held no truck with the idea of pirates. She pictured Mark in her mind – short of stature, but with a vitality and hunger for life and more, always wanting more. He was still a sexy little bastard, even though that part of their lives together was long over. Diana looked down at the laminated table top and slowly shook her head.

'No,' she mumbled.

'Can you repeat that?'

'No,' she said more clearly.

'Why?'

She looked back up at him. 'You're kidding me, right? Have you ever met Mark?'

Flanagan looked at her through narrowed eyes. 'Never had the pleasure, ma'am,' he said.

'Mark could never be that easy to kill,' she said simply. 'He's a shit, a bastard, he's... always in control of things.' She shook her head. 'No, he would never let himself be *killed*. He'll go on his own terms after he's sucked life completely dry.' She was rather surprised to hear the words out of her mouth, having not thought about the matter ever.

Diana tugged at the waistband of her jeans, uncomfortably conscious of the muffin-top which had formed there and glad of the baggy sweater that covered it. Her belly rumbled, her slice of toast having been interrupted so many hours ago. She took a tentative sip of the murk in the thin plastic cup. Bitter, but to be honest she'd had worse in her time. Many years ago.

Flanagan slowly nodded his head. 'Do you realize the situation you are now in?'

Wheels began to turn in earnest. No, she hadn't had much opportunity to dwell on it, aside from the immediate indignities which plagued her, but she did now. Mark was dead or not, disappeared at any rate. The money he had so shrewdly invested and grown over the years, the money which established their place in Baserville society, was missing according to Flanagan. It had disappeared, just like Mark. Could it be...? No, surely not, but she ran it by Flanagan just to be sure.

'You don't think Mark took the money, do you?'

He raised a single eyebrow.

'He wouldn't do such a thing!' She vehemently denied the idea. 'I mean, for him to take... *steal* everyone's money – well, we'd never be able to hold up our heads in Baserville again! He's worked too hard to attain our position... *we've* worked too hard...'

The horror of dawning realization washed over her. 'And he's disappeared, so he doesn't have to worry about it...'

Flanagan opened his mouth to speak, but Diana was now lost in her own world. Admittedly, a much more unpleasant world for her than yesterday's. A world in which she had no social standing, having lost everything she had struggled and worked for over the years.

'That goddamned bastard!' She stood as she roared, knocking the wooden chair over, the blonde Norse goddess on the warpath. She missed the flicker in Flanagan's eye, a flicker of surprise, and perhaps admiration at the strength of her passion. If she could have seen herself through his eyes at that moment, she would know how sexy she appeared in her rage, even wearing her old, ill-fitted clothes. But all thoughts about her appearance had faded for the first time in years.

Diana didn't hear the forceful knock on the door but when it burst open she turned to the newcomer as if ready to eat him alive.

The short young man with full hipster beard and man-bun stopped in mid-stride, his expression morphed from indignant to terror and he yelped softly as he started back in the face of her fury.

'Who are you?' she demanded.

His eyes behind his thick glasses darted quickly from Diana to Flanagan, then back to the raging she-demon who towered over him, as if afraid to take his eyes off her for fear she would eat him. He gulped. 'Your lawyer?'

The tension was broken by a soft chuckle from the FBI agent.

'Come on in,' he waved the young man in. 'Mrs. Quenton, meet Daniel Downey. He's the state appointed lawyer assigned to your case.'

Diana stared with horror at the dishevelled and plump man before her. He hardly looked out of his teens. She slowly sat back down. 'State-appointed lawyer?' Her voice cracked. 'I hardly think I've stooped that low, even in these circumstances.'

Dan's face drooped with hurt and disappointment and his shoulders began to sag.

She gave a short laugh in disbelief. 'If I needed a lawyer,' she continued, gaining back her momentum. 'If I needed a lawyer, I'd hire one with a bit more experience. And better dress sense.' She laughed again cruelly as she watched the young man crumple in on himself. Was that a quiver on his lip? 'I certainly wouldn't choose this specimen to represent me.'

At those words, Daniel lifted his head and visibly pulled himself together. He sucked in his belly so his shirt was not pulled so tightly and adjusted his tie.

'I think, Mrs. Quenton, I think that especially *under these circumstances*, you'd be happy to have anyone on your side,' he said. 'Anyone at all.' He stood over her and fixed her in his glare, drawing himself up to his full height. 'However, I'll not stay where I'm not wanted, so I bid you good-day,' he said with as much dignity as he could muster.

Flanagan looked as if he was enjoying the sideshow. 'Hang on, Dan,' he said. 'Don't go any-where yet. I think Mrs. Quenton doesn't realize the full situation she's in. She may yet change her mind.'

Dan hesitated, torn between losing face and los-ing billable hours. The empty wallet won out, and he carried himself to the end of the table between the two and sat himself down.

'He is *not* my lawyer,' she stated to Flanagan. She darted a glance toward Dan and barely stopped herself from shuddering.

The FBI agent nodded in agreement. 'Maybe you don't need a lawyer,' he said. 'Maybe you have nothing to do with Mark's disappearance. Pending accumulation of evidence, of course.

'The problem, Mrs. Quenton, is that you are still not free to go. Not yet. I have a lot of questions to be answered, and you're the only one who can give me those answers.'

'If you insist I still need representation and since Keith is not available, let me make a call to the city lawyers.' She refused to further acknowledge Dan's presence.

'That might turn out to be difficult for you,' he told her.

Was that pity she saw in his eyes? 'How so?' she asked, impatience coloring her voice.

Flanagan turned to Dan. 'You want to explain to her?' he asked, offering the young man a chance to show his stuff.

He nodded. 'Mrs. Quenton, there are basically two reasons preventing you from hiring a lawyer,' he said.

She continued to stare straight ahead at Flanagan with a rigid set to her mouth.

'One, you don't have any money,' he said simply and braced himself for the backlash.

He was rewarded finally with a frosty acknowledgment as Diana turned on him. '*I* have more money than *you* can ever dream of having,' she said. 'I am Diana Quenton. I own the largest mansion in the county, I have a cottage on the lake, I have a driver, I have a Mercedes, I ... I ... don't you tell me I can't afford a proper lawyer!'

Dan bravely met her glare head on.

Flanagan chose that moment to intercede. 'He's right, Mrs. Quenton,' he said. 'For all intents and purposes, you do not have access to funds at the moment.'

She whipped her head back round to the agent. 'Don't be ridiculous! Even if Mark took everything, I can mortgage the house. I'll always have access to cash. Everyone knows that.'

'But everything owned jointly by you and your husband has been seized by the Feds,' Dan pointed out gently. 'Every bank account and all your property. Face it, you have absolutely nothing.'

Diana continued to shake her head vigorously in denial. 'I have friends in high places,' she said. 'I'll call my Congressman. The Mayor. My banker. This is only temporary, you'll find Mark, or whatever happened to him, you'll find the money and we'll give it back.' She beseeched both of them. 'Right? Just let me out of here, I'll fix everything, I promise.'

'That brings us to reason number two,' Flanagan said. 'You'll probably find that all those friends have disappeared, along with the money.'

Dan took a newspaper out of his briefcase. 'Brace yourself,' he said. 'It isn't pretty.' He placed it before her so that the headline jumped up at her.

WHERE'S THE MONEY, HONEY?

It ran the whole width of the paper, just under the title, in stark black and white. She'd never seen a headline so big, such large type. So huge. So cruel.

And right under it, a photo of her. A man's hand on her head forced Diana into the back seat of the car as she twisted and yelled at Susie, her jaw out of alignment and mouth wide open and the expression in her eyes was pure rage.

'You didn't tell me there were photographers,' she accused Flanagan, her face burning with embarrassment.

He shrugged his wide shoulders. 'They must have slipped in when the gates were open and hid in the shrubberies. Such a shame.'

'This is awful!' She was referring to the photo. 'They were trespassing on my property. They had no right! You need to charge them and show them a lesson.'

Flanagan and Dan exchanged a glance – the young man wide-eyed, the older man amused.

'That's the least of your worries right now, ma'am,' the agent said, not unkindly. 'Read on.'

'I don't want to,' she said, after a pause, in an uncharacteristically small voice.

'You need to know how people are feeling,' he said. 'What you're up against.'

Diana reluctantly bent her head down to the paper again, but the words swam in front of her eyes. Loose and meaningless phrases surfaced – grand theft, fraud, disappeared and believed to have absconded, bla bla bla. They were talking about Mark.

She raced through the paragraphs until she found names of her closest friends and neighbors, searching for comfort, but there was nothing to sustain her there. Oh, they were hurt, the quotes told her, and angry, so very angry. There were even personal digs at her, Diana, and from people she held dear to her. Could Rose LeBlanche from next door truly have said such nasty things?

'I am a leader, not a bully!' Diana focused on that one quote – the rest of the article was too much to comprehend. 'Rose is a backbiting, snivelling bitch. She's been trying to be president of the Women's League for years, but she just doesn't have the support behind her. People won't dare vote me out, they know I'm the only woman for the job.'

Flanagan said nothing.

'This is all scurrilous nonsense, sensationalistic journalism at its lowest.' She pushed the paper away from her. 'Verminous rag!'

'I won't disagree with you there,' he said mildly.

She sat back in her chair with her arms crossed and a petulant expression on her face, as she did the rare times in her life when she was forced to face up to unpleasant things.

'Alright,' Diana said, after a while. 'Alright. This means war.' She grabbed the newspaper with its loathsome headline and began to read again, this time with focused care. 'Get me more coffee!' she barked without looking up. 'And make it fresh this time.'

CHAPTER SIX

After further questioning in which Diana refused to budge an inch from her claim to know nothing of Mark's whereabouts, Flanagan told her she was free to go, with the caution for her to remain accessible. He excused himself, leaving her alone in the room with the lawyer.

Dan, having nothing better to do and not having been asked to leave, remained with her. He wouldn't miss this for the world.

'So,' she said finally looking up, still lost in thought. She took a long swallow of brew and winced. That brought her back to the here and now. 'They really need to change their brand.

'But no matter,' she continued, looking directly at Dan. 'We need a plan.'

Dan Downey hadn't led a very exciting life up to this point, and coming from a middle-class suburb, he'd never rubbed shoulders with the rich and powerful or the go-getters of the world. Such was the force of Diana's personality that he felt a small thrill with his acceptance as part of her team, despite his reservations and the nasty words she'd said about him not an hour previously. He was at a bit of a loose end this morning, and with luck there might be money in it.

'So a plan,' she said. 'I'm free to go?'

'By the sounds of it.'

'Then tell Sam to come pick me up.'

'I think the vehicles have all been seized.'

'Oh. You'll have to bring me home then.'

'You can't go there.'

'Don't be ridiculous. I'm not going to let Rose LeBlanche scare me away.'

'Your home's also been taken, remember. There's the matter of the missing money. It'll be used to reimburse the investors and other stakeholders.'

'Hmph. The cottage then, we'll have to camp out there.'

'Seized.'

'That too? Have I nothing left? But... but where are the animals? My pets? Oh dear God, don't tell me they've been seized too!' Panic was showing in her voice.

'I took the liberty of inquiring,' he said. 'Mrs. Hastings has taken them to her own home.'

'Oh good. They'll be with a familiar face then, they won't be too traumatized. We can collect them on the way. Where does she live?'

'Why are you asking me that? She's been your housekeeper for twenty years. Surely you know where she lives.'

'You didn't take the time to find out where my pets were going?'

Dan puffed out his cheeks in a sigh. 'I'll inquire.'

'Good. The only problem right now is ...' She fixed him in her glare.

Dan started in alarm. 'You can't stay with me. I live in my parent's basement,' he said quickly, anticipating correctly.

'Eeuw, no,' she replied. Diana thought for a moment. 'How much money is left?'

'I don't have the details, but I assume everything is gone. It was all in either both your names, or the business?'

Diana gave a one-shoulder shrug. She had never needed to pay attention to things like that.

'We need to get out of here, at any rate. Susie, we'll go to Susie's.'

He said nothing.

'What?' she asked, turning his way. 'Don't tell me even Susie...'

'Her money was lost, too,' he reminded her. 'She may not be very welcoming to you.'

'I don't believe that for a moment.' Then she frowned as she recalled the smile on Suzie's face as she'd watched Diana being led away in handcuffs. 'But I'll give her time to calm down, just in case.'

She sat and thought for a further moment, her eyes resting on Dan the whole while. He was a smart guy, and according to him, she had nothing, no resources to her name. It wasn't true, couldn't be, there was no way everything could have crashed apart so suddenly. On the other hand, she would need all the assistance she could muster for the loose plan which was forming in her head, at least for the next twenty-four hours.

If he accepted hopeless cases like her own for the pittance offered by the state, he was probably in need of cash. Everybody had a price, after all, she just had to figure out what his was. There was no doubt in Diana's mind that she would be successful in finding her husband and have the funds to make good on the offer she was about to make. She leaned in closer to him and spoke in a low voice.

'I need your help.'

'They've dropped the charges,' Dan told her. 'I'm not your lawyer anymore.'

"I'll make it worth your while, but I warn you, it will take some time to complete.' She took up the pen and wrote a figure which made his eyebrows shoot up. 'You willing to take the chance?'

Dan looked at the paper, the quick calculations of the cost of his dreams written on his face.

'I can't do anything illegal,' he hissed at her.

'Nothing illegal about it, not on your part,' she said. 'And I'll make full restitution before anything is found out.'

He gave a quick glance around the room, search-ing for a camera, then shrugged his acceptance. 'What's your plan?' he asked.

'Can't tell you here,' she whispered. 'The walls may have ears.'

·♥·♥·♥·♥·♥·

As the door closed behind them, Flanagan chuck-led and turned off the built-in microphone in the tiny room next door. It was going even better than he'd planned.

Diana Quenton was guilty as hell and now that she thought she was buying Dan's assistance, the young lawyer had a reason to keep in touch with Diana. She was going to lead the FBI straight to

Mark, her partner in life and in crime. He gave himself a mental pat on the back.

He called Dan back for a moment, into another small room with no microphones or cameras.

'It's like this, Dan,' he said, settling on to the corner of the desk. 'Mrs. Quenton is in a situation right now.'

The lawyer looked at him head on. 'She had nothing to do with her husband's actions,' he said in a firm voice.

'I agree,' Flanagan said as if he meant it. 'But we still need to get our hands on Mark. And I got a feeling that Diana, even though she doesn't realize it, may be able to lead us to him.'

Dan shifted uncomfortably and looked away.

'She's a force to be reckoned with,' the agent continued. 'But I like the lady, and I don't want to see her getting herself into trouble.' He waited until Dan nodded agreement.

'As the charges against her have been dropped,' Flanagan said. 'You're no longer acting as her lawyer. I'm suggesting a little tit-for-tat, you scratch my back, that sort of thing.'

He held up his hand as Dan drew a breath to protest. 'Just need to know what she's up to,' he quickly assured him. 'And you know, you have a promising career ahead of you. One that could be helped with the right contacts. Like me.'

Flanagan held out his business card and winked as Dan slowly accepted it. 'Stay in touch.'

·♥·♥·♥·♥·♥·

Dan was a mess of emotions as he found himself caught up in this intrigue, working between Diana and Flanagan, and all in order to further his innocent dreams. The agent had hinted that if he went along with Diana, work would be sent his way in the future, while Diana had promised an astoundingly large sum for his assistance on her end. It was a win-win situation for him, and he could walk away anytime if he sensed his lawyerly ideals were being compromised. Right?

Anyway, it wasn't like he had much else to do at the moment. Recently graduated from law school, he was on his way to living his dream – he just wasn't quite there yet. Unlike Diana, Dan came from a middle-class background, one which was far too bourgeois for his comfort. The suburb he grew up in consisted of small enclaves of cul-de-sacs whose neighbors took turns at hosting the weekly barbeques. They all attended the same church, all their houses were built on the same plan and were all carpeted throughout. Everyone was everybody's friend, and Dan thought he might suffocate under the niceness of it all.

This fellowship of neighbors didn't understand him, either, but they were all really kind about it. His rebellion was looked upon indulgently, and they excused his beard and man-bun with the reason that he had always been artistic, and was very intelligent. He'd been top of his class at law school, they told each other. They forgave him his differences, and this was the final strangulation.

Being passionate, creative and of a romantic bent, he wanted more from life. Not wealth and riches, his yearnings hadn't been the same as Diana and Mark's. Dan needed a reason to live, a big passion in his life and he wanted a worthy cause to fight for. For that reason, he hadn't applied to article in the big law firms where he would be just another junior giving his whole in a race to the top. He was attracted to study the law because he saw himself fighting for the little guy, helping to make his society a just one and righting the wrongs. He hated the injustices he found outside his parents' safety net.

If he hated inequality so much, one must ask why on earth he was moved to take on Diana's defence in the first place. She and Mark and their present situation represented everything he, like Flanagan, found wrong in his country. The rich got richer and stole even more. Everyone was greedy and wanted more than their fair share and had excuses as to why they deserved it.

The answer of course, was that Dan needed the money, for living and working out of his parent's tidy suburban basement had never been part of the plan. He dreamed of a little store-front office in the seediest part of town where he could reach out to the people who needed him most, but even that required a down payment. He was offered this present opportunity because no-one else would touch Diana's defence. Even Dan had hesitated before agreeing to the work, but had justified it to himself by stating that he would be proving his worth, making a name for himself. He would put his all into her defence, and the upside was he wouldn't be blamed for the inevitable failure. It was really a win-win situation except for his morals, but he was quickly learning that there is compromise in every situation. He had done his homework, and was prepared to bluster on her behalf and strut his stuff.

So in essence Dan found himself as a double agent of sorts that day and although he had mixed emotions about this role, he was in the city and anything was better than returning to the endless dreariness of that happy suburb.

Besides, Diana had sparked his curiosity. Unlike Flanagan, he believed her when she claimed to know nothing about Mark's disappearance. He'd glimpsed the woman behind the wealth and infamy, and to his surprise, he rather liked her attitude despite her rudeness.

·•·♥·♥·♥·♥·

Diana, being Diana, didn't question Dan's allegiance. She had ruled the Women's League of Baserville for almost twenty years – during which time she had honed her understanding of the finer points of manipulation, and she was satisfied she had correctly judged the level of the young man's desperation.

Oh, her plan? She wasn't about to share all of it right away, for she suspected it wasn't quite legal even though it would solve the immediate cash flow issue. Largely through her own efforts, money had been raised and put aside in a trust which would help poor people spay and neuter their pets. Everyone deserved to have a pet – a little thing like finances should never get in the way, for these expensive procedures could be a deterrent to pet ownership for some. She and Susie, her trusted side-kick, had signing power over these funds.

These funds would now serve her, but she needed to have Susie on board.

CHAPTER SEVEN

By this point, the reader might be wondering about the lack of mention of Diana's family in this story so far. The twins that she had birthed twenty years previous – what of them? Had they been even informed of their father's possible death? Diana's four siblings and her mother – why were they not gathering around to provide emotional support?

Unfortunately, Diana being Diana had ensured none of the above played a part in her life, unwitting as her actions may have been. When the twins were born, she was as loving a mother as anyone could hope for. However, as they grew into independence and lost their adoration of the maternal breasts, she quickly lost interest in them and took up with the dogs. That happened around the age of two, for the twins were precocious and being the products of two strong parents, their innate personalities became apparent at a very young age. They'd been very well provided for and sent to the best schools with all the bells and whistles that befitted the scions of the house of Quenton, but other than that she was guilty of inconsistent parenting. The animals had by this time taken over her life and were far more rewarding in their affections.

The present-day whereabouts of the twins was vaguely known to her mind – Theresa was finding herself in Tibet, Giles in California, but as she could not control them, the ties that bind loosened more and more every year. As Mark was no longer believed dead, it was not an emergency to find them. Mrs. Hastings would be minding their contacts, much as she was minding the pets, for that was her job.

As to her birth family, well, they'd been left in the dust long ago. They'd learned to not look her up and ask for money. Enough said. No immediate family would be coming to her rescue or interfering in anyway, and that was how she expected it to be.

·❤·❤·❤·❤·❤·

Diana and Dan left through the main smoked glass doors onto the street where, to his quiet disappointment, there was no gamut of reporters for them to push past. The fall evening drizzled, the streetlights already on in the dusk. His rusted Corolla waited two blocks away down a narrow alley in which parking was not precisely legal, but it was free of meters.

They tracked down the abode of Mrs. Hastings through Dan's cell phone, as Diana's was presumably still at her home, seized, like everything else. The dour Scots woman lived in a crooked pre-Victorian cottage in a little village by the sea not five minutes' drive from Diana's mansion, but a world apart in every other sense. A warm light glowed through the lace curtains and as they walked up the short path to the door, there were no sounds except for the waves washing the shore and the cries of the last seagulls heading home.

The lion's head knocker on the front door brought a volley of bayings behind it, and as they waited in the rain, Diana's face wore a happy smile for the first time that day at the thought of being reunited with Cerberus and his brother Outhros, those two magnificent specimens of doggy love.

'Quit your racket, ye hounds of hell!' The front door opened inward a crack and Mrs. Hastings' nose thrust out, followed by two wet and furry doggy snouts. The two below were whining now they knew their mistress was there.

'It's you, finally.'

Diana barreled through Dan and the housekeeper to hurl herself down to the level of the dogs, her arms around them. She appeared to be wrestling the great mastiffs, but Dan could see their tails wagging and that this was a joyful game played between the three. He had no doubt as to who was the alpha in the pack.

'I'll be glad to see the backs of them,' Mrs. Hastings muttered to Dan, daring him to not take the dogs with him when he left. Not being aware of Diana's plan, he had no answer for the woman.

That gleeful welcome over, Diana turned next to the cats ranging up the crooked stairs. Celine, Mariah and Aretha – the three divas. She gave them their due, greeting each by name, nuzzling and reassuring ruffled tempers. Mrs. Hastings tut-tutted about the fur flying loosely over her hall floor.

Diana finally straightened and turned to her housekeeper. 'I'll need to stay here too,' she announced, at which news the lady's eyes bulged. 'At least for tonight.' She glanced around the tiny hallway and grimaced. 'Don't think I'll be staying longer than one night.'

Mrs. Hastings mouth was set in a grim line and she looked accusingly at Dan for bringing Diana there.

'This is Dan,' Diana said airily. 'He's my new lawyer.' This was said as if the arrangement was mutually chosen, as if the pairing hadn't been the last ditch effort of fate.

'Ah, technically, no I'm not...' Dan hastened to interject, but both women ignored him.

If Diana had understood her housekeeper better, she would know that alternative solutions were quickly running through Mrs. H's razor sharp mind, and just as quickly discarded until she accepted the inevitable.

'One night only, mind. And then you're to find alternate arrangements. I can't be having the dirty creatures here in my home. Bad enough I spent the last twenty years cleaning up after you all.'

She stumped down the hall to the kitchen, Diana and dogs following her. Dan was left standing uncertainly just inside the front entrance, wondering if he'd been dismissed for the evening.

'Come through if you're wanting tea,' he heard the screech. 'I'm not serving in the front room. And it's mugs you'll be getting, not the good china.'

He walked into a room surprisingly large yet cozy, which stretched along the entire width of the house. A huge fireplace complete with burning logs blazed along the center wall, the brick chimney running right to the ceiling. It was a kitchen that many would love to emulate in modern houses, with comfortable chairs ranged before the fire and an old oak table for eating at, and blackened beams running along the ceiling. Yet he doubted that the room had been updated much since the house's inception two hundred years before with its faded wall paper, original farmhouse sink and flagstone floor. It was sparklingly clean, despite its' great age.

He was handed a plate with a slab of ham thrust between two unevenly sliced hunks of thickly buttered bread. Diana sat eating only toast, as she was vegetarian and Mrs. Hastings kept nothing in her pantry to cater to her tastes.

'Nice home,' said Dan weakly, his middle-class upbringing requiring polite conversation to fill the silent void.

'It's small enough,' Mrs. Hastings replied with a sniff. 'Perfect size for one person.'

Diana blithely continued to plow her way through the stack of toast, now and again tossing crusts to the floor for the dogs to scarf down and lick up the crumbs.

'So you've lost it all,' Mrs. Hastings raised her voice to be heard over the crunchings. She glowered at Diana and the dogs in turn.

'No,' came the decisive reply. 'Turns out, Mark's taken the money – all of it. Everything he's invested for people, and everything that he's grown over the years. He may or may not be dead. The government has seized the property, all of it, even my personal items.

'But nothing is lost, as such,' she continued. 'I don't think Mark is dead. I just need to find him, get the money, give it back and then I can have my house again.' Diana spoke as if it would be an easy task to accomplish.

'Never thought he was dead,' muttered Mrs. H. 'You can't kill the devil that easy.'

They all sat and looked at the fire for a while longer, lost in their various thoughts.

'What's your plan then?' the housekeeper asked finally. 'After you find a place to live,' she quickly added.

Diana shook her head. 'I'll let you know,' she said. 'When I figure it all out.'

♥ · ♥ · ♥ · ♥ · ♥

She spent that evening holed up in Mrs. Hastings's parlor, forcing her host to retire early to watch her shows on the small TV upstairs. Diana frantically Googled the numbers of all her contacts, but to no avail as it seemed nobody was picking up their phones. Either that, or no one wanted to speak with her.

Annoyed, she logged into her FaceBook account to message them all, only to find the cruelest blow of all. Most of her followers had already unfriended her in a mass spate of outrage.

All those grateful owners of dogs and cats, they'd forgotten who was responsible for uniting them with their beloved fur-babies. All those price-gouging shopkeepers of Baserville whom she had supported by buying local, and how much had she lined their pockets over the years? Even the owner of the Mercedes dealership had dropped her. This was outrageous.

'Susie?' She tapped on the keys. No, Susie was still there, she saw with relief. That timid mouse wouldn't have dared unfriend her, just in case. But what she saw posted on her friend's page shocked her to the core.

A clip from the original Wizard of Oz, that horribly cheerful song 'Ding Dong the Witch is Dead'. Trumpets blared, munchkins cheered in joy. And above it was written:

This one's for you, @DianaQuenton.

It was Rose LeBlanche, of course, who had shared it to Susie's page, but it had over five thousand likes. Five thousand?

Did Diana even know that many people?

She slept that night on the pullout sofa, her only comfort the dogs and cats who squeezed in next to her, looking to share her body heat in that freezing cottage.

But sleep is well-known for its curative powers. She had seen for herself the evidence that her situation was as dire as Flanagan claimed, and only then was she able to accept the truth. She'd fallen from her lofty perch like a gargoyle tumbling from a crumbled turret, but instead of lying broken and wounded in a gutter of self-pity, she amassed her tremendous powers to call for revenge.

No, Rose LeBlanche, this witch wasn't dead yet.

·♥·♥·♥·♥·♥·

After begging gas money from his forgiving mother, Dan showed up early the next morning at the seaside village. He spotted Diana and dogs further along the rocky beach, her fair hair flying as she raced with the large dogs. The creatures splashed mightily as they plowed through the surf. He sat on the sea wall and waited until his glasses became quite misted with spray.

She came up to him, her face flushed and glowing. Diana wore a large grey anorak over yesterday's clothes, perhaps a remnant of the long-departed Mr. Hastings.

'So, the plan,' she said decisively as she sat beside him. The dogs threw themselves at her feet, panting happily as they gnawed on logs of driftwood they had dug out of the rocks. The animals smelled of wet seaweed and half-rotted fish. Mrs. Hastings would not be pleased.

'But first - see that house back there?' She twisted and pointed to a weathered salt-box behind them which peeked out through a copse of trees, across the coastal road. The land was enclosed by a rickety picket fence. The paint on house and fence, if ever there was any, had long since peeled, and the windows he could see were set in moldering sills. There was a faded 'For Sale' sign hanging by one corner off the tilted fence.

'It's empty,' she said. 'I'll take it.'

He blanched, the lawyer in him horror-struck. 'I don't think you can just 'take' it,' he said after clearing his throat. 'I'm sure it's somebody's property. They may not look kindly on that.'

Diana laughed out loud. 'I mean I'm going to rent it,' she said. 'Find out who owns it and make the arrangements for me.'

He had seen pictures of her mansion (he had thoroughly done his homework after receiving the call the previous day) and he compared the two structures in his mind's eye. Dan eyed the old salt-box doubtfully. 'I think you'll find it's not quite what you're used to...'

Diana shot him a glance of fierce determination, her blue eyes as dark as the sea.

'Dan,' she said. 'Dan, you don't know me. I've lived in much worse in my time. I've already looked – it seems to be furnished. Besides, it's only for a short while until I find Mark and retrieve the money.'

He sighed. He had given the matter much thought on his drive to the village that morning. After a night's sleep away from Diana's dynamic influence, common sense had started to creep in and he was having second thoughts about his career as a double agent.

'You know,' he began. 'You might want to leave that job to Flanagan and the FBI.' He felt her stiffen beside him and he girded his loins and took his cue from Mrs. Hastings, who had no fear to confront Diana with nasty truths. 'I mean, they have resources, and you... well, you have nothing, let's face it. Can you even afford to rent that cottage?'

A light drizzle started, moving in from the sea.

'I have, as you put it, resources,' she said slowly. 'However, I will need a loan till I can get my hands on that sum of money.' She looked at him square-ly. She didn't bother putting up the hood of her anorak, and her hair began to glisten with wet. 'You have a credit card?'

She waited until he slowly nodded his assent. 'Good. It will all be paid back within a short time.'

And the needy animals would just have to wait for their neuterings, she added silently.

CHAPTER EIGHT

Dan did as he was bid, albeit with many misgivings, and soon the keys for the decrepit house overlooking the beach were in Diana's hand. She moved in with the five animals that same day, much to Mrs. Hasting's loud relief. The housekeeper hadn't been overjoyed at Diana's close proximity, but was last seen vacuuming with gusto and scrubbing every corner of the spotless house anew once she was finally rid of the pets. After, Diana directed Dan to drive her to the nearest large supermarket to buy pet food and treats, along with sheets and bedding and new clothes for her.

He watched as she chose sweaters and jeans and heavy socks from the discount store's aisles. This was a far cry from the fancy designer wear Diana was accustomed to wearing, he knew, but she didn't appear to be put out at all. She hummed happily as she marched through the store with a cart piled high.

He watched in apprehension as her fingers played over the display of pre-paid cell phones and when they paused over the iPhones, he coughed discreetly.

'What?' She turned on him. 'I need a phone – I feel naked without one.'

'I thought you didn't have any friends left to call,' he muttered.

That earned him a nasty glance, but she settled for a flip phone. 'This *is* the cheapest model,' she pointed out unnecessarily.

He cringed at the check-out, for his card had never been stretched so far. It had lots of bounce still in it, as a law degree was a ticket to extended credit in the eyes of the bank, but he personally hated to put anything on plastic without being certain that he had the funds to cover it.

'Now,' she said as they brought the last of the bags into the house between them. 'Now, for the plan.'

He waited, but she still wasn't sharing the details with him.

'We need to go to Susie's,' she directed.

'What good will that do?'

'She's my best friend,' Diana replied in explanation, and prepared to leave the house again.

Dan stopped on the threshold. He had found time to read all the evening papers online last night after returning home, with all the interviews from the residents of Baserville who'd lost their savings and investments through Mark's disappearance, Susie amongst them. He, too, had creeped them all on FaceBook, and seen that none of the comments were complimentary to Diana – in fact, they were even angrier and they raked her over the coals, damning her to hell. He found it especially odd that all their distress was aimed towards the wife, he noted – Mark escaped with very few curses. He feared that Diana would find Susie was no longer her friend.

'What exactly do you hope will come from this visit?' he asked, turning the key in the ignition of the rusted Toyota. It began with a cough but, true to form, ran smoothly enough.

'She's my 'in' to Baserville,' she replied, omitting any reference to the trust and her need of Susie's signature to release the funds. 'Despite what she wrote on FaceBook, Susie's the one person in the world I can count on.' She saw the incredulous look he gave her.

'That's only Rose's influence,' she said, defending her erstwhile friend. 'Anyway, back to my plan. You see, Mark is a creature of habit. You know how a criminal will always return to the scene of a crime?'

He shook his head. 'That only happens in novels,' he said. 'It's a useful ploy for writers with a weak plot. It doesn't necessarily happen in real life.'

She brushed this objection aside. 'Mark will return, if only to gloat over the damage he's done. I need to have ears and eyes in the town to alert me, so I can get ready to pounce.'

He drove the short distance to Baserville in silence, reluctant to point out how Mark was now a wanted man and, if he had any sense, would not be crossing borders just to gloat. If he were still alive, that is.

They finally drew up before a fine colonial house with a gracious yard, not a single leaf marring the perfect green lawn. The gardens had long been put to bed, with not a withered stalk in evidence, and the rose bushes were all tucked up in their burlap coats.

'Drive up around the corner, and wait for me there,' she commanded him as she got out. 'I don't want her thinking I drove here in this rattle trap.' She slammed the door on his protests that this

junk heap was presently her only mode of trans-
portation, totally missing the expression on his
face.

The woman was reaching new heights of rudeness. Dan closed his mouth and set his jaw and hid
the car from view as she commanded, even if he
did so reluctantly.

She obviously didn't plan on including him in the
visit to Susie's, but curiosity won out and he crept
into the yard to hide in the shrubberies shielding
the house from the street. From here, he had the
perfect vantage overlooking the front entrance.

The wooden door with beveled glass swung inward silently. There, standing before Diana, was
Rose LeBlanche, her ex-neighbor and worst ene-
my. Dan recognized the tall woman with the sleek
short hair from the photos in yesterday's papers.

'Well, what have we here?' he heard the woman
drawl, as she leaned against the doorpost, a vicious smile lighting her face. 'Why aren't you in
jail?'

Diana's back stiffened. 'What are *you* doing
here?'

'Consoling my friend,' Rose replied. 'Because of
what you and your husband did to this town.'
The woman's eyes travelled up and down Diana's
body, noting the cheapness of her clothing and her

rubber boots, then finally coming to rest on her wind-blown hair. 'My, how the mighty have fallen,' she smirked from the step above. 'What happened to your Louboutin's? Oh right, they've been seized! Hopefully the auction will raise a bit of money to repay what you and your filthy, no account husband stole.'

'Get Susie here,' Diana ordered. 'And take yourself away.'

Rose laughed. 'Susie is... not at home for you.' She didn't budge an inch.

Even from this angle, he could see the color rising in Diana's face. 'You rotten witch!' She was beginning to lose it.

Hang on there, Di, he found himself almost saying aloud, don't let the bitch push your buttons.

The stand-off was cut short by the appearance of Susie at Rose's side. Petite with her blonde hair cut in a cutesy bob, the woman stood and looked unhappily up at Diana.

'Tell her, Suze,' Rose purred. 'You can do it, girl-friend.'

'Diana, you need to go away,' Susie stammered in her squeaky voice as if reciting lines, looking half frightened to death as she did so. 'You are no longer my friend. You stole all our money and... and you're a bully!' Her eyes popped open wide as if surprised at her own boldness.

'Susie,' Diana cried. This was not good. 'What's gotten into you? How can you throw our friendship away over... over mere money?'

The two women gaped at her, even Rose thrown off balance.

'This is just a glitch,' she told them quickly. 'The money will be returned. I'll find Mark, don't worry about that. Have I ever let you down before?'

Susie appeared to be wavering, uncertainty written on her face. She'd been bossed about by Diana for so long, it was almost natural to cave and let her take the reins again. Rose firmly stepped in.

'Suze, you're not taking her seriously? Remember how she's bullied you and ordered you around for years? Never taking into account your opinion, or thinking that you have feelings?'

'It's true Diana,' Suzie said, nodding her head. 'You've pushed me around for years and... and I'm sick of having to pick up your dog's poop from my lawn!'

'Susie, I order you to send Rose away. She's not a good influence on you.'

'I'm a person, you know! You can't order me around like your dogs. *You* go away!'

'Why are you doing this?' Diana demanded of Rose. 'Do you hate me that much? What have I ever done to you?'

'You even need to ask that?' Rose asked back, her voice cool now. 'Goodbye, Diana. You're not welcome in this town anymore. Nobody likes you anyway.' Rose and Susie linked arms as Diana admitted temporary defeat, slinking off towards where Dan had hidden the car, dejection in the slump of her shoulders.

She looked at him with anguished eyes as he stepped out of the shrubbery.

'You heard that?'

He nodded. They got in the car in silence.

Sorry as he felt for her, Dan was still miffed at being ordered to hide himself and the vehicle which had brought her here, at her not wanting him to be seen by her old associates, so he might be forgiven for probing her fresh wounds.

'That didn't go so well, did it?' He darted his eyes over to her. 'I told you so.'

Silence from her side of the car.

'Some friends.'

'Shut up.'

'What were you thinking?' he asked finally, as they pulled up to a red light. 'Oh, your plan, your big plan. What did you really think was going to come out of this? That Susie would forgive all? That you'd be welcomed with open arms? Your husband stole all their money, and they don't know that you weren't involved in that.' He thumped his hands against the steering wheel. He liked Diana, he admired her force, and he really wanted to help her but she wasn't making it easy for him. He was also very worried about that credit card bill.

'Look,' he continued in a softer voice for he wasn't brought up to be mean. 'I'm really sorry. What happened back there? It sucks. But you have to face reality, and we have to come up with a real plan, something, if it's at all possible...'

The trust money was evaporating in front of her. It had been her only salvation, her one hope. If she could just get to Susie, she knew she'd be able to talk her round, but Rose wasn't allowing that to happen. So frustrating. And for Susie to turn on her like that.... It all hurt too much, and Dan being nice about it just made her want to cry. So Diana did what any wounded animal would do, and bit the hand which reached out to her.

'You don't have to be here,' she said to him in her nastiest voice. It helped keep the tears at bay. 'In fact, I don't see you being any use at all. I don't need you – you're just a wanna-be lawyer living in your parents' basement. Go back to your video games! And shave off the god-damn beard and cut off the man-bun, neither of them suit you. Grow up and get a real job.' She crossed her arms and slid further down in her seat. It hadn't worked - she didn't feel any better after saying all this.

Dan, being a young man of intelligence, had few illusions about himself. He knew himself to be short of stature, and not slim, with thick glasses and red hair to boot. But he was proud of his ability to grow this red hair when other men were haunted by thinning scalps and wispy facial hair. He was proud also of the statement it made to his suburban neighbors, how it set him apart as different and interesting. He liked how the tidiness of his man-bun told the world he was a man to be reckoned with, yet a sensitive soul too. For her to attack the one aspect of his appearance he took pride in, well, that was just too much.

'Screw you!' he shouted as he took the turning into the village far too sharply, the money she owed him temporarily forgotten. 'After all I've done! I'm trying to help you and all you do is tear me down. No wonder you don't have any friends!'

He jerked the car to a stop in front of her house. 'Get out! I never want to see you again.'

She slammed the door and thumped her way up past the rickety gate post, not looking back. He could not see the tears which were dripping down her cheeks.

'Go get yourself a 'real' lawyer,' he muttered as he performed a perfect three-point turn with bald tires screeching on the pavement. 'Good luck with that!'

CHAPTER NINE

Like a hurt wolf who snarled at any offers to help, Diana needed to slink away to a dark cave and lick her wounds in quiet. But the silence of her new home pressed in on her, the unfamiliarity of the walls boxed her in. The sofa whose dented seat was adjusted to someone else's bottom, the kitchen with the cups chosen by someone else's taste, these all served to remind her that she now had no home and no friends. Only the dogs welcomed her, but even they couldn't stop the torrent of thoughts which threatened to engulf her. She couldn't stay in this house a moment longer.

The wind had been rising all the while, and was now rattling the loose windowpanes in the old house and whipping the waves to high whitecaps on the ocean outside her window. It suited her bleak mood. So Diana, being Diana, sought escape from the horrid truths thrown at her from all sides that morning in the hurricane-force winds and rain along the shore.

Battling the winds occupied her body and allowed her mind to wander away from the rotten present. There had been a time once, many years ago, when she had felt this dejected, it may have been the last time. Their marriage was still young and she was pregnant with the twins. Mark was establishing himself, working long hours and schmoozing with potential clients when he wasn't at the office, convincing the men of Baserville to let him show them his magic.

Yet in the early days the doors of Baserville society had stubbornly refused to budge for his wife. Diana may have changed her name and her hair stylist but they all knew she was still the poor girl from the trailer park and beneath their notice. Diana's application to join the Women's League was rejected out of hand.

Mark had come home to find his wife sprawled on the sofa in the darkened living room, curtains drawn against the world and tears streaking her face.

'You're letting the likes of them get you down?' His voice was gentle as he stroked her hair. 'It's gotta be the pregnancy hormones. This is not the Diana I married. And you know why I married you?'

She sniffed back her tears and turned to look at him, desperate for his soothing words.

'Because you're just like me, darling,' he told her. 'We have enough smarts and we know how to use them. The first time I saw you, do you know what I saw? I saw an Amazon, a fucking amazing Amazon of a woman. And I thought, I thought to myself, if I can have this woman by my side I can conquer anything. You have power like I've never seen in anyone but me.'

He hugged her and gave a small chuckle. 'Just you wait, in five years' time, no in three years' time, all those old bags will be hollering at our door, desperate to be included in your inner circle. I know you, and I know you can do anything you set your mind to. Diana, you make a difference.'

Coming back to the present, she found she was striding down the beach, racing the wind and the dogs, and feeling much better. Mark had been right, as he often was, and together they had made it to the top of the heap of Baserville society. She *had* made a difference there, look at the Animal Sanctuary she had founded. Entirely due to her own efforts, the greater Baserville area was the best place to be a stray dog or cat. People would

even drive a hundred miles to drop off their unwanted pets in this county, knowing they were giving them the greatest chance of life.

It felt good to remember that she made a difference wherever she went. She looked at her new
surroundings with a critical eye and another plan
began to form. Just a temporary plan, for it wasn't
her intention to live in this dowdy village for long.
But she would make her mark here, and in years
to come the villagers would remember her with
fondness for changing the face of their home.

After that restoring romp on the beach and endless games of catch into the ocean, Diana and her
dogs found themselves at Mrs. Hastings' doorstep.
Dear Mrs. Hastings, the rock in her life, the one
person who knew her better than her own, long-re-
jected mother. It was a beaming Diana, flushed
with love, to whom Mrs. Hastings opened her door.

'I've been thinking,' Diana said as she made
her way down the hall and into the comforting
warm kitchen, not noticing the scowl on her former
housekeeper's face.

She sprawled herself into the floral chintz comfy
chair. 'I'd love a cup of tea,' she told Mrs. Hastings.
Not that she even liked tea, not really, she'd kill
for a Starbucks coffee right then, but tea was the

quaint beverage Mrs. Hastings drank, so she was prepared to be amenable.

The dour woman thumped the kettle onto the old electric range, and made a kicking motion at the dogs under her feet. They missed her, truth be told. Diana was their mistress and they had great fun with her when she was around, but Mrs. Hastings was the being who kept the hearth warm and the food bowls filled. She was the constant in the lives of both the dogs and Diana.

'So I've been thinking,' Diana repeated as she munched on the butter cookies offered, never minding the crumbs. The dogs were happy to take care of those. 'What this village really needs is a draw for tourism. You know, we can get that beach front cleaned up, should only take a few man hours. It's a disgusting mess right now. And we can create a walk up to the falls – they are totally unknown, and people would love to have a destination.'

It might be called the 'Diana Quenton Walk', but really, it was a bit soon for that. And she would wait for the suggestion to come from the people in an organic sort of way. She knew how to nudge people in the right direction.

Mrs. Hastings hesitated with the kettle of boiling water. Perhaps the thought of throwing it over Diana crossed her mind, but she didn't act on it. 'I don't want tourists over-running the place,' Mrs. Hastings said in horror. 'I like my quiet village just as it is, thank you very much.'

'We also need some sort of tea-room, you have to cater to the walking crowd,' Diana looked over at her, speculation in her eyes. 'That might be just the thing for you, now you're out of a job.'

'Haven't had much of a chance to enjoy my retirement yet,' the other woman muttered. 'Thanks to you.' She poured the hot water into the old brown teapot, frowning as she did so.

'You really are the best cook I know,' Diana acknowledged, licking her fingers before she reached for another biscuit. 'This could be big.'

Mrs. Hastings left off with the tea and seized the broom, furiously sweeping up loose dog hair which already threatened to stick to the kitchen floor as the large mutts scratched their flanks and drooled with great abandon, so at home did they feel in her company.

Diana stopped and gazed around her with a critical eye. 'This would be perfect for the tea-room, but you could really do with a lick of paint in here,' she noted. 'It's looking a little run-down. I can pick the color for you, I know just the thing.'

She broke off as she became aware of Mrs. Hasting standing over her, broom held high and an unaccustomed color flushing her face.

'Get out!' the Scotswoman cried. 'Get out of my house and take those hounds with you! I'll not be having my peace interrupted with your blathering and your mess any longer.' She shook the broom for emphasis. 'There's the door – mind you don't slam it on your way out!'

Diana really had no choice but do what the good lady insisted. Hurt and rejected for the third time that day, she fled through the door with her tail between her legs and quickly over to her own cottage, dogs yelping at her heels.

Back in the safety of the cold house, finally she had to face it. The entire world had turned against Diana Quenton, and she had possibly had a hand in her own downfall.

'Am I that horrible?' She looked at the cats purring around her ankles, oblivious to her distress. 'You like me, don't you?' She sat heavily on the uncomfortable sofa. Celine and Mariah immediately vied for the lap, and she put her arms around both together. 'Nobody else does. Just my cats. And my dogs.'

With that she sat and cried out all the hurt and confusion building over the past two days, howling to herself till she fell into a deep slumber on the sofa, surrounded and comforted by the five warm bodies who still depended on her and loved her in their various ways.

And it was in this manner that Flanagan came upon her, having ascertained her new address earlier that morning via a phone call from Mrs. Hastings. The dogs, tuckered out by their long romps in the waves and happily snug around her body, hardly batted an eye between them when he entered the dwelling.

Flanagan looked down on the sleeping puddle of fur and human. If she could have seen the soft light in his gaze, she would have felt comforted and known herself to be well-regarded by at least one other person in this world, but alas she was snoring with the pets, the whistles and the rumbles from the sofa a musical and peaceful chorus.

He cleared his throat, and with that all awoke, first Cerberus and Outhros, the two hellish hound brothers, and then the divas and finally Diana herself.

She rubbed the sleep from eyes that were still reddened and swollen from her tears as she sat up.

'Have you come to tell me you hate me too?' she asked drearily when she realized who was there.

'You needn't have bothered, I'll just take it for granted. It's easier on me that way.'

She shushed the dogs and stood up, stretching as she did. She missed the appreciative glance from the tall man as he admired her form. Diana in sweater and jeans, with no makeup on her face and her hair in a messy simple pony-tail – well, this Diana was looking almost human.

'You were supposed to leave word of your new address,' he told her gruffly. 'We still have questions for you.'

She shrugged and rolled her eyes. 'Like I've got somewhere to run to? I don't even have my passport. You seized it, along with the rest of my life.'

He held out a paper coffee cup, at which her eyes widened. 'You brought me coffee?' He could almost swear that tears rose to her eyes before she took the cup and turned away.

'Didn't think there'd be much on offer here,' he said roughly in his deep rumbling voice.

'Good thinking on your part.'

He also passed her purse over. 'You'll be needing this,' he said. 'The credit cards and bank accounts won't work of course.'

Diana led the way to the kitchen, where the sun almost warmed the air.

'Why don't you turn the heating on?' he asked.

She looked around her, at a loss. 'Because I'm not sure where it is?'

There were no electric thermostats on the walls of the decrepit house, something she hadn't realized when she demanded Dan make her arrangements for the rental. There was, however, an old wood stove with logs stacked by it, and Flanagan soon had a roaring fire within.

'That's so much better,' Diana said, holding her hands to the blaze. 'Thank you.'

'As a matter of interest, how'd you swing the rental?' he asked. 'I know you're hurting financially...'

Diana stiffened. 'A... friend was good enough to help me out.' She silently rolled the word around in her mind. Friend. Dan had been a friend, for that short period of time. The money he loaned her seemed to her a very small amount, but perhaps it meant more to him. After all, look at the car he drove. She felt the discomfort of an unaccustomed twinge of guilt in the area where her heart lived.

'I need to ask you some more questions,' Flanagan began, keeping a careful eye on her for any reactions she might show. 'While I'm pretty sure you don't have anything to do with the money and Mark's disappearance, I want to go over some things again.'

She sat back and let the strong coffee revive her, answering the now familiar questions almost by rote. No, she didn't know where he went while she was in Paris; she thought it had been somewhere in Mexico or that part of the world. No, she had no inkling that he might be planning something, there was nothing in his behaviour to raise her suspicions. Of course, their paths rarely crossed, so there nothing new in that.

'Amaryllis...' Flanagan began, and Diana's hackles stood on end.

That bitch. She remembered the first time they'd met – Amaryllis was newly hired as Mark's PA and he'd brought her along to Rose's bash, the grand 'pool-warming' party to celebrate that gaudy half-Olympic size pool she'd just put in her back yard.

She didn't mind him bringing his secretaries everywhere he went – it was a necessary evil as Mark never stopped working. But this particular time had been different.

While Diana appeared to be a confident woman, she had one fear, and that was of deep water. She was scared to death to go in over her head, so she'd never learned to swim. Growing up on the wrong side of the trailer park, this rarely was an issue in her life before Mark, and even during their honeymoon on Aruba, her husband had not made a big deal of it, just went on in the water himself. Later, he had encouraged her to take swimming lessons, but she could never get the hang of floating so had given up.

But the day of Rose's bash with his new PA at his side, Mark had needled her, almost jeering her in public, pressuring her to get in the water and show everyone how well she could swim. She'd had to make up a story that she'd just got her hair touched up that day and couldn't possibly get it wet, and then spent the whole party feigning interest in Susie's scrapbooking efforts, while Mark and Amaryllis frolicked like dolphins in front of everyone.

She had no love for that woman.

'What about Amaryllis?'

CHAPTER TEN

'What about her?' she snarled. Diana was aware that Amaryllis usually accompanied her husband on all his business trips. Mark's secretary (or PA as she called herself more accurately, as she had not been hired for her secretarial skills) wasn't the sharpest knife in the drawer. However er she had other attributes, one of them being a former Victoria's Secret model, skinny little Barbie doll that she was.

'She's taken his disappearance very hard,' he noted.

'That woman prefers to take things hard,' Diana thought, only realizing she'd said the words out loud when she saw Flanagan's jaw drop. She pasted a sweet smile on her face, but Flanagan wasn't fooled. He gave her a small crooked grin.

'How close are they?' he asked. 'Apart from the obvious, of course.'

Diana shook her head. 'Don't tell me, she's vowing undying love for him? Heartbroken about his death?'

Flanagan lifted an eyebrow in acknowledgement.

'She'll live to find another sugar daddy,' Diana told him with absolute certainty. 'And if Mark did engineer his own disappearance, I doubt whether he would have brought her with him. She's too stupid. She's got a good nose for money, but she's hardly his intellectual equal.'

Diana and Mark had drifted apart over the years, but she knew they had once shared something real. He was a shithead, true, but one with a powerful mind. Diana was certain he would never have taken Amaryllis seriously, and that wasn't just jealousy speaking. 'Amaryllis would only be a hindrance to him right now.'

'She wasn't on the boat the morning he disappeared,' Flanagan told her. 'She said he'd arranged for her to have a special spa day as his early birthday present to her, and they were going to meet for a slap-up night out because he had a big surprise planned. That's what she said, anyway.'

That did sting a little, she had to admit. When was the last time Mark had gotten Diana a present to note any occasion? Well, one that she herself hadn't picked out and arranged to be delivered.

'By the way,' he continued in a casual tone. 'Amaryllis wants to be allowed into his home office. She says she wants to have a memento of him.'

'What – she wants his chequebook to remember him by?' Diana scoffed. 'What on earth could she ever want? There's nothing of him in his office. His golf trophies are kept in the city, as if anyone would be impressed by them, and at home, there's only copies of the framed photos of him and the famous people he's met.'

Mark must have made a point of keeping very little of himself in the Baserville house, she realized as she spoke. Even the old laptop, the one that had died just before he left for Mexico, even that object had been ordered to be removed and destroyed. And Mrs. Hastings was nothing if not thorough about removing useless items from her realm. She'd even tried to get rid of the cats, once.

A distant bell rang in the far reaches of her mind. The laptop. That was it. Computers were used to connect with the outside world. To make plans, arrangements for flights. And to explore other realms, possibilities, look for information on places to hide if you were planning to abscond with your neighbors' money. A laptop in your home where your PA wouldn't see your plans if you weren't planning to take her with you...

Would there be any evidence of Mark's plans on the old laptop? But it was gone surely, long gone, like this morning's dog hair in Mrs. Hastings' kitchen. Or was it? She needed to find out. Perhaps she should tell Flanagan.

Or perhaps not.

'So, speaking of that, what are the possibilities of returning to the house?' she asked. She tossed the question off lightly.

Flanagan noted the gleam in her eye. 'What exactly did you have in mind?'

'Oh,' she trilled with innocence. 'Just personal items. My make-up, for example, I'm feeling quite naked without it.'

She pursed her lips flirtatiously and attempted to bat her eyes at him. Unfortunately, her lids were still swollen from her crying jag and she couldn't carry off the bad imitation of a seductress at that moment.

'Perhaps some clothing?' She pressed on. 'I can't live in these cheap rags forever. I may need to go out in public at some point!'

'Make out a list of everything you need. We'll see what we can do.'

'Oh come off it!' she said, with a little of her old bossiness rising. 'It's my house. What do you think I'm going to do, steal the crown jewels?'

He narrowed his eyes as he looked at her. 'Your jewellery is off limits. That is presently being appraised.'

'What?'

'The money has to be returned to the investors some way,' he said. 'That's what happens when items are seized. Everything is being appraised and will be sold at auction. This shouldn't come as a surprise.'

Yet Diana felt as if he'd socked her in the stomach. Yes, she knew the house and its' contents had been seized, along with the cottage and the cars and all their investments, but she'd only seen this as a temporary situation, more like a hostage taking until the money was returned. This... this was more like a rape and pillage.

'You can't do this!' she squawked as she sat up straight. 'That's my *stuff*! It's *my* stuff. You have no right. We'll get the money back to you, I swear, if it's the last thing I do. Just leave all my things alone.'

Suspicion showed in his eyes and he pounced. 'How do you propose to do that?' he asked. 'What are you not telling me?'

Diana clamped her mouth shut. They stared each other down.

'You're not out of the water yet, Mrs. Quenton. Not by a long shot,' he said carefully. 'I suggest you be very open with me. We should not have secrets.'

He leaned forward menacingly and held his hand up, thumb and ring finger a mere inch apart. 'You are this far away from being incarcerated. I am the one person standing between you and jail. Do we have an understanding?'

Mutely, she nodded. This close to him, the spice of his scent wafted over her and she breathed in a little deeper to catch it.

Tell him about the laptop, a small voice inside her whispered. *Now is the time, quick.*

'I'm not hiding anything,' she denied, jutting her chin in the air.

He nodded slowly, his disbelief evident. 'We'll see about that,' Flanagan said as he rose to leave. 'Here's my card. Call me if you remember anything that might help the investigation.' He passed it to her directly, his hand almost caressing hers as the card changed hands, and all the time his eyes were hard on hers.

He had almost reached the door when he paused and turned back to her. 'I'm keeping a very close eye on you, Mrs. Quenton. Remember, I want to know where you are at all times.'

'I doubt if I'll be going far,' she retorted. 'Do you remember I have no money or credit cards? I'm stuck here, in this pit of a village. Mark has left me with nothing.'

Flanagan turned away, then stopped short and smacked his forehead in a theatrical way. 'That reminds me - how could I have forgotten?' He turned again, reaching into his inside jacket pocket. 'The safety deposit box contents.'

What? Mark had never believed in safety deposit boxes – he preferred to keep anything of importance under his own eye in the office safe. He wouldn't pay a bank to do what he felt he could do better.

Flanagan dangled the large white envelope between his two fingers. It gleamed dully, caught in a beam of the late afternoon sun breaking through the clouds. She could see it had been expertly slit open along the top and knew that Flanagan had already examined the contents, not even bothering to hide the evidence of his nosiness.

What would be so important that Mark would trust to a bank?

She grabbed for it but it danced out of her reach. 'Ah ha, not so fast,' he said. 'Do you have any idea what this is?'

Diana took a deep breath and stepped back, 'I'm not playing your games, Mr. Flanagan,' she said as she folded her arms and stared him in the eye. 'You obviously want me to have this. You can either give it to me or not.'

A light of respect showed in the smile he turned on her. He wasn't so unattractive, not really, his brown eyes with a hint of gold in them. Flanagan nodded and passed her the envelope.

'Mark's life insurance policy,' he said. 'All five million dollars' worth. To be paid out dependent on his death, natural or unnatural.'

Five million dollars. What she couldn't do with that money. The sun broke clear of the clouds, shining on Diana's blonde hair and her blue eyes sparkled in the light. 'Five million...' she whispered, then caught herself and her eyes hardened. 'What's the catch? Who... who is the beneficiary?'

'You are, Mrs. Quenton.' His tone was gentle, and she was too busy staring at the blank envelope to see the quizzical expression that flitted over his face.

'He left me five million dollars...' That son of a bitch. He stole her life from under her feet, had probably faked his own death while he ruined the lives of all those around him, yet had the foresight to leave her not totally broke. He had cared. She clutched the envelope to her breast, mixed emotions playing therein.

Suspicion won out. 'But... but the Feds will take this money on me, won't they?'

'No, he said. 'That's an interesting point about insurance payouts. If you get a good lawyer, they can argue this settlement is outside the period of confiscation, after the fact. It would be all yours.'

A dazed smile began to form on her face.

'Of course,' Flanagan said, clearing his throat. 'Of course, you getting the payout is dependent on proof of his death.'

'Proof? What kind of proof do they need? We can get the Mexican police report, they didn't hold much hope for his survival.'

'I don't think that'll cut it. You know insurance companies,' he said with a shrug. 'What would satisfy them enough to hand over that kind of money? His heart in a casket, or head on a silver platter? They want irrefutable proof, or you won't see a dime of it.'

He gave a cocky salute, then walked out the door with the confidence of a man whose plans were set in motion.

⋅♥⋅♥⋅♥⋅♥⋅♥⋅

For five million dollars, they would get proof of that shithead's death all right, even if Diana had to kill him with her bare hands to get it. She tore the policy from the white envelope. Yes, that was Mark's signature alright, signed three years ago almost to the date.

Three years ago. He'd been planning this move for that long. The documents Flanagan had shown her and Dan that first day, the ones with her own signature that made it seem as if she was in on the scam, that was three years ago also. Diana even remembered the day.

He had tossed down the papers lightly on the dining room table, and had a 'talk' about the need for her to be more involved in the business, that he could no longer do it on his own and needed her perspective. They needed to be partners again, like in the old days.

She'd been thrilled, fool that she was. Mark needed her again, and she had fallen for it without even bothering to read the bloody documents she was signing. Full of renewed confidence, Diana had even started planning for a quick getaway to Aruba, hopeful their romance could be re-kindled at the site of their honeymoon.

That plan had fallen through shortly thereafter, and she'd been so hurt she hadn't even remembered to ask what was the importance of those papers. What a fool! And here she was left holding the bag.

The insurance policy was a joke. The Mark she knew had never had any intentions of dying, and certainly would never have had a thought to those he left behind in the event of such an unnatural occurrence. What was the reason for this? She thought long and hard until finally a glimmer came to her.

How devious. He left the insurance policy to dangle in front of her like a carrot on a stick, enticing her with the idea of five million dollars so she would spend her time and energy trying to get it out of the insurance company and in so doing forgetting the larger picture, which was the portrait of Mark and the missing millions.

It wasn't till then that she remembered her purse lying on the kitchen table where she had left it. She lifted the soft leather of the Hermes bag to her face. It was warm against her skin and held a whiff of the perfume of her former life. She breathed in deeply and knew why she hadn't told Flanagan about the laptop.

For she needed to hold on to something, anything. She'd lost so much control over her life in the
past two days, was it three days? She'd lost track.
She needed to wrest some of that control back.
Through his actions, Mark had ripped everything
away from her, everything she held dear, everything which defined Diana Quenton to the outside
world. Even at this moment, FBI agents were going
through her very closet, fingering her lingerie and
putting a price on her life.

It was Mark's fault and she would get him back for
this. That's why she didn't tell Flanagan about the
laptop. Mark would pay, and justice would be all
hers. The five million dollar insurance policy? That
was peanuts, she was going for the whole shebang.

'Too bad, Mark,' she said. 'I'm on to you, and
I'm going to find you. And I'm going to make sure
you're finished for real.'

CHAPTER ELEVEN

The only problem was that Diana didn't have a clue how to go about wreaking her revenge. Financially, she had nothing, unless... She quickly poured the contents of her purse onto the sofa and checked through the wallet and all the pockets. Her passport had been returned to her, and aside from the loose change and a few hundred Euros from the aborted Paris trip, she also found hidden inside an inner pocket of the bag a roll of fifties, a thousand dollars' worth. Who knew she had so much on her at any one time? In fact she didn't even recall tucking away that much cash. That time in Rio? No, that was before this purse was purchased. Strange that Flanagan had allowed her to keep this large amount, but perhaps he'd missed it, tucked away as it was.

At any rate, she would not draw attention to this oversight. This money would help her find Mark. Somehow.

She shoved on her rubber boots and gave a piercing whistle. Cerberus and his brother immediately gave up their prime fireside seats to the cats in anticipation of another rollicking good time on the beach but alas, they were to be disappointed in that. Diana only had intentions of going as far as the village store, for she might not yet have a plan, but she knew she was hungry.

And as she walked, an idea did start to form loosely in her head, for Diana was always an organizer and a doer. Her plan went something like this. A) Get the laptop back from where Mrs. Hastings had consigned it to. B) Get it fixed. C) Figure out where Mark had gone through his browser history. D) Find him and make him give the money back. Yes, it was a loose plan, but she had utmost faith in herself. It had to work out.

But for all this it would help to have a partner in crime, as she had no vehicle. Her only options at this point were Mrs. Hastings or Dan, both of whom were not speaking to her at the moment. Diana ruled out Flanagan entirely, as he would only want to take control of the plan. She was on her own.

Unless she used the dollars to pay Dan back the money she owed him and guilted him into working with her. That might work.

Thinking was a hard business, as was walking, and hunger was setting in. There wasn't much of a selection in prepackaged food in the local store, but she did score the last dusty carton of potato leek soup. The dogs snuffled around the corners of the display cases, in the places where years of accumulated dirt had been shoved by infrequent moppings. It was a new and exciting world for them.

'I need to find some phone numbers,' she said to the woman behind the counter, who waved her over to an old pay phone half hidden behind a tall rack of cut-rate DVDs.

'Oh, they still make phone books,' Di said. 'I can't remember the last time I saw one.'

The store-keeper was already re-immersed in the soap opera playing loudly in the corner. So much for the friendliness of village stores, Diana thought to herself.

She was sure Dan had complained about the sub-urb his parents lived in, yesterday in the car while they searched for Mrs. Hastings. Ah yes, Middle Springs, that was it. Downey was his last name. She quickly looked down the list of D's, but the print was small and the store was ill-lit, and she could not pick out the words or numbers. The solution was easy – Diana ripped out the page and stuffed it into her pocket.

'Thank you!' she called cheerily as she left, but was pretty sure she was still being ignored.

.♥.♥.♥.♥.♥.

A light shone through the tiny window in Mrs. Hasting's door, and Diana paused. She clearly remembered instructing the housekeeper to get rid of the old laptop, and was pretty sure Mrs. Hasting's would have complied for that was one woman hated who clutter. If it had been sent out to the trash, Diana wouldn't have a hope in hell of getting it back. Perhaps, though, it hadn't made its way to the garbage. Perhaps it was still at her house. Her real house. In which case, she had every right to get it back.

And there was only one way to find out. Surely Mrs. Hastings would have gotten over her snit by now.

She made her way up Mrs. Hasting's path, followed by the dogs who barked with joy when they realized where they were.

'Mrs. H?' Diana called as she opened the front door. Cerberus pushed past her, followed by

Outhros the younger brother and they raced noisily down the hallway each wanting to be the first to greet their old friend, not having seen her since the morning.

'Bloody hell!' The clang of a pan dropping to the floor followed this exclamation.

'You're home, then?' Diana entered the kitchen.

The air smelled of freshly grilled sausages and fried potatoes, a heavenly scent except that Diana was vegetarian these days. The dogs weren't though, and they happily helped clean up the floor of the wayward sausages and grease.

'That was my supper!' Mrs. Hastings was still in a very bad temper after all.

'Well you can't eat it if it's been on the floor,' Diana pointed out. ''At least it's not being wasted.'

'It was in the pan before that lot came in and knocked it over.'

She might have a point, but Diana didn't have time to spend arguing it. Before she could ask her question, Mrs. Hastings continued on with her complaints.

'Can you not wash those poor creatures? They're stinking to high heavens.'

Without Mrs. Hastings' daily ministrations, the dogs were quickly reverting to their natural doggy state. Rolling in rotten seaweed and fish had hastened this deterioration, something which Diana did notice now it was pointed out. She sniffed the air tentatively. 'You might be right, they're getting a bit pongy. You can give them a bath, if you want. I think they miss you.''

'They reek! And I'm not your housekeeper anymore, so I'm not messing up my bath tub on their account again. Take them out of my house!'

'I just have a quick question.'

'Out!'

'Wait, wait. Just... the old laptop, what happened to that, after?'

Mrs. Hastings stopped in mid-squawk. Diana could have sworn her eyes shifted uncomfortably and a strange look washed over her features before she turned away.

'Which laptop would that be?'

'Mark's, remember? I asked you to toss it just before I left for Paris. He said it was broken and that he had no doubt you would dispose of it properly.'

'Well, then, I imagine it was disposed of,' Mrs. Hastings said to the dogs, refusing to meet Diana's eye.

'You don't sound very sure,' Diana said slowly. This behavior was not typical of her former housekeeper. As Diana had controlled the society of Baserville, so Mrs. Hastings had controlled everything to do with the house. If she'd been college educated, the woman might have majored in the finer points of garbage, compost, and recycling. 'What exactly did you do with it?'

'I can't remember everything I did at that house!' Mrs. Hastings changed the subject. 'It was bad enough keeping on top of the animals, let alone your mess too. Don't be bothering me, now. I've got to go and cook another batch of sausages.'

Diana hesitated.

'And no you can't have some,' Mrs. Hastings continued. 'You're vegetarian, and thank God I haven't to cook bloody lentils anymore. Now get out and take the hounds with you.'

Yet again Diana was evicted from Mrs. Hastings' cottage.

·♥·♥·♥·♥·♥·

Hands in her pockets, she thought hard as she walked back to her new house. Mrs. Hastings was on her mind. She'd never seen her act so strangely, so secretive... so guilty. As Keith had been Mark's conscience, so to speak, Mrs. Hastings had been hers for the past twenty years, always letting her know when she'd overstepped a mark, or needed to apologize to someone, send the twins birthday presents – all those things that smoothed the way and kept the other people in her life happy. Mrs. Hastings always told the truth, even if she was a little harsh sometimes.

And that was it.

Mrs. Hastings had been lying to her just then. And not being used to deception, the Scots woman was a terrible liar.

All of this pointed to one thing, in Diana's mind.

'Ah ha!' she cried out as she turned up her own garden path. '*Mrs. Hastings forgot to throw out the laptop!*' Her housekeeper had not wanted to admit she wasn't as thorough as she pretended to be, that she was imperfect and had neglected that duty. That she was, in fact, human.

The first obstacle in her plan was removed. The laptop was still in the house, and she would retrieve it tomorrow, even if it meant breaking in to her own home.

The next obstacle was easily overcome, too, Diana realized over her toast and instant coffee the next morning. She had no vehicle to take her to her mansion, and she had even less knowledge of public transport. But there was an old bicycle in the run-down shed attached to the house.

'I biked around the Netherlands on my fifteenth anniversary,' she boasted to the dogs. 'For hours and hours every day. I can do the five minutes to Baserville no problem.'

She had of course forgotten that while the Netherlands was a fairly flat landscape, the road from the coast up to Baserville was anything but. Also, the used bike was not a modern model built for racing or hills or even off-roading, but a simple old-fashioned type of bike older than herself. Diana ended up pushing the rusted machine much of the way.

During this long walk more than ever before, she felt the loneliness of her situation. She was a social creature at heart, even though she tended to drive away the people in her life as she stepped on them and insulted without cease, yet she also thrived on the company of others and needed them. This complexity of character might explain why people like Susie and Mrs. Hastings tolerated her. They sensed her need and were too soft-hearted to abandon her completely. Except when they were pushed too far.

She didn't feel sorry for herself for too long, for her natural exuberance returned as she moved in the fresh air. Although she did wish she'd taken the dogs for company, she began to enjoy the terrific exercise of the long uphill climb in the fall sunshine and she started to take notice of her surroundings.

The road levelled off as it entered the outskirts of Baserville, past the trailer park on one side and the horse stables on the other. Few cars passed her, but there seemed to be a preponderance of white sedans going back and forth. She climbed back on the bike as she reached a little used road which led to her enclave. It was important not to draw attention to herself and from this lane, she could easily get to the wooded area in the back of her own home. The wrought iron gates at her house's entrance were only at the front, for show.

Nobody was around on this fine day. This late in the season even the gardeners were finished with their tidying, and it was too chilly for anyone but the help to be out walking dogs. They wouldn't come back here anyway, it was private property, and her neighbors respected ownership. She just had to make sure she wasn't spotted by Rose next door as she lurked through the undergrowth.

There was very little evidence of a police presence around the grounds, Diana saw as she hauled herself out of the brambles. She left the bike behind the growth of bushes.

'I could have just walked up to the front door,' she muttered, but she wasn't too put out because this had been a fun adventure so far.

A basement window opened easily to her touch, she was horrified to note. 'Jesus, what the Feds don't get, our friendly neighborhood robbers will,' she said aloud. Diana realized she was talking to herself too much these days, it was a bad habit, and it might be an early warning sign of senility or something ghastly like that. This would be a lot more fun if there was someone to share it with. Susie would have... well, maybe not. Susie didn't really have much of a spark, did she? Susie would have made it less fun, worrying and twittering about getting caught doing something illegal. Susie wasn't actually that much fun at all, come to think of it. She just did what she was told, which was really boring.

But now Dan, he would be more useful in this kind of venture. He was a sidekick who had a brain and gave back as good as he got. She could laugh about their little spat now that she was in a better frame of mind. Sure, he needed a strong person like herself to give him direction but the kid had potential. She would get back in contact with him and pay him his money. Whatever he was mad at, like herself, he'd probably gotten over by now. Yes, she'd find him and continue this marvellous adventure.

At least Susie would have been able to squeeze into the window with no trouble. Diana suspected Dan would have had just as hard a time as she was having. The window was far too narrow for comfort, but if she just sucked in the belly a bit and pushed.... And she was in.

CHAPTER TWELVE

The basement was unexplored territory – this was Mrs. Hastings' realm, and Sam's when he was in gardener mode. Sure was a tidy space, she thought to herself as she looked around. The concrete walls and floors were painted a uniform gray and the entire space was open and, after checking all the numerous cupboards, Diana had to conclude the laptop was not down here.

Where would Mrs. Hasting have stored the old laptop before disposing of it?

Perhaps it had never left Mark's office, but if that was the case, the police would definitely have removed it already and she was going to be out of luck. Going up the basement steps, she paused at the burglar alarm by the back door. There were no lights blinking – it hadn't been activated. So windows unlocked, no alarm on – how inefficient were these FBI guys anyway? Five days ago she would have been loud in her condemnation of such lackadaisical actions, but today Diana the newly born criminal blessed her luck.

She checked in Mark's study just in case, but no laptop there. He kept very little personal stuff here in their house, except for his shrine of photos of him with famous people. He'd had many copies made of each, and liked to hand them out to friends and clients as Christmas presents, especially the one of Mother Theresa. The saint was in earnest conversation with a local bishop, with Mark photo-bombing the pair, popping his head up between them in an idiotic grin. God knows how he'd wormed his way into that meeting, it was probably taken right before he was ejected from the room. She gave a cynical laugh.

The laptop wasn't in the library, the living room, not even the kitchen or pantry or the little room Mrs. Hastings called her sitting room. Perhaps Diana had read the housekeeper wrong. If the Feds hadn't removed the laptop from Mark's desk where he left it, then Mrs. Hastings must have disposed of it after all.

It wasn't upstairs either, in Mark's bedroom or his dressing room. Disappointing, yes, but she lingered in her own roomy walk-in closet, fingering the silks and velvets hanging there. Surely they wouldn't miss one or two items? These were, after all, her personal items of clothing. Lingerie didn't take up too much space, and it's not like anyone would buy used underwear at an auction. Maybe just enough items to fill that small Keep-all....

She settled on a slightly larger piece of luggage, the Louis Vuitton carry-on with the tasteful brown and gold monograms that Mrs. Hastings had not had a chance to unpack after her return from Paris, and she threw all the dirty clothes in it to the floor.

'Let Flanagan deal with the laundry, if he insists on taking all my stuff,' she said with a bitter laugh. She replaced the items with clean ones.

Before she left, she paused at her desk as the makings of an idea passed through her mind. Perhaps all was not yet lost for her temporary financial situation. If Susie wouldn't help her, she could help herself. How hard would it be to forge her signature anyway? She grabbed the folder of trust papers and stuffed them in the outer pocket.

The zipper wouldn't go over the fancy cheque-book with its hard edges, so she hauled it out again and ripped out a few cheques for her use, then tossed it back into her desk drawer. Who used cheques these days anyway? So quickly things become archaic. Diana had never even seen a chequebook before she met Mark. Her mother had preferred to work for cash when there was work available, so as not to mess up the Social Security payments, and all of the Trust's financial work was done on-line these days, she was pretty sure.

Hopefully her cheque with Susie's forged signature would pass.

Back down in the basement, Diana realized she may have been a bit too greedy, for although the luggage fit easily into the First Class lockers on a jet, the case was almost the exact size of the basement window and threatened to remain stuck, no matter how she pushed and pulled and tugged.

One final heave though, and it was wrested from her hands, as it flew through the window and landed upright outside. No-one was more surprised than Diana.

'Damnit, woman, why didn't you just use the back door?'

The pair of sturdy black boots in the window was joined by Flanagan's handsome face as he bent down to glare at her through the open window.

'You do know you're trespassing?'

'Well, help get me out of here then,' she said. And with some more pushing and pulling, between the two they got her out of the narrow space. She brushed off her jeans, then grabbed the suitcase and held it behind her, as if trying to hide it.

'I told you I'd be watching you,' he said. 'Don't look so surprised.' He looked down at the suitcase behind her legs. 'And what you got hiding in there?'

'Just some clothes. Winter's coming, you know!'

'You got a fur coat stuffed in there?'

'No.'

'Flannel nighties?'

'Don't be ridiculous.' Diana drew herself up to her full height and put on her imperious face, a trick which usually worked to subdue any society ladies who were getting out of hand. It didn't work with Flanagan, though. He stepped closer and looked down at her, forcing her to look up if she wanted to keep the upper hand.

She met his glare head on. 'You can give me a ride back to the village, since you're here.'

'Not before I have a look through that fine piece of Louis Vuitton,' he said. 'And see what's caused you to break and enter.' He held out his hand.

'It's raining,' she said. It was true, cold moisture was coming down, a harbinger of the snow which would surely arrive in the not too distant future. 'The silks will be ruined.'

He reached his arms around her, almost but not quite touching her in the big woolly sweater. 'You want to give it to me, or you want me to take it?' Flanagan was almost playful. The rumbling in his voice reverberated through her. All of a sudden the day was warm again. If she were nearing menopause she could have sworn she was having a hot flash, and she could feel a hot blush starting below the sweater from her ample breasts and rising.

Diana stepped out of his reach, hoping he didn't misinterpret the flush rising through her face. 'Take it then, look for yourself,' she said as she held it out in front of her. 'Don't worry, I'm not hiding anything valuable.' The papers for the Spay and Neuter Trust were in the cleverly concealed zippered outside pocket. She would not be able to explain the presence of those documents easily, true, so she stuck out her chin in defiance.

'I know that look on your face,' Flanagan said, narrowing his eyes. 'As my children are well aware, you can't hide deceit from me.'

He had kids? Now that was a surprise. Poor sods, she thought, conveniently forgetting her own half-hearted attempts at mothering.

Flanagan made her open the carry-on luggage right there by the bushes. She held her breath as he inspected it carefully, fingering the new Dior black silk suit, and her shoes, making a mental inventory of each item until he came to the matching underwear and bra confections. His fingers lightly brushed the lace and satin as if considering, before he closed the case.

'Okay, you're clear,' he said. He sounded disappointed. 'I'll let this pass.'

'I told you so,' she muttered as she bent to do up the zipper.

'Now, let's get that bike of yours into the trunk, and I'll give you a ride down the hill.'

'How did you know how I got here?' Diana hauled the ancient bicycle out of the brambles where she'd hidden it and followed him out the back gate. He waited by a white sedan.

'Oh,' she said. 'That was you. I thought there were just a lot of white cars in the area.'

'You don't notice very much do you?' he asked, loading the bike then shutting the trunk lid.

CHAPTER THIRTEEN

She didn't invite him in, but trundled the carry-on and bike up past her rickety fence with a curt word of thanks, and waited to hear his car drive away before she let herself in the door.

Well that wasn't such a waste of time, she thought as she opened the case and drew out her beautiful clothes and shoes. There were only iron wire hangers available in the rental house, so she folded everything lovingly away into the old wooden bureau in the upstairs bedroom overlooking the ocean. The case she stored into the empty closet of the room. Diana looked at it fondly. The Louis Vuitton had accompanied her on all her trips over the past twenty years, and it still looked as good as new. That was quality for you. If things got too rough, she could always sell it, although it would feel like selling off a member of her family.

She wasn't any closer to getting that laptop, though. She sat on her sofa in thought, the dogs snuffling around her, hoping to remind her how much she enjoyed a good romp on the beach. They were out of luck.

'I need to talk with Mrs. Hastings again,' she told the dogs. 'And I don't think she wants you guys in her house. You got a very chilly reception yesterday, remember.'

Flanagan had implied that she couldn't see beyond the nose on her face, but he was wrong. She knew her ex-housekeeper well enough to have seen that Mrs. Hastings was hiding something yesterday, she knew that, and she knew it was something to do with Mark's computer. And if it wasn't that she'd neglected her duty by not disposing of the laptop, then, she had disposed of it, but not necessarily in the expected manner.

Would Mrs. Hastings have stolen the laptop for her personal use?

Diana tried and tried, but she couldn't fit that into her image of the woman. Why, if she'd wanted an old broken computer (which she didn't – she herself had used the efficient stream-lined one in the woman's parlor the other day) well, Mrs. Hastings would have outright told her she was taking it, and used the opportunity to scold her for wastefully throwing away a perfectly good piece of equipment. That's what Mrs. Hastings would have done.

But why, oh why had she looked so shifty? Diana had to get to the bottom of this, so she marched down the road without the dogs and knocked at the front door before she opened it. She was slowly learning consideration for other people.

'I am so sorry to bother you again,' she began as she walked down the short hall, planning to snow her prey with apologies and thus disarm her before Mrs. H could throw her out.

There was that look of guilt on Mrs. Hasting's face again, she realized, as she took in the scene before her. And well she should look guilty, too, because her companion was the loathsome Dan, and the pair were sitting at the oak table drinking tea out of fine china cups and saucers. And looking quite conspiratorial while they were about it.

'What's going on?' Diana looked at the pair so cozily huddled over a plate of scones, Dan with embarrassment written all over his face, but only because she caught them at it. A horrible feeling of exclusion came upon her, that feeling that had haunted her all her life beginning in high school when the popular and rich girls had decided she wasn't good enough for them. She hadn't felt that way for a long, long time, but it had left a scar which still motivated her throughout her adult life. 'Dan, what are you doing here?'

And why is the best china out for you, but never for me?

Dan was the first to speak. He hurriedly stood up. 'Diana!' he said. 'We were just... talking about you.' He quickly looked at Mrs. Hastings for back-up.

The guilt quickly changed to a glower on her face. 'We were indeed,' she began.

'And saying why don't we invite Diana to join us,' he cut through, his middle-class niceness attempting to smooth the situation and prevent hurt feelings. 'Right?'

'No, we weren't,' the ex-housekeeper said, shaking her head. 'We weren't saying anything of the kind.'

Diana slumped into the chair across from Dan.

'Dan here was wondering how he was going to get his money from you, the money you owe him.'

Dan, his face very red, attempted to brush this aside. 'It's okay, no rush. I just happened to mention that there was an amount outstanding, such a small amount really...'

'Five hundred dollars is no small amount,' Mrs. Hastings retorted crisply.

'Oh, right!' Diana said, happy surprise in her voice. 'I have the money here.' She opened her purse. 'How much was it exactly?'

Dan's face turned even redder when he saw the thick roll of fifties. 'Really? How'd you get that much money?' He clapped his hand over his mouth once he realized what he'd said.

'Oh, Flanagan gave me my purse back,' she said. 'I had no idea I carried that much cash.' She quickly counted out six hundred. Mrs. Hastings intercepted the wad and carefully counted each bill before passing it on to Dan.

'There's money for gas there too because you've been driving me around so much,' Diana said, casting a smug look at her former housekeeper. And extra cash might help him agree to drive her again, she felt pretty sure.

'Thanks,' Dan said, still bemused as he carefully placed the money into his wallet.

'Now,' Diana said, looking at them both in turn, then resting her gaze again on Mrs. Hastings. That generosity had bought her the upper hand in this little group and she was going to make full use of it. 'The laptop.'

If squirming uncomfortably was in her nature, Mrs. Hastings would be twisting in her chair right now. But Mrs. Hastings preferred upright honesty in all matters, so there was relief in her voice as she confessed. 'I gave it to Sam,' she said.

'Who's Sam?' Dan asked.

'You didn't want it,' she pointed out. 'To you and Mark, it was a broken piece of rubbish. To Sam, it was worth a lot of money saved, because he has the knowhow to fix it and he needed a new computer.'

Diana stared at her, not knowing whether to be ecstatic or annoyed. The trouble she could have been saved, if only she had known of this, but now it was within reach. 'How do I find Sam?'

'You'll not be asking him to pay for it,' Mrs. Hastings scolded her. 'I know you, you're all about money, especially when it's someone else's.'

'Who's Sam?' Dan asked again.

'With him out of a job thanks to your husband's doings, and a new bairn and all.'

'I don't want money from him! Jesus, what do you take me for?'

'The least you can do is let him have an old laptop that you don't want anymore.'

'He can have the stupid thing!' Diana stormed. 'And if he's fixed it, all the better. Come on, we need to go there. Now!' She stood up and looked expectantly at the others. 'Who's going to drive?'

'Who is Sam, and where does he live?' Dan asked Mrs. Hastings.

'Dan will drive,' Mrs. Hastings decided. 'I believe he's parked in the back lane.'

He had indeed parked behind Mrs. Hastings' house, not wanting his car to be spotted by Diana as he conferred with Mrs. Hastings about how he could get his money back. They all climbed in and drove down the old utility lane hidden behind trees and then out on to the coastal road.

CHAPTER FOURTEEN

Under Mrs. Hastings' direction, they went back up the hill and turned into the trailer park. This was not just any trailer park – it was the very same place Diana (or Debbie as she was then) had spent her formative years. Her heart sank as they drove down the familiar roads, and she tried to keep herself low in the passenger seat. She was pretty sure she still had siblings living around here even though they'd had no contact for years. It was a stark reminder that she hadn't come so very far in her life, after all.

They drew up before a tidy double-wide trailer, a vintage Volvo station wagon parked in the drive. Two white plastic chairs and a matching table sat on the tiny front lawn. The landscaping was minimal but pleasing with native shrubs dug up from the nearby woods.

It was a far cry from the decrepitude Diana had grown up in. Sam lived in the west end of the park which had always been a step up, socially, from the eastern end. Yet she still pulled a scarf over her hair as she exited the car and donned her sunglasses despite the drizzling rain. Mrs. Hastings nodded knowingly as their eyes met.

'Oh, shut it,' Diana muttered to her.

Sam came to the door, a baby on his hip. He was a gangly man in his early thirties, his brown hair in waves that crowned his intelligent face, and he wore a ready smile for Mrs. Hastings which faltered when he recognized Diana behind her disguise. She took off her sunglasses. Funny, she'd never noticed he had such warm brown eyes. But then again, she rarely saw his face from her perch in the back seat of the Mercedes.

'Sam, this is Dan. He's helping Mrs. Quenton,' Mrs. Hastings explained the lawyer's presence.

'Not in a legal capacity, of course,' Dan interjected.

The baby gurgled when she saw the Scots woman.

'Ooh, my little Amelia, how she's grown,' Mrs. Hastings cooed. 'Let me take her. Come to Aunty Fiona, then, my darling lass.'

Diana started in surprise to learn Mrs. Hastings' first name. Of course she'd known the woman had a name, everyone had a name or two, but it had never crossed her mind to wonder what hers might be. This was turning out to be a day of firsts for her.

Anyway, all this baby talk was getting on her nerves for there was a mission that needed to be completed. She couldn't contain herself as the talk droned on and on about the milestones reached since Mrs. Hastings had last seen the child the previous week, and the cute things the child had done. It was a baby for God's sake, it can't have been doing that much. She let out a huff of impatience.

'Would you like to hold her?' Mrs. Hastings turned to Diana, putting the child in her arms before she could object.

Of course she didn't want to hold the child, Amelia had nothing to do with her mission. Diana just wanted to get on with the task at hand.

And then Amelia smiled at her, and the baby goodness quite melted her heart.

'Oh,' Diana said. 'Oh, she's beautiful. She's.... she's cuter than a kitten.'

Her memory strayed to the days when the twins were this little, so perfect and sweet, and all she had wanted to do was mother them and love them and hold them forever. What had happened to those days? Where had she lost them?

The baby gurgled and emitted a large belch. Diana hastily passed the child on to Dan, who looked like he'd been given a hot potato.

'The laptop,' Diana began immediately, unwrapping the scarf, turning in time to see the stricken look in Sam's eyes at her words. She had the uncomfortable feeling of being accused of being a nastier person than she felt she was. 'No, I don't want it back, alright?'

'It's true,' Mrs. Hastings told him, nodding. 'She just needs it for... what *do* you need the laptop for?'

Diana looked around at the faces all directed towards her. She realized she owed them all an explanation. At that same moment too, it occurred to her she might need a team. And as none of these three had anything better to do, this could work out well for her.

She indicated they should all take a seat at the small formica-topped table. Dan hastily gave the baby back to the father before sitting as Diana began to explain her plan with regards to the laptop.

'I think you'd better tell Sam what's happening first,' Mrs. Hastings interrupted her. 'All he knows is that he's out of a job. He deserves to know what's going on, and you're probably going to need his help. You're useless with the computers.'

'I know my way around computers!' Diana objected, then thought again and graciously conceded.
'But perhaps you're right. Sam may know more
about this than me.'

'Sam, you're aware that all the money Mark invested has disappeared, along with Mark,' Diana
began.

He nodded. 'It's all over FaceBook. There's even
a page set up for the people who lost their money.'

She winced. No doubt Rose had a hand in that.
'Right. Well, at first it was thought that Mark had
died down in Mexico,' she said. 'And then it surfaced that the money everyone invested had disappeared.'

Diana looked around the table. 'It's pretty certain
that Mark engineered the whole thing,' she said.
'And I want to find him, and get the money back.'

'The FBI is looking for him,' Dan pointed out.

'And I think they'd be far more likely to find him
with their resources,' Mrs. Hastings added. 'Why
don't you just let them do it?'

Diana paused, and looked at each one of them
again in turn and spoke carefully. 'This is personal.
Mark took everything from me. My home, my place
in society, my security – everything we'd built up
together over the years. Sam, Mrs. Hastings – he
took your jobs.' She didn't mention the insurance

policy that required proof of Mark's death – that was nobody else's business.

The tiny kitchen was quiet. Even Amelia was wide-eyed and raptly looking at Diana, back in her father's arms.

'And how about the animals?' she continued. 'No-one is going to support the clinic now – I know that. No matter how good a cause it is, the whole set-up is tainted with the Quenton name, and all the work that's been done is for nothing. By his actions, Mark has single-handedly ruined the sanctuary!'

She looked down at the table and saw that her own fists were clenched tightly. She willed them to relax and watched as they uncurled. 'And because of this, I want to return my name, I want to pay back all the people he stole from, I want to keep on helping the animals. And... I want revenge.' Diana looked up at the others again almost shyly, uncertain of how they would respond. She wasn't used to baring her heart.

Dan had a glimmer of a smile dancing behind his beard and was the first to speak. 'Social justice. I can get on board with that.'

'This has the makings of a great story,' Sam said, excitement in his voice. 'Can I use this? And hey

– if you find him, can I write the account? We can negotiate movie rights!'

'You can do that,' Diana said generously. 'We'll discuss royalties later.'

Only Mrs. Hastings put a damper on Diana's mood.

'I'm quite happy in my retirement,' she said with a sniff. 'No more dogs and cats and mud and fur and keeping that behemoth house in order. Mark did me a favor, if anything. I say let him stay where he is, and good luck to him.'

Diana gave her a measured look. 'You really want to let him get away with this mess he's created?' she asked her. 'You're not itching to tidy it all up, put everything in its proper place?'

Mrs. Hastings cocked her head and gave it a second thought. A small smile lit her face. 'Oh, go on then. Count me in.'

CHAPTER FIFTEEN

'But just how do you propose going about finding Mark?' Dan argued. 'The FBI have the resources for this job. You really should let them do it.' No matter how hard the young lawyer tried, sometimes he just couldn't escape his middle-class worries.

Diana brushed the objection aside. 'I have one advantage they don't,' she said. 'I know Mark better than anyone else does. I know the deviousness of his mind. And best of all, I know what choices he would make, so that will narrow down my search a lot.'

She cut Dan off just as he opened his mouth to ask the question. 'I can't know what he's chosen, until I find out what choices he had to choose from.'

'So the laptop?' Sam asked. 'You think this will help.'

Diana nodded. 'It's the last one he was using before he disappeared, unless there's a computer in his city office. But the FBI will already have appropriated that one.'

Sam nodded. 'Yes, any web sites he visited will show up in his browser history,' he said. 'Unless of course, he erased the history. But that's no problem, really.'

Diana paused. 'You can find deleted history?'

'With a click of a button.'

'Oh. I didn't know that.'

'Cheer up,' Sam said. 'I can get around it. Nothing really disappears on the internet or on a computer, not if you know how to look.'

Now Diana beamed. 'Great. Let's get started.'

With one hand to steady Amelia, Sam reached behind and brought out the laptop and laid it on the table. It had been top of the line when it was new, but that was at least five years ago. The black leather was scuffed with dust ground into the various scratches on the surface and it no longer looked like something a man of Mark Quenton's financial stature would use, except for the gilt initials pasted on the top.

'Wait a minute,' Dan objected. 'There's something bothering me about this. Why are you so sure there's anything on this laptop? It doesn't look like it's been used for years. Perhaps it would be a waste of Sam's time to go hunting through the guts of this.'

Diana smiled in triumph. 'And that, my friends, is the reason I'm the person to lead the search for Mark,' she said. 'You see, Mark specifically requested that this laptop be disposed of. *Properly*, he said.'

She turned to look at Mrs. Hastings. 'Does that sound like something Mark has ever done before?'

'God no,' the Scots woman said. 'He doesn't even bother flushing the toilet.'

Sam's face blanched. Amelia giggled.

'Too much information,' Dan murmured.

'I have to go through his socks and underwear every six months and remove the ones with holes in them,' Mrs. Hastings continued. 'If he's finished with a thing, he just leaves it where it is and expects someone else to deal with it.'

'Exactly my point,' Diana said. 'So why was he so hell-bent on getting rid of this lap-top? And why did he ask me to make sure Mrs. Hastings disposed of it?'

'Because he wanted to make sure it was gone,' Sam said, excited. 'He expected her to bring it to the electronics recycling, or at least throw it in the garbage.' Amelia was beginning to fuss, so he jiggled her on his lap.

'That's right, I am very efficient at disposing of unwanted items,' Mrs. Hastings interjected. 'God knows the place would be piled high if it wasn't for me.'

'So he wanted to make sure it was gone,' Diana said. 'Which can only mean that he had something to hide.'

By now Sam had opened the laptop and was busy clicking keys. 'You know, I've already gotten into the guts of this, and changed it over for my own use. It seems to be working fine alright,' he said. 'But to get into Mark's account... any idea what his password might be?'

'Try his own name,' Diana suggested. 'That's usually his go-to password.'

Sam tried that one, and various others that Diana could think of, but nothing opened the screen.

'Can't you just hack into it?' Diana burst out finally. She hated to see her good ideas fail and for such a simple reason. 'You're a geek, this shouldn't be a problem.'

'There's got to be another combination,' Sam retorted. 'If you know him so well, you should be able to come up with it.'

Amelia was by now starting to be a little cranky and voicing her discomfort.

'Hush, hush, my darling girl,' Mrs. Hastings crooned as she reached over to take the child into her arms. 'Ooh, look, she's talking. What a clever wee thing.'

'Am-ma!' The baby was showing a fine set of lungs.

'Och, she knows her own name.'

Diana stared at the child, her face slowly draining of color.

'Oh, no,' she said. 'He wouldn't.'

Dan was the first to notice. 'Wouldn't what?'

Diana's mouth was set in a grim line. 'Try it,' she said to Sam. 'Try... her name.'

'Amelia?' He looked doubtful.

'No, course not! That slut. Amaryllis. Try that.'

A series of keyboard clicks and the Windows screen gave its jaunty notes to indicate success. All eyes turned to Diana and apprehension was thick in the air.

She slowly let out her breath. 'Alright. Let's get this bastard.'

♥ · ♥ · ♥ · ♥ · ♥

It was surprisingly easy to track Mark's movements from his browser history, almost as if he'd laid a trail of neon breadcrumbs into the deep dark woods.

'Bogota!' Dan said. 'That's in Colombia.' They were all looking over Sam's shoulder by now. The blue sky and sunlit buildings on the screen contrasted to the dreary cold outside in the trailer park.

'And this.... this would be his hotel,' Sam said.

'The W Hotel Bogota,' Diana said. She had a sour look on her face. 'Only the best, of course.'

Sam hesitated. 'Want me to see if I can hack his email?'

'Oh, yeah,' Diana said. 'I want everything.' She drew out the last word, savoring it. 'Try his g-mail. The Feds would already have gotten to his work account.'

The screen filled with the airline and hotel confirmations. It appeared that Mark had booked the Super Wow Suite at the most expensive hotel in Bogota. How absolutely tacky.

'So...' Dan said, looking over at Diana. 'What now?'

I will go to Colombia. I will rip him limb to limb. And then I will set fire to Amaryllis and throw her from that pent-house suite.

Diana quite surprised herself by the depth of her feeling at that moment. Anything that her and her husband had shared was long since dead, and she'd known about his other women for years, so this should come as no shock. What really hurt, what was really tearing her apart was his use of his girlfriend's name as his password. Mark had never had a shred of romance in him, not even in the early days of their marriage. Theirs had been a passion based on mutual ambition and recognition of kindred spirits. That Mark could have a heart, and that he would waste it on... her, that skinny bitch, that was just cruel beyond comprehension. Much as she hated him, she had still respected their equal footing. But the events of the past few days had changed everything in her life.

Or maybe Diana was finally waking up.

·♥·♥·♥·♥·♥·

The party didn't last too long after that. Diana needed to be alone with her thoughts to formulate a plan. She took the laptop with her, for this could be construed as evidence by Flanagan and she didn't want any of her friends to get in trouble with the law on her behalf.

The dogs needed a romp, and she needed a good long think in the strong ocean breeze, so the three set off along the shore.

She had her passport, and now she needed enough money to get to Bogota. There was only four hundred dollars left in cash, and even combined with the euros, this was not enough to get her there. Could you even buy airline tickets with cash in these days of suspicion and terrorism? She'd deal with that later. And what she was going to do once she got to Colombia, she couldn't yet see. But as Diana had known all her life, once you have enough money, everything else falls into place.

The trust fund was her only option. She needed to borrow from that.

Susie's cooperation was out of the question, even if Diana could wrest the silly idiot away from Rose's influence. She used to be so easy to get along with, back when Diana was the queen of Baserville. The only option she had was to forge her former friend's signature. Susie was forcing her to commit a criminal act.

Diana Quenton, nee Debbie Sears, had been accused of being many things in her forty-five years on earth, and many of these weren't very nice, yet unfortunately they were often accurate. However, no one had ever had cause to accuse her of anything illegal. Oh, sure she bent the rules sometimes, but these were either her own rules or else they were stupid rules which didn't suit her purpose. Not actual laws, though, never anything actually illegal. This was a line she'd never crossed before.

And now she was considering forgery in order to steal from the very ones who needed her most. She only needed Susie's signature – she'd given her friend that authority when the Trust was set up, for Diana herself couldn't be bothered with the daily minutia of the financial side. She'd known full well Susie would never abuse it for the woman didn't have a spark of imagination in her skull.

'No, not steal!' she told the dogs. 'I'm just borrowing. It's a temporary measure. The animals would do the same for me!'

And Diana vowed she would only take as much as she needed to get her down to Bogota. How long would it take her to route out Mark? Was he still there in the hotel? He had tons of money so he could probably live there for the rest of his life if he chose.

It was the only clue she had, there were no other leads. She had her passport. She had to figure out how to buy the ticket online, as every travel agent between here and the city would know her name and turn her in.

Which brought her to the next set of problems. In order to buy a ticket on-line, a credit card was needed. How was she to transfer the funds from the Trust to a credit card? All hers were cancelled of course, or she wouldn't have this problem in the first place. Come to that, how was she even going to transfer the funds? Her bank would never release money to her. The bank manager had been one of Mark's clients.

It was to Diana's credit that she didn't want to involve any of her new-found friends in her scheme. The whole thing smacked of illegality even if her intentions were good, and it wasn't fair to taint them with her crimes. Too bad she didn't have any choice. She just had to figure out which one of them had the least to lose.

'Okay, Dan, new plan,' she said on the phone. 'Come over here. I need your help.'

CHAPTER SIXTEEN

Special Agent Flanagan of the FBI hated only one thing more than rich and entitled people. He hated bosses who didn't trust his brilliance. He liked to think of himself as a bit of a lone wolf. Unconventional in his methods, he always got results, but only if he was left alone to do it his way. That was the real reason he'd left the Marines, but he didn't like to spread that information around because it made him seem flakey to the people that mattered. But he knew his own mind, and he'd learned to trust his instincts and didn't like having to explain himself before the results happened. So far, the FBI had suited him just fine.

So when the newly appointed Deputy Assistant Director of the Criminal Investigation Division (Special Operations) Hillier ordered him into her office for an update on the Quenton case, he cursed quietly under his breath. He didn't have time for this. Hillier, or he should say Dr. Hillier, for she held a PhD in Criminal Investigative Psychology, had sailed up through the ranks on the wings of her formal education but with little real experience or understanding of the human psyche, before being dumped into her present position from which she was unlikely to leave, not having the skills to move upward and being too loath to take a pay cut to take work that suited her talents better.

'Ma'am,' he said, presenting himself at her door.

The Deputy Assistant waved him into the room without looking up and proceeded to ignore him for a full three minutes as she continued to read the papers in front of her. He could hear the rustle of her starched blouse as her button nose followed the words on the page. The top of her head showed a crisp straight parting of mousey-brown hair which hung dead straight.

There was no doubt in his mind that she was trying to intimidate him and show him she was boss – he'd used this tactic himself on numerous occasions. What she was succeeding in was pissing him off royally, but he continued to stand at ease before her desk.

Finally Hillier looked up. 'Have a seat, Flanagan,' she said. 'No need to loom over me.'

He waited as she shuffled the papers on her desk into a neat pile to the right. That task completed, she folded her hands in front of her and looked at him with a moue of distaste on her mouth.

'Diana Quenton,' she began.

Here it came. He couldn't help but let out a silent huff of air, frustrated at the time he would have to spend arguing his case and the reasons for every action.

'Diana Quenton,' Hillier repeated. 'You had her. Why isn't she still locked up?'

'Ma'am,' he said, to acknowledge her superior rank before dumbing down his explanation. He was still certain that Diana was her husband's accomplice in every way, but that would require a long and convoluted explanation to his boss. It was easier to stick with the story he'd given Diana. 'After thorough questioning of the lady, it is my belief that Mrs. Quenton played no part in her husband's disappearance.'

'So?' He could hear the eye-roll implicit in his boss's voice. 'As per Section 145, we need to keep her in custody. All the better if she's innocent (which I truly doubt) because then we have a chance that Mark Quenton may return, in order to free her.'

This was so far off in left field that Flanagan was left momentarily speechless. Hillier had read the transcripts of the interview and the field notes, and had an advanced degree in psychology, yet had not picked up on the supposed enmity between the husband and wife. He himself was confident that Diana would be joining her spouse shortly and would lead him right to the thief. He quickly regrouped and mustered false enthusiasm in his voice.

'That's exactly my plan! But if she's locked up in security, he would never be able to reach her,' he explained, his eyes wide with sincerity.

'Oh.' Hillier chewed on this for a moment before she could follow the train of thought. 'Right. We need to leave her out in the open, so he can contact her.'

'I agree,' Flanagan said, nodding slowly. 'So we can quietly keep a close eye on her and nab him when he shows up.'

She put her head to one side and her finger to her lip, deep in thought. 'That might work,' she said. 'But it's cheaper to leave her inside. How many man hours are you talking?'

Always the budget. How did she expect to catch criminals and right wrongs if she let the departmental finances dictate their actions? He scratched his head and pretended to think.

'Well... How about if we only use my team?' he asked, inwardly loathing the fact that he had to spell things out for her. 'They're all on salary anyway, and there's not a lot else to occupy them at the moment. And Quenton is a pretty big fish, remember. The boss guys at HQ will be mighty happy to see this settled.'

This brought a small smile to her face. The combination of not stressing the budget further along with the prospect of scoring brownie points with her bosses appealed to her.

'Okay,' she said, nodding with satisfaction. 'You get on that, then.'

As he was leaving, he paused at the door.

'Perhaps given a long enough leash, Diana Quenton may even lead us right to her husband,' he threw out, as if it were an afterthought.

'Excellent thinking,' Hillier agreed, already turning back to her paperwork before her mind registered his words. 'Wait! Just how long a leash are you talking about? I'm not okaying travel costs!'

But Flanagan was gone, out of sight thus officially out of earshot.

·♥·♥·♥·♥·♥·

It didn't take Dan long to speed down to the village. He was dubious at first, and then downright negative as the details of the plan were revealed.

'No, no, no,' he said. His bourgeois roots were throwing up walls in every direction. 'No, you just can't do this.'

'I need to get to Bogota. This is the only way.'

'Seriously, what are you going to do there? Knock him over the head and drag him back?'

'That might work, but it would be a problem getting him through Customs.' Diana had previously considered this option. She thought about it a little more. 'But... I can lure him to the Embassy, and once there they can hold him. Then I don't need to worry about getting him here, they'll do it for me.'

'Why don't you just tell Flanagan what you've discovered, then you can cut out a few steps? Like, the steps which involve forgery, theft and you leaving the country illegally?'

'But Dan, don't you see? Mark would expect the FBI to be out looking for him. He'll be keeping a cautious eye out for agents,' she said. 'He would never in a million years expect to see me!'

'Diana, you said you know him better than anyone else in the world does,' he pointed out.

'Doesn't it stand to reason he knows you too? Surely this is what he would expect of you.'

'How do you mean?'

'He knows you're a ... that you like to take charge of a situation,' Dan said. 'Wouldn't he expect you to go charging down there? Are you sure he's even there?'

'No,' she said, not liking his argument at all. 'I mean, I know he's there. You don't understand. Mark lives for Mark, everyone else is just an add-on to his life. It's all about Mark – he doesn't know me at all.'

Dan was reaching the end of his arguments and the end of his rope. 'Diana, you just can't go to Colombia!'

'Why not?' She raised her voice to match his and clenched her fists. 'It's the only way!'

'Because...' Dan swallowed. 'Because it's dangerous, there's drug lords and cartels and gangsters.... And because I'd worry about you.'

She stopped in mid-rant. That might be the nicest thing anyone ever said to her. 'Really?'

He shrugged and looked down at the floor. 'Probably. A little. You have a knack for rubbing people the wrong way,' he said. 'I'd hate to see you step on the wrong toes. That could be really dangerous down there.'

She quickly did the sums in her head. Might as well be hung for a sheep as a lamb. The trust fund could cover his ticket as well, and if Dan went along with this, then his cooperation in the financial matters would be a done deal. She would appeal to his chivalrous side.

'Maybe you should come with me. For protection,' Diana said. 'To stop me from putting my big foot in it too deeply.'

Dan looked doubtful as to how he could stop Diana on any path she chose. He drew a deep breath, and she could see he was marshalling his arguments against the sense of her travel.

'Oh come off it, Dan! This is your chance to see a bit of the world. You have a passport, right? Have you ever used it?'

She hit the jackpot. Dan had never travelled outside his own country before. The road trips in the Downey mini-van had been to the family-friendly standards that defined middle-class American life – the Grand Canyon and Yellowstone Park, the Liberty monument of Washington, Disney Land, and even one daring trip to the dangerous New York, New York. He had never been allowed to stretch his wings further afield, to see the real world outside his parents' enclave, and couldn't yet afford to do it himself. She could tell by the gleam in his eye that she had caught his imagination.

'Here's the plan. First, I need to forge Susie's signature on the cheque,' Diana said as she hauled a large envelope out of her Louis Vuitton bag. Inside the envelope were all the Trust's documents and most importantly for her purpose, the cheques. 'That won't be hard, she still writes like a little girl, all roundy and cute. I had to make her stop dotting her 'i's with hearts, it was just too embarrassing.

'We'll make the cheque out to your business,' she continued. 'You'll deposit it and... What now?'

Dan's eyes were enormous behind his thick spectacles. 'Oh my God, you can't do that.'

'And how else are we going to fund the trip to Bogota?' she asked with sarcasm in her voice. How quickly she could forget how just moments before, Dan had touched her heart with his concern for her.

'But this involves my business! I'm a lawyer,' he said. 'That won't look good. Can't you just make it out to me personally?'

Their eyes met over the table, hers in disbelief. 'Yeah, you're right,' he said. 'Okay.'

'Be quiet now while I concentrate.' She practiced a few times on a scrap of paper, then confident she had the intricate curlicues of Susie's childish hand down pat, proceeded to make out the cheque. She handed it to him with a flourish. 'Now, you deposit this, as I said, and pay off your credit card balance. It'll take a couple of days to clear, but you should be able to move the funds around electronically.'

He took the cheque into his hand as if it was a death sentence, eyes bulging at the amount.

'You do have enough credit to carry it off, right?'

Dan nodded as he gulped. 'I'm really not comfortable with this,' he hesitated.

'Oh, get over it,' she barked. 'Imagine how I feel – I've never done an illegal thing in my life. You're a lawyer. When you start billing you're going to be robbing people all the time. Get used to it.'

He stuffed the paper deep into his coat pocket as if to hide it away.

'Now, go!' she ordered. 'I'm going over to Mrs. Hastings' to book the tickets online. She's got WiFi.' As he was heading out the door, she stopped him.

'Credit card,' she said, holding out her hand. He handed it over without a murmur albeit with great reluctance, thus sealing his fate as an accomplice.

'Just one thing,' he said as he lingered at the door. 'Have you given any thought as to how you're going to make it past Airport Security, Diana? The FBI will have your name on a 'no-fly' list or whatever they call it. Before you buy the ticket, shouldn't you think of that? In fact, you have to give your name when your purchase the ticket, and your passport number. You may not even be able to buy the ticket!'

He could be such a wet blanket. She hadn't thought of that, and now her plan was dissipating in front of her eyes, dissolving into a thin film of gray. Diana couldn't bear it, for this plan was her only hope. She couldn't trust the FBI to catch Mark or find his body. If she wanted something done right, she had to do it herself.

And she had to do this, she didn't have a choice. But she couldn't do it if she didn't believe in Diana, and for that she needed one hundred percent agreement from all those around her.

'Why do you have to be so negative all the time?'

'Not negative, just pointing out that...'

'You ruin everything! Stop overthinking it, you're not in charge. This is *my* plan, and it's going to work!'

'Diana, this is ridiculous! You're not going to get anywhere. Your plan is flawed. Just let the FBI do...'

She drew herself up to her full height, towering over the lawyer, daring him not to go along with her.

'Oh, fine,' he mumbled. 'Have it your way. I just don't see how...' The rest of his thought was lost to the slamming of the wooden door behind him as the unhappy Dan stalked off down the garden path, his shoulders set stiff.

'It's going to work, it has to work.' This was her mantra as she turned away, set on getting her plan in action. She did not watch him walk away from the house.

Diana took the laptop from its hiding place beneath the stairs, preparing to run over to Mrs. Hastings' house for her internet connection. First though, the dogs needed to be let out into the fenced back yard or they would want to follow her. She had to keep on Mrs. Hastings' good side.

'Out you go,' she told them, opening the door and herding them through. 'You won't be welcome where I'm going.'

CHAPTER SEVENTEEN

Dan was a mass of nerves when Flanagan found him just outside the short path to Diana's house.

'I can't do this,' he said immediately, his face ashen as he looked up at the agent. 'I cannot be a partner to her crimes.'

'Woah, wait there just a moment,' Flanagan said, placing an arm around his shoulder. 'Here, come back to the car and tell me about it.'

Inside the white Lexus, the lawyer spilled everything without missing a detail, from the laptop to the forgery and the planned flights to Colombia.

'The minute she tries to book a ticket, your side will clamp down on her,' he said finally. 'And she wants to use *my* credit card! I am going to be in so much shit.'

'Hey, I got your back,' Flanagan assured him as he thought quickly. 'You know what? You go ahead with this. I'll fix everything at my end.'

'But she'll be putting herself into so much danger,' Dan said. He shook his head in despair. 'She doesn't know what she's doing.'

Flanagan had no doubt the lady knew *exactly* what she was doing, and he admired her hutzpah in planning a trip out of the country even though she was supposedly not allowed to leave. To his mind, there was no way Diana could not know that Dan was working with him, he'd made it so obvious by calling Dan aside before leaving the FBI Headquarters. And so, she must know that he would come to Flanagan and tell all, thus ensuring the agency's cooperation in her flight.

No one married to Mark Quenton for that long could not be a master at intrigue, and he was pretty sure Diana was one step ahead of him all the way. The depth of her criminal mind floored him, while it also excited him immensely. He had found his match, his soul mate in deviousness.

And if he wasn't mistaken (and he rarely was) the attraction flowed both ways.

His only sorrow was that he would have to put her behind bars for the rest of her life. He sighed when he thought of the great things they could have accomplished together. What a team they could have made.

Perhaps he would give her another chance to come clean.

·♥·♥·♥·♥·♥·

The thudding on the old wooden door continued, barely heard above the barking of the dogs who had been thrust outside into the cool wintery air. They weren't used to being barricaded from Diana – only Mrs. Hastings ever locked them away.

'Goddammit, hold on,' Diana muttered as she slammed the back door on the dogs. In the front hallway, she grasped the knob and flung the door wide open, fully expecting to see Dan with another reason against the viability of her plan. 'Just do what I said and don't argue with me!'

But it was Flanagan who waited on the doorstep. She shut the door again in a hurry and shot the bolt. The laptop – where was it? She'd left it on the kitchen table. Okay, he wasn't getting past the parlor. Or the hallway if she could help it.

She drew a deep breath before unlocking the door then remembered what else was on the kitchen table, lying in full sight. The cheques for the Foundation! Oh sweet Jesus she couldn't even let him in the front door – that man would sniff them out. Diana opened the door again, just a crack this time.

'Agent Flanagan,' she said, staring him full in the eye as she peered round the door.

'Ma'am.'

The pause was getting a little uncomfortable. 'How can I help you?'

'Why don't you let me in, and we can discuss that?'

'I'm on my way out,' she replied, risking a quick glance behind her to make sure the kitchen table hadn't moved through to the hallway while her back was turned. All she could see were the two dogs standing on their hind legs, watching her through the back door window, intent on her every move. Cerberus woofed to ask what was up.

'I'll only take a moment of your time,' he said, shifting his hands to his hips to take up more space. If she was thinking of making a break for it, she wouldn't get past him.

'Oh, come in then, if you must.' Diana opened the door and stepped back, blocking the hallway to the kitchen. 'Into the parlor.'

He paused as the dogs let out a welcome volley at the sight of him through the window of the back door. They rather liked Flanagan, despite Diana's feelings about the man. Perhaps they could sense that, just like their mistress, he wasn't in the least intimidated by their size or their noise, and he would make a darn good master.

'Yo, dogs,' he said to them in greeting, and made to move into the kitchen but Diana thrust herself firmly into his personal space.

'The parlor.' She pointed to the room on his right.

'Yes, ma'am.'

Diana remained standing at the doorway of the room, her arms crossed, ready to prevent him from getting into the kitchen should he make a sudden lunge for it. 'What can I help you with?' Her voice was as tight as her body language.

'Why don't you come in and get comfortable? Take a seat. Like I said, this will only take a minute.' He sat on the sofa and patted the cushion next to him.

Diana slipped into the armchair closest to the door, dislodging Celine with a loud yowl. Her hands clutched the armrests, ready to push herself back up at the least movement from him, and she stared at him. She was getting nervous. The longer he stayed, the greater the chance he might make it into the kitchen and see the evidence of her wrong-doings. The laptop was emblazoned with Mark's initials in flashy large gilt letters against the battered black background, and the Trust cheques had the unmistakable image of Diana surrounded by animals – the logo she had insisted was appropriate for the Sanctuary and that was a familiar sight to anyone in the area with all the advertising they'd done over the years. Flanagan would immediately recognize what she was up to.

And then he'd haul her off back to jail, and she'd never get a chance to find Mark and the money.

·♥·♥·♥·♥·♥·

'I think your dogs want your attention,' Flanagan said, raising his voice to be heard over the baying from the back yard.

'Never mind them,' Diana said. She strove to make her voice normal as if she always spoke at high decibels. 'They're always barking. What is it you want now?'

'I have a suggestion,' he began. 'I've been thinking.'

'What?'

'I've been thinking,' he yelled. 'That you were right.'

'I'm always right,' she shouted back, affronted. The dogs increased their volume, hearing the raised voices.

'We need to... we need ... Oh for God's sake can't you shut them up?' Flanagan was roaring by this point.

It was a bit much, she realized. She had to go let the hounds in, for they would never shut up till they got to greet Flanagan properly. 'Okay,' she said.

'What?'

'I'll let them in,' she shouted. 'But... you just stay there, alright? Don't move.'

'Are they going to bite me?'

'No, just don't... follow me.'

She dashed up out of the armchair and into the kitchen. With one swoop she grabbed up the laptop and the papers and shoved them into the cupboard beneath the sink, and like a ballet dancer, swivelled on one foot back to the back door and let the dogs in, keeping an eye on the kitchen entrance at all times. Cerberus and Outhros rushed past her at full volley to leap into the living room. Once there, they quieted considerably at Flanagan's feet, panting and gleefully looking up at their mistress.

'That's a damn sight better,' Flanagan remarked with relief.

Diana slid back into her chair, eyes on him at all times. 'So? You wanted to talk to me.' She folded her arms across her chest. Her secrets were all hidden now, she had nothing to fear.

'As I was saying,' Flanagan continued from his previous thought. 'You were right – you know Mark better than anyone.'

She nodded.

'You want him found, I want him found. We both want the same thing.'

She nodded again, her eyes narrowing with suspicion.

Flanagan leaned forward. His brown eyes were warm and open. 'Let's work together. You and me.'

Diana let that thought pass through her mind, tried it on for size. Just give up and let this guy run the show. Allow those strong arms to steer the boat, and she could sit back and enjoy the journey and the arms. She had no doubt Flanagan would find Mark, with all the legal resources at the man's disposal. She could call Dan and tell him to cancel the plan, and pretend she'd never forged a cheque, she would get the insurance policy (or probably not, because Mark surely wasn't dead) but she would see justice served.

Yet, on the other hand - justice being carried out would *not* mean that she would get all her money and her stuff back. Mark would go to jail for years and years, true, and would get what he deserved. But how about Diana, would she also get what she deserved? No. She would be in the exact same situation she was now, no money or house, no social standing, no freedom, and all their estate would be tied up in the legal wrangle. Even if there was something left over after the lawyers, it would take a long time to trickle its way back to her.

Diana looked around her at the little house. This was only ever meant to be a temporary situation, there was no way she could ever live here for any amount of time. Of course, she had no doubt she would bounce back even without her millions, but where was the satisfaction in that?

She was so angry with Mark, she wanted to chew him up and rip him to pieces, and she wanted the joy of the hunt. He had broken his vows – no, not the marriage vows, she had little faith in them having broken a few herself. But he had broken the promise that they were a team. The formidable Quenton team, rulers of Baserville. Untrustworthy little bastard.

Working with Flanagan would ensure success, at least. Maybe, just maybe it wouldn't be a bad idea...

'What do you say, Diana?' Flanagan was still leaning forward, confident in his pose. 'We could be a team...'

She was brought to earth with a start. 'What did you say?'

'We'd make a great team, you and I,' Flanagan repeated, sitting back on the sofa, a smile on his face. He relaxed now, stretching his arm across the back of the seat.

Right, a team. This was unbearable, yet another man who wanted to use her, promising team work indeed. She'd tell him where he could stick that idea, she'd let him know she wasn't to be misused in that way again. Right, they'd be a 'team' while it suited him, then he'd take all the glory for himself. A 'team' of convenience. She'd... Wait. Two could play this game.

'A team, huh? And how do you propose we act together as a team in looking for my husband?' Diana opened her eyes wide.

Flanagan leaned forward with an air of success, obviously pleased he had won her over to his side. 'Like you said, you know Mark better than anyone. I propose you work with me on the investigation.'

She leaned forward also, as if seriously thinking this through. 'You going to pay me for my time?'

'Eh, I'm sure we'll work something out.'

'I'd need my own office.'

'No, that's not going to happen. I didn't mean *officially.*'

They stared at each other, blue eyes on brown. 'Okay mister, you got yourself a deal.'

He nodded, satisfied.

'Just one thing,' she said. 'I can't start right away.'

'Time is of the essence,' Flanagan said, a frown beginning to crease his brow. 'We need to get at this today.'

She shook her head. 'I have to go away for a bit, straighten out my head.'

'Nope, not possible. You can have a vacation after we find Mark, you'll have lots of time then.'

Diana forced her eyes wide and made a sad face, an old trick she'd learned when she was hanging out in Broadway in the early days way before Mark, when she was trying to be an actress. The sad face always brought tears to her eyes, it never failed. She let a sob escape from behind her fist.

'This is... this has all been too much,' she said, softening her voice as she wiped an eye. 'I just need some time, a little time, maybe just get away for the weekend with a friend of mine.'

Flanagan was staring at her, his face unreadable.

'And where are you proposing to go? I thought you had no friends left.'

'I have friends,' she replied shortly. 'Of course I have friends. There's.... there's my friend Morris in New York. I need to go visit Morris.'

Yes, Morris was the answer. Or Maurice, as he had preferred to be known these days. How had she forgotten him? She could pretend to be visiting him when she was actually down in Colombia routing out Mark.

'Fine,' Flanagan said slowly as he stood up. 'Fine. You go to... New York for the weekend. But...'

She quickly moved the handkerchief back in front of her mouth to hide her small smile of triumph. 'But?'

'I'd appreciate it if you kept in contact.'

'Okay, no problem,' Diana replied. She hustled him to the door through the mass of dog bodies who were loath to miss any action. She was running out of time, those tickets wouldn't book themselves. Once he was gone she rushed into the kitchen to reverse her actions, grabbing the laptop out of the cupboard under the sink, laying it on the table and turning her energies into herding the dogs out the back door again.

But in her hurry, she hadn't given the front door the necessary push to engage the lock and amid the noise of the creatures, didn't hear Flanagan return to add another thought to their conversation. She totally missed him eyeing the laptop and nodding to himself.

'I'll need your New York address.'

Diana slammed the back door and whirled around, her eyes automatically darting to the laptop. His followed. She jumped over to place herself between the table and Flanagan. Unfortunately there wasn't a lot of room in the old kitchen with that massive old-fashioned furniture, and she found herself invading his personal space to an uncomfortable degree. Diana leaned backwards as much as she could in a belated attempt to hide the laptop.

In place of the computer, Flanagan's eyes were now drawn to her generous bosom mere inches away. This might have distracted him from his suspicions that Diana was playing him, but only momentarily. His eyes travelled up the length of her body to her face.

'The place you'll be staying in New York,' he reminded her, his deep voice vibrating through the air between them.

'Umm.' She was unable to move out of his space for fear he would grab the laptop, and thus she found herself also unable to break their eye contact. They remained at this impasse for another long moment, neither one budging. He was taking all the air in the room, sucking out all the oxygen in the short space between them.

'I'll text it to you,' she said finally, running out of breath, her fingers finding the leather case behind her and holding on for dear life.

Yet another endless moment passed before he gave her a curt nod.

'You do that.' And he was gone, leaving a cool draft in place of his presence.

CHAPTER EIGHTEEN

How could she have forgotten Maurice? Perhaps her one true friend in the world, although truth be told their friendship had survived the tests of time only because Maurice was as self-absorbed as herself.

And Morris would cover for her. He was her oldest friend, they had met when she was fresh off the bus in New York City, ambitious to begin her career in the footlights of Broadway. Her first audition, and his too, they had won the parts in an off-off-Broadway production staged in an old warehouse. There hadn't been much competition as there was no budget for the show. Diana had played a gravestone, and Morris a snake, and it had only run a couple of shows. She'd never understood what it was all about, but Morris had pretended to grasp the concept, and that's maybe why he had been able to forge a career on the fringes of Broadway over the years. He had been Artistic Director for a now defunct anti-dis-establishmentarianism Art House and had naturally moved on to become a very popular gossip columnist. He especially liked to be at the forefront of all pretentious twaddle, which made him the darling of the over-educated, under-utilized Ladies Who Lunch set, and the academics.

Morris had gained a mid-Atlantic accent during the time he'd served in the trenches of the New York theatre scene, along with a stoutness of belly that came from a diet of hors d'oevres and no exercise other than sprinting for cabs. She had no worries that Morris would turn her back on her during her time of need, for the juicier the scandal, the better, and he would dine out for weeks on his connection with the Quentons. Yes, Morris would cover for her.

A knock sounded on the front door just as she was closing the back on the dogs yet again. She placed the laptop on the kitchen table, hesitating as she did so. It had been a light knock, not Flanagan's heavy fist, so she didn't bother hiding the evidence thoroughly.

The door was the old-fashioned type from early in the last century – solid wood slats which precluded a peek at who was standing on the other side. Diana opened it.

A vision of loveliness was before her, a woman tall and thin to the point of skinniness except for the fake boobs which stuck out and gave her some much-needed curves. The perfect brunette wore widow's weeds, all in black, and her perfection was marred only by the reddened nose.

Amaryllis.

Before Diana could slam the door in that perfect face, Mark's mistress threw herself across the threshold and into Diana's arms, sobbing unconstrainedly.

'So awful,' she cried. Tears were spouting from her eyes and leaving damp spots on Diana's hoody. 'Such a waste. We must be strong.'

Diana could see some passers-by look curiously up the walk to the old house, wondering what the loud caterwauling was in their usually peaceful village.

'Oh for God's sake,' Diana muttered. 'Get inside.' She hauled the vision in and slammed the door. At this rate she would never get the tickets booked. 'What are you doing here?'

Amaryllis looked around her at amazement. 'Oh, so... cozy,' she said. 'I would never have thought this was your style.'

'It's not my 'style',' Diana said in a defensive tone. 'This is the result of circumstance. Brought about by your bo... boss, I might add!' She'd almost said 'boyfriend', but that was too good a term for Amaryllis and Mark's relationship.

'Anyway,' she caught herself. She had no need to defend herself to Amaryllis of all people. 'What do you want?'

The younger woman looked at her with round eyes reddened, the picture of sympathy. 'I came to commiserate with you.' Her eyes slid around Diana, continuing on to examine the raggedy carpet on the stairs and the scuffed linoleum on the hall floor. She grabbed Diana again in her arms and, catching the heavier woman off guard, swung Diana so she could see into the living room to the right.

Frustration that she was yet again impeded from her mission to get those tickets booked, mixed with the tiniest bit of jealousy, for she was still smarting from Mark's use of Amaryllis's name as a password for the laptop, and perhaps this meant that Mark really did love the woman, all this translated into an expression of anger for Diana, for she was never one to name her emotions.

'Get off me!' Diana threw Amaryllis against the cupboard door leading under the stairs. 'And get out of my house!'

The lovely eyes of Amaryllis almost bugged out of her skull at the force of the blow. She gasped and put her hand up to the back of her head, and this movement allowed her to look into the kitchen where the laptop waited on the old table. The bright gilt letters shone. The dogs had resumed their volleyings outside the back door and scrabbled at the door.

'That's Mark's laptop! What are you doing with that?' Her voice was shrill.

'None of your business,' Diana yelled back in fright. 'He's my husband, why wouldn't I have it?'

Amaryllis leaped towards the black leather case but Diana threw herself in the way. The two tussled. Even though Diana outweighed her by many pounds, Amaryllis appeared to be fueled by desperation.

'Leave me alone, I need that,' the younger woman grunted as she struggled and grabbed a hank of Diana's hair. She pulled hard. 'It holds the proof.'

The ancient back door couldn't hold against the excited weight of the dogs anymore. The latch clicked and they jumped into the melee.

'Ouch!' Diana shoved her palm over the woman's face, pushing her away, almost tripping over Cerberus as she did. 'What proof?'

'Proof that he loves me!' Amaryllis screeched in her ear. She let go of the hair and attacked with her clawed hands, aiming for Diana's eyes.

'He doesn't love you!' Diana hooted even as she deflected the other's hand and elbowed her in the jaw for good measure, sending the other backwards. Amaryllis stumbled over Outhros, her hands still outstretched and unable to save herself, she landed on her back with her high heels in the air.

'Get out of my house!' Diana yelled as she grabbed the laptop and held it high over her head, victorious. The dogs pounced, slathering the downed woman's face with kisses of good intent. They scrabbled with their muddy paws all over her designer widow's weeds, each vying for the best position. They loved wrestling.

Amaryllis had never been much of an animal lover, not even at the best of times, and she screamed with terror at the attentions, hitting blindly at snouts and wagging tails in her efforts to be free.

Finally she crawled over to the hallway door and the dogs, still barking, turned their love on to Diana in the hopes of enticing her into a round or two. Amaryllis hauled herself up by the doorjamb and delivered her parting shot.

'I will leave,' she announced, panting as she attempted to straighten her dress. 'But you haven't seen the last of me, Diana Quenton.'

'I could be that lucky.'

Amaryllis's eyes narrowed as she paused by the door. 'I know you killed him,' she hissed. 'Somehow you engineered the whole thing and stole the money. You knew he wanted to marry me and you couldn't bear to lose him. I will get you Diana Quenton, if it's the last thing I do.'

With that Amaryllis disappeared through the front door in a cloud of perfume and diaphanous black material.

·♥·♥·♥·♥·♥·

Did that just happen? Diana wondered as she leaned against the door after firmly shutting it. Her husband's whore thought *she* was the mastermind behind his disappearance.

This cheered Diana up tremendously, and she laughed as she walked the short distance to Mrs. Hastings' home, dogs still barking in the distance as she left them behind.

'Too funny,' she said aloud and giggled again, feeling light as a feather.

For this could only mean one thing – Mark had had no intention of bringing Amaryllis with him on his nefarious disappearance. He may have promised to marry the skinny bitch, but he'd been lying, of course he'd been lying! It meant nothing that he'd used her name as his password. Amaryllis knew nothing about his scheme and was not part of his plan. Diana was triumphant, for he hadn't proved her wrong after all. She still knew Mark Quenton better than anybody else in the world, and she knew there was no room in his shrivelled heart for anyone but Mark.

She did so love to be proven right.

It was surprisingly easy to book the tickets to Bogota, and if her guard hadn't been relaxed she might have been suspicious at the ease at which her passport number was accepted for international travel.

Mrs. Hastings not so much. 'But you're a person of suspicion in a major FBI investigation,' she pointed out. 'Everything's computerized today, there's no way they'd let you out of the country. Your name has to be flagged in the system.'

'Well I guess *someone* didn't do his job properly,' Diana answered, smug as all get out to have put one over on Flanagan. 'And by the time he realizes, I'll have gone and come back with Mark or at least the money.' She sat back, quite pleased with how the afternoon was turning out.

They waited as the printer clattered out the ticket. Dan had thought it best to buy his own so no-one could link the two travellers.

Mrs. Hastings shook her head, a look of doom and gloom on her face. 'I do not have a good feeling about this,' she said.

'Oh, don't be such a misery-pants,' Diana scolded her. Really, the woman could be such a wet blanket sometimes. 'We'll go down to Mark's hotel, confront him, either get him or the money, and fly back. I'll be taking Mark by surprise, because he's sure I'm flapping about the insurance money and spending my energy getting hold of that five million. I tell you, he is *not* expecting me to show up on his doorstep. Flanagan won't even know I've left the country. What can possibly go wrong?'

﹒♥﹒♥﹒♥﹒♥﹒♥﹒

They took the train down to Manhattan, Dan's credit card covering the lot. She'd always loved trains – first class of course – the luxury of sitting back and being carried to a destination that was not home. Europe had the best trains, she informed him.

'The Europeans have mastered the train journey,' she said, fondly reminiscing. 'Travelling through the Alps on a sunny winter morning, being served the best coffee, champagne suppers, you should really try it some time.' She looked over to her companion who was staring at her almost nervously, his fingers drumming a tattoo on his legs.

Poor kid, she thought. His first international flight, he's a mess of nerves. She continued on her happy stream, trying to soothe his nerves.

'You see that Louis Vuitton up there?' She pointed to the overhead compartment. 'That has travelled with me everywhere I've gone for the past twenty years. All over the world. It's a part of me, really.'

Her stream of triviality didn't seem to be calming his mind, so she laid it on thicker.

'I know exactly what I can fit into that case, I've developed packing down to a fine art,' she noted. 'For example, all my toiletries in special little bottles. I only take three pairs of footwear no matter where I'm going. The first is my regular heels, like these.'

She extended her foot to show him. He looked down, bemused.

'These babies will get me anywhere, and always look great. I can walk in them for hours. The other pair of stilettoes – well, they're for special occasions, the times when I just have to look fantastic and there's no effort required on my part.' She paused again to admire her shoes, and added advice for him. 'Always buy quality, it'll last you forever. These shoes and the Louis Vuitton, that's almost all I need in life.'

'And the third pair?'

At least she'd distracted him from his fears of flying. 'Oh, they're the get-away sandals. I always pack them just in case.' She laughed it off.

'In case of what?'

'Oh, you know,' she said. 'Something might come up, where I'll have to actually walk a distance. It happened to me once, on Santorini. No taxis, the funicular was broken, I had to walk all ten thousand steps up from the old port. Well, I wasn't going to get on a donkey, was I?'

He shook his head in agreement.

'So ever since then, I pack one small pair of sensible sandals,' she said. 'Never used them since, but you never know.'

He looked at his watch.

'What I'm trying to say is, you're in good hands,' she said, smiling as she leaned forward, magnanimous in her sensitivity towards the young man's obvious nervousness.

He looked down at the phone he held in his hands. 'Excuse me,' he said and jumped up and down the narrow corridor.

Dan did this a couple more times. By the third time, Diana was losing patience.

'Do you have a nervous bladder or what?' she asked, rather annoyed at any sign of weakness as he plumped himself heavily into the seat across from her.

'No!' he said too quickly, then realized his cell phone was still in his hand. 'No, just had to make a call, business you know...'

'Your business right now is my business,' she told him as she snapped her fingers. 'Keep your mind on the task at hand. Now, when we land in Bogota ...'

'Have you ever been down there?' he cut in.

'No, not as such. But one foreign city is much like the other. That's not worrying me. Not at all.'

'I'm still not sure this is a great idea...'

'Oh shut it, would you? You're such a nervous Nellie, it's starting to get on my nerves.'

Dan did shut it, but before the train pulled into Central Station, he excused himself once more.

CHAPTER NINETEEN

M orris was delighted to see her, as always, even more so with the scandal of Mark's disappearance. He ushered them into his squalid loft in Harlem, made all the dingier by the heavy velvet curtains hung everywhere, on the windows and the walls themselves and as room dividers. It would have given the large room a feeling of being in the circus, if the place had been better lit.

'I've been hearing so much about you, Diana my sweet,' he said. He was a slightly built man with a bulge around his middle, and the years had been kinder to Diana than to him. His hair was quite gray with age (distinguished, he insisted) yet grew with abundant large waves which were trained to stand off his head as if he constantly faced a strong wind. His trim goatee worked with the deep lines on his face to give him the air of a wooden marionette, a painted smile always on his face. Maurice drew his silken smoking jacket closer around his narrow body. 'Your photo splashed all over the news, your husband run off with his mistress and taking all the money... You must tell all.'

'He didn't run off with that skinny twig,' Diana spat. 'He left her behind, she was totally unaware of his plans. What he did do was to take off with all my friends' money, so now everyone hates me.' She sat in the nearest overstuffed armchair, an antique from the last century, the raised velour pattern nearly rubbed off and the horsehair padding showing through in spots on the armrests.

'Not I, Di,' he replied. '*Au contraire.* I am the sympathetic ear.'

'Morry, you're perhaps the last friend I have left who's speaking to me,' Diana agreed.

'Maurice, dear, I go by Maurice these days,' he answered her, his voice just a little sharp. 'I think I've told you that before.'

'Yeah whatever,' she replied. 'Thing is, I need your help. Just a little thing.'

'Why don't we have a drink first, then you can tell me all about it,' Maurice said. He gave a predatory leer at Dan, pausing at the young man's luscious red hair, but when he reached the expression on Dan's face, he sniffed and dismissed him.

'Thing is,' Diana said as he poured three glasses of sherry. 'If anybody asks, you have to say that I've been here all weekend. Nursing my wounds in the comfort of friendship, that sort of thing.'

'And your little friend? Though I don't think he's really your type.' Once dismissed as beneath Morry's attention, it was as if Dan were not even in the room.

'This is Dan. He's my lawyer,' Diana said, accepting the tiny cut crystal glass from him. 'And you haven't seen him.'

'Technically, no I'm not...'

'Oooh, Diana's asking me to lie?' Maurice cut in over Dan. 'You do know there is a price attached to that sort of request...'

'Listen, you'll be the first to have all the details when it's done with, and then you will be free to tell the tale wherever and whenever you please,' she said. 'But until then, you need to keep it under your hat. If word gets out, the FBI will be down on me so quick there won't be a story to tell. They'll probably arrest you for being an accessory if they think you know anything.'

'I can't say *anything*?' He looked quite dismayed. 'Not even a hint? Oh Diana dear, you know that's too much to ask of me.'

She relented a little, for she had to make it worth his while. 'Listen, you can quietly spread the word that I'm holed up in your apartment,' she said. 'For verisimilitude, in case the FBI go sniffing. Cause that's what I'm telling them. And then when it's over and I have the money back, we could maybe take a nice trip to Venice next spring... Compliments of Mark's estate, of course...'

Maurice gasped. 'The Palazzo Venart?' He closed his eyes in delight, his gray goatee quivering. 'Oh Diana, you know that's the thing I want most in the world.'

Trust him to know the most expensive luxury hotel in every major city.

'A whole week, Morry,' she said, leaning towards him. 'But only if I can get Mark's money back, and that means my plan has to work and in order for that to happen you can't leak it out.'

'Mum's the word, darling,' he said, winking at her devilishly. 'Mum's the word.'

·♥·♥·♥·♥·♥·

Dan insisted they enter JFK Airport separately. 'There's cameras everywhere,' he whispered as they got off the train. 'We can't be spotted together. And I think we're being followed...' He darted glances around them as if he was looking for someone to pop out behind a pillar, and was sweating profusely by this point.

'Keep the faith Dan, dear. No-one is looking for you. Flanagan thinks I'm nursing my wounds in Morry's scummy Manhattan apartment, and I'm sure he would never guess that you've got the courage to go looking for Mark in South America,' she told him. 'Besides, Flanagan doesn't know that I have access to the funds from the trust, so as far as he's concerned, I don't have the means to travel. I have him fooled.'

'You're not worried about getting through security with your passport?'

'I have a plan, and the plan will go through successfully, Dan,' she replied haughtily. Mark had taught her that, have your eye on the goal and never waver, and everything will happen as you visualize it. He had helped her grow her perfect confidence in herself. Like way back when they were freshly married, he had foreseen the obstacles to her acceptance by Baserville society, had instructed her on every little matter like which fork to use and who to place where at her lavish dinner parties, so they couldn't fault her on any minor etiquette mishaps.

That was something she missed these days, Mark and his confidence. They had been such a great

team, in the early days. She pulled herself together.

'It's still not too late to back out,' he said, almost
pleading. 'You don't know what you're doing Diana. You're out of your depth. Let the FBI handle
this. Flanagan will help you, he even wants you to
work with him...'

'Did I tell you that?' Diana asked him, cocking her
head. 'I don't remember passing that on.'

She shrugged. 'Never mind, let's go. We'll approach separately, as you insist, and pretend we
don't know each other on the plane, as you also
insist. When we land in Bogota...'

'I'll text you,' he said, a little more firmly. 'I'll be
behind you the whole way, making sure you're not
being followed.'

'No one knows we're going, Dan,' she said, the
exasperation making her voice shrill. 'No one is
going to be chasing us.'

'Mark may have been mixed up with drug lords,
you don't know,' Dan replied, cautiously, then bit
his lip.

'Where are you getting all this from, Dan? Mark
may be a scumbag, but he's not mixed up in drugs.
He stole the money from our friends, not some...
Mexican banditos!'

'We're not going to Mexico, Diana,' Dan told her in his worried voice. 'Oh! Before I forget, give me your money.'

'What? If we're splitting up, I'm not giving you my cash.'

He reached into his carry-on. 'I'm not going to take your money. I've got something for you.'

She reached into her wallet and withdrew the euros first.

'Thanks,' Dan said as he drew out an object and placed the money inside. 'I borrowed this from Mom. Place it around your waist and it'll keep everything safe.'

Diana stared aghast at the fluorescent orange plastic in his hand. 'That's a fanny-pack! I'm not wearing that.'

'Yeah, it's a fanny-pack.' He looked at her, puzzled. 'They're the best thing for keeping everything close. Practically thief-proof. Bogota is a dangerous city, you know.'

She drew herself up with all of her years of entitled living. 'I have travelled the world and managed not to get robbed once, I'll have you know,' she said. 'And never once have I needed a... fanny-pack.'

'Yes, and you travelled in a bubble of safety the whole time, your money ensuring no bad elements could get near,' he retorted. 'Just take it, and put it round your waist before we land. And don't forget to put your American dollars in too!'

'Oh for God's sake!' She shoved the offensive item into her purse, flicked her long scarf around her neck and turned towards to the entrance. 'I'm going in, and I will see you when we land in Bogota.'

'Just don't draw attention to yourself, okay?'

She ignored him and swept through the automatic doors, trailing her Louis Vuitton behind her.

Diana kept her large sunglasses covering her face as she waited in line with the hoi polloi so as not to risk being spotted here in the lineup, if she had any friends left to recognize her. Still, there were always reporters. That awful photo of her being arrested still haunted her, and she hadn't looked at a newspaper since. Not that it was likely anyone would recognize Diana Quenton in an Economy line-up.

The line dragged, and she looked around her, bored with nothing to distract or take her attention. She didn't even have a smart phone for entertainment, only that cheap pre-paid Dan had forced her to purchase. Although, standing in a line-up *was* a bit of a novelty in itself. She looked around at the masses of people on both sides, but there was no sign of Dan. He hadn't chickened out at the last minute, had he?

And of course there were no issues getting through security. She laughed to herself, for Dan had been worrying about nothing. The FBI were pretty slack in their jobs, for they had totally forgotten to alert the airlines not to take her onboard. Must be the bureaucracy slowing everything down.

She passed through the scanner and waited patiently as a guard buzzed her up and down. Loud beeps sounded as he passed over her chest, but he was used to the positioning of underwires in women's clothing and ignored the alarms. The tense moment came as another guard scrutinized her passport and looked up with something like recognition in his eyes.

'I must ask you to remove your sunglasses, ma'am,' he said.

She placed them on top of her head and stared him down.

He signalled to another guard, and Diana felt a burly presence behind her, blocking any escape.

'Please wait right here, ma'am,' he said. 'Don't move an inch.' He disappeared into an office at the back of the room.

The crowd behind her whispered and fidgeted, their impatience growing, but the guard was back in no time flat.

'You can go on,' he said with a slightly puzzled air as he handed back her passport and boarding pass.

She found the gate and boarding came not too long after. She walked the endless white tunnels with the other people, much like a herd of sheep till they came finally to the entrance of the plane.

This was one of the older models of planes which hadn't had the First Class seats updated into pods yet. Diana automatically began to scan the first rows for her seat number, but was hurried on by the steward.

'Towards the back,' he said, motioning her to hurry on past the comfortably laid out seats, past the curtains to the main body of the plane, where the commoners sat.

Steerage. This was another novel experience.

Well, at least she had a window seat. Diana harrumphed and the woman who would be her neighbor slowly wrested herself from the seat to allow Diana to pass.

'This is an adventure,' Diana told herself as she settled. 'This is not forever. I will get that money and never have to travel like this again.'

She caught sight of Dan's red hair further up the aisle. He was being ushered into the middle of the central row, so that allowed her to feel quite smugly better about everything. He was going to have to travel squashed between two people, without even the benefit of a window to give him the illusion of space. She didn't have it so bad in comparison.

But before the seatbelt warning came on, that same steward who had denied her access to her natural environment of First Class leaned over the seats to Dan, and taking his bag, led him away up to the front of the plane, past the barrier designed to keep the great unwashed masses out of the peace and airiness of the greener pastures.

'Hey!'

Dan looked back quickly and made a cutting gesture across his throat and just as quickly turned his back on her before disappearing behind the thick curtain.

The little bastard. That should have been her being escorted to First Class, he knew that. Why didn't he act like a gentleman and offer the space to her? Diana Quenton sat back into her inadequate allotted seat and fumed as the plane took off into the skies. Her elbow pushed her neighbor's off the armrest, and she glared, daring the woman to complain. Her neighbor merely sighed and tucked her arms into her body.

It just wasn't good enough. Shame on Dan! Once the plane was safely in the air, she knew she had to confront him on it and whine until he changed seats with her. On the pretext of looking for the toilet, she pushed past her seat-mate and sashayed up the aisle.

Peering through the curtain with one eye, she spotted him, deep in conversation with a man whose back was turned to her. The woman in the seat behind them wore a hat so large that it quite hid the view of Dan's companion; she could only see that he took up a lot of space.

'Psst!'

No-one could hear her over the roar of the jet engines.

'Dan!'

The only person who heard was the large-hatted woman who looked up then quickly looked back down again, studiously ignoring the intrusion. Diana sighed. She was going to have to break the class barrier and go through the curtain.

'Excuse me, ma'am, can I help you?'

'Ah, ha,' Diana said. 'Just looking for the washroom.'

The steward firmly pointed toward the back of the plane, blocking the entrance through to First Class and any chance that she might get Dan's attention.

'Mmm, yes. But the soap is better in the one up there,' replied Diana. 'I have very sensitive skin...'

It didn't work. Diana was firmly escorted to the back of the airplane to sit and stew in the tiny cubicle considered adequate facilities for the cheap seats.

But after a glass of wine or two, (which she had to pay for, there was no end to the humiliation in Economy) she felt slightly better. It wasn't Dan's fault, after all. He couldn't let anyone know they were together, so could not possibly have offered his good luck to an unknown woman. That would have drawn attention to her, and that was the last thing she needed. And besides, when would the likes of Dan Downey, with his dreams of serving the poor, when would he ever get a chance to travel First Class again in his life? She could let him have this one.

Because she was now an international investigator, travelling incognito in Economy. Removing the laptop from the carry-on and settling back into her too small seat, she opened it up and began to make notes on the 'case' so far. Flanagan was going to be so surprised when she presented him with Mark.

He thought she was having a recovery week-end in New York City before starting work with him, when she was actually forging ahead to do his work for him. Ha! She'd show him.

And Sam would really appreciate this for the screenplay. She would play herself, that was a given, for who better could understand the role of Diana Quenton?

Writing the notes was cathartic, and she found herself letting loose a stream of consciousness onto the screen. Pausing for a moment to look out the window at the blue sky with the soft white clouds below and the waters of the Gulf peeking through, her mind went back to the last time she'd passed this way. Diana had travelled lots in her life, but never back to the Caribbean after the honeymoon so long ago. So much had happened since that time, the twins born and raised and the marriage grown embittered.

Did Mark ever think back to those days, the time when life was fresh? On that beach on Aruba, and the island in the distance, soft and hazy and welcoming, like a metaphor for the dreams they had, the future which would unfold for the formidable team of Diana and Mark.

Did he ever buy that island, she wondered idly.

She sat up in her chair as the thought hit her. That island was in the neighborhood of Bogota, well, a few hundred miles away perhaps, but surely accessible by boat somehow. *If Mark is not in Bogota, check out the island off the beach in Aruba,* she typed in as a note to herself and asterisked it for importance. It was a long shot, but maybe...

CHAPTER TWENTY

As he was sitting in First Class, naturally Dan disembarked the plane before Diana. She found herself stuck behind the huge crowd of people all rushing to take their bags from the overhead compartments only to wait patient in line. Frustrated, she craned her head to find him but her view was blocked by that stupid woman's large hat. It was a lovely hat, something familiar about it, she was sure she must know the designer. But still, it was really rude of the woman to continuously wear it and thus prevent people from seeing past her.

'She's probably still pissing herself that you got sent to First Class while she was stuck back there,' Flanagan drawled with a smile as he hoisted up his briefcase and prepared to depart the plane. 'Hey, why don't we have some more fun with this?'

Agent Flanagan was still feeling just a tad annoyed that Diana had chosen to deceive rather than work with him when offered the chance. He wasn't normally a spiteful man, but he had an itch to bring her down to size.

Dan looked worried at Flanagan's words as he followed him off the plane. 'What do you mean by fun?'

Flanagan paused to allow Dan to catch up with him at the portal into the tube, allowing the woman in the large hat to pass by. 'I just want to mess with her mind a little,' he confessed in a low voice, then laughed again when he saw Dan's reaction. 'No, nothing serious. We'll have her in our sights the whole time, I promise. No danger will come to her.'

'She doesn't know this city at all,' Dan said, not feeling good about this. He couldn't help it, he still felt guilty about ratting her out to Flanagan even though it had seemed the best option at the time. 'She needs our help.'

'Like I said, we'll be behind her every inch of the way,' Flanagan said. 'She'll be very safe in our hands. I just want to take her down a peg or two...'

The FBI agent admired Diana greatly, yes, and found her an extremely attractive woman physically. He appreciated her spirit and strength, yet her entitled attitude still rankled him, perhaps more so because of that spark of attraction between the two. He was still the son of the Presbyterian minister, and a man who hated the financial inequality he saw around him and the investment bankers who fanned the flames of greed, and he found it difficult to reconcile these beliefs with his desire for the woman.

Flanagan was an imperfect hero, for he didn't even recognize these conflicting emotions within his own breast.

'Let's go in through here,' Flanagan said as they drew up to a door marked *Entrada Prohibida*.

'I think that signs says no,' Dan replied in a cautious voice, unwilling to point out his new friend's ignorance of Spanish.

'Not for us,' Flanagan said as he sailed through the forbidden door, his FBI ID card ready to show. The sentry inspected it, and let them pass without issue.

Dan said nothing, not even to point out how much Flanagan's arrogance could be a match for Diana's any day of the week, as the agent outlined how they would go about taking Diana down that notch or two. Just for fun, mind.

·•·♥·♥·♥·♥·

It never failed, every time she stepped out of an airport into a strange land she felt that thrill of excitement. The feeling was different somehow, maybe it was the air... she sniffed. Warm and moist, muggy even, so different from New England. The faint smell of exhaust always brought her back to that initial arrival in New York City all those years ago, stepping off the bus for the first time from the confines of the Baserville trailer court which had imprisoned the young Debbie Sears.

Possibility, that's what it promised, that heady big city smell, and with this youthful excitement pulsing through her veins she paused to regroup and look for Dan. He was nowhere in sight.

Her phone buzzed.

You're being followed. It may be the FBI. We need to keep apart and not let anyone know we're together.

His texting was immaculate, his punctuation precise.

Don't worry. I won't let you out of my sight.

She felt her first moment of panic as she texted him back. *What am I going to do?*

Take a bus into town, get off at the central bus station. We'll meet there.

Diana looked about wildly. A bus? Bad enough she had travelled Coach on the way down here. She hadn't taken a bus since that first trip to New York, and here people didn't even speak English. *How do I take a bus?*

There was a pause as Dan digested her question, then a curt reply.

Take a cab then!

You've got the credit card, not me.

Use your American dollars?

That was probably a good idea, and one she felt comfortable with. The taxi lineup was some twenty bodies long, it would take forever. Fixing her sunglasses over her face again, she quickly nipped into the head of the queue. That stupid hat-woman from the airplane didn't appear to notice Diana cutting directly in front of her, for she was intent on watching something across the road and had her face turned away, though there were grumblings from the folks further behind.

Where am I going?

Dan?

Answer me goddammit.

But Dan didn't answer at all. She was on her own and her turn was up at the taxi line. The smiling man offered to take her carry-on, but she held it close with her purse. Once in the cab, she checked her phone again, but Dan still hadn't responded. Best to revert back to Dan's original plan and meet him at the bus station, for that was where he was most likely headed by now.

The cab driver claimed not to speak English, and did not understand the phrase 'bus station'. 'Hotel? You wan' hotel?'

'No, BUS STATION,' she said, speaking louder so he would better understand, but it still wasn't working.

'Hotel Bus?' he asked, looking uncertainly at her in the rear view mirror.

'No,' she replied, and gave a sigh of frustration. The other taxis were now blowing their horns at him, telling him to move on. 'Bus! Station!'

He pulled into the traffic, spouting a stream of Spanish, looking a little annoyed.

'Don't you speak English at all? What's so hard to understand about Bus Station?'

He answered her in a fashion. These Latin types were so dramatic. If everyone just spoke English, their lives would be so much easier.

They drove into the heart of the city, him pointing to hotels as they passed and her refusing, still trying to get him to understand the concept of a bus terminal, their voices both growing in volume.

Finally, he pulled quickly to the curb in front of a large but seedy-looking building. It looked to be a couple of hundred years old, and any other time she might have thought it quite charming with its narrow wrought-iron balconies and wooden shutters.

'Hotel,' he said, pointing up. 'Good hotel.'

'Oh for God's sake,' Diana muttered. She looked around, there was nothing that looked the least like a bus station. But... could it be?

Oh, this was truly serendipitous! Across the road and up the block a ways, there sat the W Hotel in all its glass fronted glory. This made far more sense. She had to find Mark at this hotel, after all, and she only had the weekend to accomplish her grand scheme. Why mess around? The bus station was probably nowhere near the most expensive hotel in the city, anyway, and she was right here.

'Okay,' she said, and climbed out of the back seat. Setting her carry-on with the laptop on the ground beside her, she opened her purse and withdrew the wallet.

'How much?' She stooped into the passenger window.

'*Qui?*'

'How much!' She shouted at him and shook her wallet in his face.

He may have told her the amount owing, but she still didn't understand.

'American dollars,' she said. 'I only have Amer-i-can-o. HOW MUCH?'

He gestured permission to take the proper amount out of the wallet, for he obviously didn't even know the basics of one, two, three in English.

'Yes, fine,' she said. 'Take the right amount out.'

With that, he snatched the wallet and quickly pulled back into the road. Diana had a split second to remove herself from the window so she wasn't dragged along with him, and then another split second to realize what had just happened.

'Thief! He took my wallet!' She looked around but no one was paying attention, nobody was leaping up to come to her rescue. She turned back to get the license number or some identifying feature on the cab, but he was long gone down the road and around a corner. It was useless to give chase.

'Shit,' she said, collapsing onto her Louis Vuitton. 'He took my wallet, and all my money. What the hell?' It took her a moment to digest, for nothing had ever happened to her like this before. Well, excepting Mark and his disappearance. She knew she needed to regroup. And she needed a coffee.

·♥·♥·♥·♥·♥·

'We lost her! You said this wouldn't happen.' Dan was white-faced. 'You promised it was just a bit of fun and she'd be in no danger.' They were standing outside the airport, about to embark into the car provided by the FBI. Diana was nowhere to be seen in the taxi line-up.

'Relax,' Flanagan said, brushing aside his worries. 'She can't have gone through the line-up that quickly. She's probably still in the can.'

Dan searched the line-up again with no success. 'She may not have bothered waiting in line. You know what she's like.'

The agent laughed. He was enjoying the warm breeze on his face. 'How much trouble can she get into? Check the phone again, has she gotten back to you?'

'Hmm,' Dan said as he scrolled through his phone. 'She's wondering where to meet me, and she sounds a little pissed.'

He looked up from his phone. 'Yeah, she skipped the taxi line. And now doesn't know where to go.'

'We wait then,' Flanagan replied. 'And see where she ends up. That's where we'll go.'

⋅♥⋅♥⋅♥⋅♥⋅♥

Change of plan, she texted to Dan. *I'll meet you at Mark's hotel instead.*

She had no money left save for the few Euros still in the hated fanny pack. Diana stood with her bag on the sidewalk, looking up across the road at the towering luxury hotel which took up the whole block, but whose doors were quite closed against her means, and she almost screamed aloud at the unfairness of life. Perhaps she could just get a room here, and worry about the bill later. But no, they would demand to see her passport. Which was in her stolen wallet. She checked the phone, but there was still no more word from Dan.

She began to get an uncomfortable feeling that something may have happened to him, and that it would be her fault for dragging him down here to Bogota against his will. But this uncomfortable-ness soon passed, for it was Dan's fault she was left here without a credit card. He was really quite an-noying, disappearing like this when she had been robbed of her money.

'I'm at least going in for a coffee,' she said aloud. 'I deserve that, and I can afford that.' And she set off through the tall glass doors, sweeping past the concierge as if she still belonged in this rarified atmosphere of gilt and sparkling chandeliers.

It was the right move, for the coffee was divine and the armchairs comfortable, just what she needed. She closed her eyes, and tried to think of her next plan of action. A missing passport had to be reported to the Embassy, yet at the same time she wasn't supposed to be out of the country. Hoo boy, as Susie would say, this was a bit of a pickle. Best to let Dan know what had happened.

He'd have to know about the wallet sometime, and it was easier to say it through text rather than face to face. By the time Dan caught up with her, he would have had time to calm down. *Wallet and cash stolen. Having a coffee at hotel. Will wait for you.*

'Diana, my darling,' a deep, accented voice greeted her as she hit the send button. 'Finally you arrive! You keep me waiting so long, you naughty you!

CHAPTER TWENTY-ONE

It took a moment for her to register who had enveloped her in a huge bear hug, his bronzed arms strong and delicious, for she had no reason to expect to see her lover Jean-Luc in Bogota. She had left him still in bed in Paris, crooning to his new Cartier watch, was that just last week?

She stood up, the better to feel his full embrace.

'You had me worried,' he said, his face smothered in her long blond hair. 'I thought they might have gotten you.'

'Who? What? Jean-Luc,' she said, still not believing. 'Why are you here?'

'Because you asked me to come,' he said, his warm eyes puzzled but playful. 'You sent me the ticket and booked the room here.'

Well, this was pretty strange. And very disquieting, she realized quickly. But...

'You have a room here?'

'Of course.'

'All right,' she said and flicked her head towards the entrance to the cafe. 'Let's go up there, now.'

He hugged her again, suggestively this time, and groaned luxuriously. Several people looked up from their coffees at this loud display of public affection.

'Yes, *ma cherie*,' he murmured. 'I missed you too. I missed your...'

'Cut it out,' Diana whispered harshly, then relented. 'Later, time for that later.'

She indicated her bag for him to pick up.

'I'm absolutely starving. Order me a *croque monsieur* and fries to be sent up to the room,' she said. 'And a milk-shake. Then let's go up. I need to shower.'

As they rode the silent elevator up to the twentieth floor, her mind worked on overtime. She had no idea who had sent Jean-Luc here, or who was paying for the room (and the room service, she intended to make full use of that comfort) but it was an answer to her prayers. There would be time to worry about all the details later.

A nice hot shower and sandwich and a bit of reunion later, she lay on the bed with Jean-Luc massaging her back.

'I have to confess – it wasn't me who sent for you,' she told her lover.

His hands paused for a brief moment, then his fingers resumed their deep thrusting into her muscles.

'I don't understand, *cherie*,' he said smoothly. 'Of course it was you. I have no other lover, you know that.'

He was such a handsome liar, but that was unimportant right now.

'No, I'm not suggesting that,' she replied. 'I'm sure it's not another woman who brought you over here. But the thing is, who sent the ticket and booked the room? No-one knew I was coming here.'

'Eh, I received the ticket two days ago, and I have been here waiting, alone, waiting for you ever since I arrived. This bed is too big for one person, my darling.'

'Two days ago?' She squawked and jumped out from under him. 'But I only just found out about Bogota two days ago!'

She stared at him. What did this mean?

'And besides, no-one knew about our relationship,' she said, slowly now as the thoughts raced through her head. 'No-one knew about you, or where you live, or even where to find you.'

She could only find one possibility, and as she thought aloud, she was reaching a conclusion.

'It's got to be Flanagan,' Diana said. 'Only he could possibly have the resources to reach his nasty fingers into my life and find you.' Not that she and her lover had been particularly circumspect in their dalliances through Europe, but she was willing to bet that no one back in Baserville, not even Mrs. Hastings who nosed into everything in her life, no one knew about Jean-Luc. Dan had texted that she might be being followed by the FBI. It had to be Flanagan. But why? And how had he found out?

'What dastardly plan does that man have?'

CHAPTER
TWENTY-TWO

H er phone buzzed. Diana distractedly looked at the incoming message.

WHERE ARE YOU???

Dan. She'd almost forgotten about him while dallying with Jean-Luc. Oh well he was an adult and he would understand. Besides, he was outside keeping an eye on the FBI, while she had wormed her way right into the heart of Mark's hotel.

She probably should warn him that the FBI were paying for this fabulous room with its round bed and mirrors on the ceiling (really – how tacky) and the room service, and that her presence in Bogota was not the surprise she'd planned it to be.

FBI have set me up.

Turned out she didn't need Dan, after all, for now that she was in the hotel, she merely had to slip upstairs to the Wow Suite and nab Mark. There was lots of time to enjoy another round with her lover and perhaps a proper meal this time. Face it, Dan would only be in the way. Imagine his surprise when she strolled out the doors of the hotel with Mark handcuffed and subdued at her side. Yeah, she got this one.

Okay, so maybe it wouldn't be *that* easy. But before she took action, she had to figure out what was going on and now that all her appetites were satisfied, her brain kicked in.

The FBI obviously knew her husband was in the hotel, so why this big set-up? If Flanagan had known she was coming down here and arranged for Jean-Luc to be flown in, he had to have a reason for it.

And then she knew, or thought she knew. The FBI agent hated her, he'd shown that at their first meeting when he told her she was left holding the bag. He wanted to catch her red-handed with her husband to make it look like she was part of the plan all along, and had pretended to let her go so she would be caught with the big fish, Mark. How devious. How cruel.

How mean. She had been sure they'd had a rapport, that she had fooled him. But there he'd been, encouraging her to join forces with him when he was only setting her up for a fall. Somehow, this hurt more than the mass-unfriending she'd suffered on Facebook.

How could she work against this and save herself?

Through all this, she began to feel a tinge of guilt at getting Dan involved in it all. He was a young lawyer with the rest of his life ahead of him, and if the FBI knew he was working with her, his chances of future success back home might be ruined forever. Best keep him on the outside, for his own safety.

She added a second text.

Best not contact me. They may not know about you. Will text you when the coast is clear.

Somehow, she must make this blow up in Flanagan's face without letting the FBI know Dan was here.

She lay back against the pillows watching Jean-Luc drift off in a cat-nap, beautiful even in his sleep.

Come to think of it, he was a much better partner for this business of the undoing of Mark than Dan could ever be. The W Hotel was more the Frenchman's natural environment, an expensive tacky hotel with every luxury on offer. He could manoeuver around the staff and gain access to Mark's floor, while Dan would only stick out like a sore thumb in his sports jacket and man-bun.

She sat up, lost in thought. Yes, Jean-Luc was way better suited to crime fighting, because who knew what they were going to come across? He was fit – in case they had to make a run for it somewhere, and he was European – that made for a much better cohort than an American suburbanite.

The Frenchman might have a hard time believing this whole story, she certainly did herself, but she did have the proof on the laptop which she had slipped under the bed. Mark's golden initials on the black case along with the browser history would be enough to convince him.

DIANA I KNOW YOU'RE IN THAT HOTEL. WHAT ARE YOU DOING???

She stared at the phone. Dan was so... so plebian and middle-class. Jean-Luc was ... sexy, and good in bed. He looked great in a tuxedo, like Fabio playing James Bond. Her mind was made up. She was ditching Dan in her adventure and bringing her lover on board. It was for Dan's own safety.

Poor guy. She had brought him down here for nothing. His first time out of the country, he was probably feeling a little lost without her to guide him. Scared, even. She relented and quickly sent the text.

On second thought, talk with the FBI, tell them all. I have the situation under control. This would ease his mind, and might buy him some grace with them if they wanted to press charges.

'Jean-Luc, I need to tell you something,' she said to the recumbent form next to her as she turned the phone off and shoved it out of sight under the sheets.

He shifted his head to look at her. His hair was charmingly disheveled and his eyes still soft from sex. He lifted his arm to pull her close and nuzzled her neck.

'I'm pretty sure Mark is still alive.' She started to tell him all the events of her life in the short time since she'd left him in Paris, about the laptop whose trail she was following. She'd get back to Dan later. Meanwhile, he was probably busy enough yelling at her through texts, but he'd get over it once he wore himself out.

'Well, what makes it even more amusing is that the FBI seem to be involved now,' she added. 'I think they're the ones who got you down here, so you're mixed up in it too now.'

Her lover continued to gaze at her. 'No, not the FBI,' he said with certainty. 'That is too... too fantastique. You are dreaming, the FBI are not involved in this.' He indicated with a wave of his hands the luxurious room around him.

'Well, I'm sort of on the run from the FBI right now,' she told him, just a little miffed that he was not impressed. 'And I promised to work with them, but I snuck off down here to find Mark first.'

Jean-Luc jumped out of the bed as if he'd just discovered a shark under the sheets. He grabbed the top sheet and held it to him, looking around the room wildly.

'*Sacre bleu*, Diana!' he said, along with a lot of other French words which were beyond her comprehension. 'You are not working with the FBI!'

'Jean-Luc – it's okay. Trust me darling, I have it all under control. I gave them the slip. You don't have anything to worry about.'

Turned out, though, that Jean-Luc (or Pierre Duchamps as he was also known as in his native France) did have things to worry about with the FBI and Interpol and various other international policing agencies. He spat out the more salient details of the time he'd kidnapped the beloved Persian cat of the North Korean Ambassador, dressed it up in beret and French flag and demanded a ransom. Somehow, this childish stunt had ended up as an international incident involving threat on a nuclear level, and he'd been keeping his head down ever since. He hurriedly threw on his clothes and stuffed what he could in his suitcase.

'So you have a past! Who cares?' Diana sat up in bed. 'This is not about you, Jean-Luc. They don't care about you, they just want to get their hands on Mark. As do I! Look, I know the guy in charge of the case, I'll convince him to ignore you if I can get him to Mark. How does that sound?'

Her lover mumbled under his breath as he searched under the bed for his missing sock.

'Don't run away from me! I need you now more than I've ever needed you before,' Diana wailed to his fine ass sticking up by the side of the bed. No no no, this wasn't the plan! She required the handsome and debonair Jean-Luc by her side. She pulled on her own panties and took the bra off the bedside lamp. 'Help me with this thing would you, lover?'

He got up and deftly, if roughly, clasped the lace behind her back. She bent forward to let gravity bring everything into place.

He had his shirt on his shoulders and was stuffing his feet into his loafers.

'Calm down a moment, Jean-Luc,' she said, her voice rising in desperation as she stood over him in all her glory. 'Don't lose heart, we can pull this off.'

She didn't catch what he mumbled into his shoes.

'Marriage, Jean-Luc!' This was a last-ditch attempt at persuading him to stay, they both knew it. 'We'll find Mark, get his millions back, and live happily ever after!'

By this point she was so hysterical she almost drowned out the sounds of heavy knocking on their hotel room door.

They both turned to stare as the door burst open and three heavy-set swarthy men in camouflage khaki strode in. They all had guns in their hands and none of them looked happy.

'Oh, really?' Diana stood facing the men in her underwear, hands on her full hips. What the hell was Flanagan thinking? Had he followed her all the way down here just to arrest her for leaving the country before they even had Mark in their hands? 'Send in the big guns, why don't you, Flanagan?'

The men paused just inside the door, as if uncertain.

She grabbed at their uncertainty, confident she could bully her way out of this.

'Put those guns away already,' she demanded. 'And vamoose! You can just tell that boss of yours that he's never going to get his hands on Mark this way. I do have a plan, you know.'

'I don't think they're FBI, Diana,' Jean-Luc said quietly, his face set and eyes watchful. She'd never seen him so serious in all the time she'd known him.

'What? Who are they then?' She whirled to face the head honcho.

Jean-Luc said something in a foreign language. Was it Spanish?

The men paused in what they were doing and laughed, seeing real humor in his words. Jean-Luc smiled too, and added something which sounded disparaging. The men roared.

'F-B-I.' The lead guy repeated, which only set them all off more.

'Where's Dan?' Diana asked them, less sure of her ground now. 'Dan will explain. He's my lawyer.'

'Lawyer.' The guy to her right repeated the word, no doubt understanding the English word from watching American cop shows. That just set them all off again, even Jean-Luc. Diana was getting a little tired of not seeing the joke, and suspected she might be the butt of the humor.

But the joke was over before she got it. A stream of their foreign language was aimed at Diana and while she didn't understand the words, she grasped what the man meant through his gestures.

'Do you mind?' she said, as she held her linen pants to her body. 'I'm naked.'

One man grabbed hold of Jean-Luc and held him with a gun to his head.

'He says get dressed now, Diana,' Jean-Luc said to her in a surly voice. 'Or he'll kill me, and then you.'

She hauled on her pants and then took a loose cotton long-sleeved top in her hand.

'You won't get away with this, you know,' she said, her voice only wavering a bit. She stuck out her chin to stop it quivering as she pretended not to be afraid. 'If you're not the FBI, well, the FBI are keeping a very close eye on me, they're probably right outside that door!' She looked at the door as if expecting the cavalry to burst in, Flanagan at the helm with Dan right beside him. All the men in the room followed her lead, but when nothing happened the gunmen all laughed.

The first man barked out again, and thrust his gun into her lover's ribs.

Jean-Luc groaned. 'He said don't worry about being modest at this time,' Jean-Luc told her, and then received another poke. 'He says you're a *putana*, anyway, and oh, no, I can't say that.'

She didn't know what a putana was, but she did as the man instructed and dropped all pretences, concentrating only on getting her flesh covered. She paused before putting on the shoes she'd worn from the airport, realizing that this occasion might call for something a little more sensible, like if she got a chance to run away from these dudes, since they weren't FBI, she wouldn't be able to do it in heels.

So she dug around the floor by the suitcase and found her walking sandals and sat on the bed. As she did so, her hand brushed the cellphone lying unseen in the sheets, now silenced. Could she dare? Yes, if she didn't think about it. It quickly slipped into her the deep side pockets of her linen pants.

'Just do what they say,' Jean-Luc told her. Was that a note of impatience in his voice? 'It's not a fashion show. These guys mean business.'

The moment she'd finished the last strap, Gunman Number Two grabbed her from behind and snapped a plastic tie on her wrists as they had done to Jean-Luc, then marched her out of the room. The group quickly made their way down the hallway to the service elevator.

'Please someone come up,' Diana prayed fervently. Surely there would be a housekeeper or bell boy coming through who would witness this abduction and call out the alarm.

But no hotel staff was about, having been well paid to remove themselves and not see anything, and to keep all other guests away too. The elevator descended uninterrupted to the basement parking level, where a huge black SUV waited, engine running.

The men bickered amongst themselves as they bundled Diana and her lover into the back seat of the vehicle and forced their heads down. The windows were tinted black, but these guys weren't taking any chances. A black cloth bag was forced over her head.

'Fucking 'ell, Diana,' Jean-Luc whispered inches from her ear. 'What the fuck have you gotten us into?' His charming Parisian accent was slipping into a rougher patois lined with grit but she didn't have the head space to notice that. Her mind was racing, searching for anything that could help get them out of this mess.

'I don't even 'ave my phone,' he complained.

The phone. Had she turned it off completely, or had she merely silenced its angry buzzing? If it was only turned down, then perhaps the FBI would be able to trace her through GPS signals. Did a cheap prepaid phone send out GPS signals? She had no way of knowing that. Sam would know, perhaps even Mrs. Hastings would from watching her endless crime shows every evening. But Diana had never bothered to find out that sort of information, as she'd never foreseen a need to know it in her world. Did everyone in the world except her watch those stupid shows?

They drove for ages and, unable to see anything at all, she had no way of telling which direction, even if she had known Bogota and the surrounding area.

If the FBI had set her up and flown Jean-Luc over from Paris (unbeknownst to him of course) surely they would have had the foresight to set up surveillance in the room, too, right? A discreet camera, a mike hidden beneath the bed table and in the bathroom. They would be aware of everything that had gone on, and would be following them right now.

Perhaps this abduction was staged, all part of the plan to find Mark and return him to justice in the States? But the men had roared with laughter at her suggestion they were working for Flanagan, and she was pretty sure that any FBI operatives would at least understand English. So who were these guys, if not from Flanagan?

Jean-Luc was pouring more vituperative nothings in her ear as they travelled, but it was all in French so could safely be ignored as Diana had never bothered with foreign languages, either.

Could her lover even be playing a role in all of this? No way, she came to the conclusion, judging by his reaction when she mentioned the FBI. That was real fear in his eyes, the fear of someone who had been locked up once and vowed never to be in that position again. Having grown up on the wrong side of the trailer park, she was familiar with that look in men's eyes.

Could Mark be behind it all? No, she brushed that thought aside too, because although their marriage was the merest whisper of a sham, she still knew Mark. And there was no way her husband would ever do anything for Jean-Luc her lover, even if he was aware of him. He wouldn't fly him across the ocean to stay at a luxury hotel, because Mark was too much like her in that way.

For all that Diana despised her husband, the fact of Amaryllis still rankled, and she knew he would feel exactly the same way about Jean-Luc. It was territorial, really – the old 'just because I don't want you anymore doesn't mean anyone else can have you' reasoning behind many an operatic plot.

Mark would sooner take a hit out on Jean-Luc than fly him over to Colombia. And besides, Mark had gone into hiding.

Diana wished there was some way she could reach into her pocket and turn the cell phone on, but with her hands latched together behind her back it was impossible. Her arms were beginning to cramp up.

But wait! Her ever optimistic mind alighted on the fact that Dan knew she was in the hotel, he'd said that in his final text before she'd shut him out and brushed him off. He'd known the FBI were following her, and she had let him know about the set up. She almost laughed at the simplicity of it all. Dan and the FBI would have hooked up together and they were probably following the black van right now. Diana relaxed, as much as she could in the circumstances, with the assurance that events would work out as Diana Quenton desired them to. She would emerge victorious, and as ever, always on top.

But she wished they would hurry up and get about the business of saving her. This smelly black cloth was hot and making her scalp itch.

The vehicle was slowing now in order to make a wide right hand turn. It rolled on for a short space then stopped. As the back door finally opened, she was still unable to see a thing, but the black bag let in the impression of a bright sun outside and she could feel the heat of it beating on her body. The men forced her to stumble across a long gravelled drive. Pebbles scrunched underfoot, which made for unsteady walking as she couldn't hold herself erect with her hands still caught behind her.

She could hear the jungle beyond, the bird-song and the squawks of unseen animals, and could smell the green in the air through the stink of the black bag.

At last the man holding her arm forced her up some shallow steps, and then into blessed cool darkness. The way the men's voices bounced off the walls, she could tell this was a large space they had entered, perhaps a two-story entrance hall, with that peculiar soft echo that only comes from marble.

More words of Spanish were said, and then the bag was ripped from her head, taking some blonde strands with it.

'Ouch,' she said with the confidence of someone expecting rescue at any moment. 'You could be a little gentler, don't you think?' She drew herself up to her full height, as much as she was able to with her hands behind her back, and looked imperiously around her.

Her gaze was met straight on by a dark tanned man, a man who looked for all the world like her husband in his bearing and his height, even in his baldness.

But this was not Mark. This man was built as if hewn out of solid rock, with the broad shoulders and thick neck to match. This man wore the scars on his face like hard won war-medals, with pride and as a warning to his adversaries. His black eyes burned into Diana.

He was standing on the second last step of a grand sweeping staircase, bathed in the glow coming from the stained glass windows behind her. His suit was of such an impeccable cut it could only have come from Savile Row, while his shoes gleamed with the unmistakeable Italianness of their origin.

She had been expecting they would be brought into a dark dirty cave, or a sub-basement that had never seen the light of day, at least some location in keeping with the sordidness of her kidnapping. She had never expected these grand surroundings, and was almost cowed by the grandeur. But not quite.

Diana was fully intending to start yelling and kicking up a stink at her mistreatment, shouting her loudest to let Flanagan and Dan know they were here, create confusion to allow the pair and their team (surely there was a whole team of FBI agents ready to storm this palace) to break down the doors and rescue her.

But the man was so ... civilized. And mesmerizing, that dark gaze silently and slowly sizing her up. Running his eyes up her body, pausing to take in the generous bosom, and then up to her face and tousled blonde hair. She had been about to demand an explanation for this rough handling and abduction, when a small smile of appreciation lit his face.

Her bosom grew a little in acknowledgement.

And then his gaze turned to Jean-Luc beside her, his shirt still unbuttoned and waxed chest showing, with a profusion of dark stubble on his face. The man appeared to like this this vision, also.

She felt Jean-Luc draw shoulders back and preen, much as she herself had done. 'Give it up, you little slut,' she whispered out of the side of her mouth as she poked him with her elbow and shot a glare at her lover.

The man before them spoke a quick stream of Spanish aimed it at her abductors and she felt the shackles behind her back cut loose, and her arms were free. Ouch, her hands were numb by now and she rubbed her wrists to encourage the blood flow to return.

He spoke again, this time to the pair in front of him, and Jean-Luc answered. He might be dumb, but he'd picked up various European lingos over his career as a model and whatever else he had done in his life. She looked at the man before her uncomprehendingly.

'Diana Quenton,' he stated, in perfect English with just a touch of the foreign underlying it. 'Wife of the delightful Mark Quenton, yes?'

She stood her ground and stared at him. Any moment now, the FBI would be bursting through that fine upsized grand entrance.

'But where are my manners? Hector Vargas, at your service.' He gave a slight bow in her direction. 'Thank you for accepting the invitation to my private home. I am more than honored to receive you.'

'Didn't seem like we had much choice in the matter,' Diana observed, pulling herself up to her full height.

'I do apologize for the enthusiasm of my men,' the man replied, shaking his head. His bald head glowed in the reds and blues from the stained glass window. 'But I thought you might not accept a formal invitation, under the circumstances.'

'And what circumstances would those be?' she cut in rudely, folding her arms against her chest.

Hector Vargas stopped and looked at her for a moment. 'My name means nothing to you?'

'Should it?' Always answer a question with a question when you weren't sure of your ground or didn't know what the hell was going on. Diana had learned that gem long ago. This tactic gave you the upper hand and didn't let anyone bully you.

He raised a dark eyebrow while he stared at her. 'Peculiar. Yes, so peculiar. If you knew who I was, you would be very afraid right now. Obviously, you really have not heard of me before, or you are a very good actress.' He sucked in air between his teeth, and then let out a sigh between pursed lips, shaking his head. 'This may turn out to be rather awkward, I'm afraid.'

She tossed her hair, and remembered that it hadn't been brushed since before the hot reunion sex with Jean-Luc and the bag over her head. She was bursting to pee, too, so she was very firm in her manner towards the man. 'Awkward or not, I have no idea what you're talking about or who you are, or why you abducted me at gunpoint and allowed your goons to manhandle me. But I'm willing to let that go for the moment. If you don't mind, I'd appreciate the opportunity to refresh myself.'

Stall for time, that was the new tactic. Give those bumblers Dan and Flanagan a chance to regroup and break in. Meanwhile, she meant to take advantage of her captor's civility.

The man's eyes closed in what looked a spasm of ecstasy. 'Ah, you are every bit the grand lady that Mark said. I look forward to getting to know you better.' He turned to the henchmen still surrounding Diana and Jean-Luc, and fired off a rapid scolding. They melted away into the shadows.

Mark? This man knew her husband? The name Hector Vargas was ringing a faint bell in her mind, but she couldn't remember Mark ever mentioning him. Her husband rarely spoke of his business contacts.

'Please, I will show you to the room I have prepared for you, Senora Quenton,' he said as he gestured up the stairs. He walked beside Diana as they mounted the staircase, and Jean-Luc followed. 'You will find everything to your satisfaction, I dearly hope. If there is anything missing, if I have not anticipated your every desire, Maria will be present at all moments.'

In other words, a jailer would be keeping an eye on her. For all Hector's fine words, he was reminding them that this fine mansion was a prison and they weren't going anywhere. She threw a glance backwards. Jean-Luc had a thoughtful and calculating look in his eyes as he met her glance. Perhaps he was hatching a plan to get them out?

CHAPTER TWENTY-THREE

Meanwhile, in the hastily abandoned hotel room, eyes were examining the aftermath. Hector's men had made a fine mess in their futile search for whatever they were searching for, but the lovers were not the tidiest to begin with even in the short time they had been there. Deft hands sorted through the mess, creating even more havoc in the room and the bathroom in the hasty search, throwing the pillows from the bed and brushing the pile of towels to the floor.

Finally, success. The laptop slowly slid out from beneath the bed accompanied by a definite grunt of satisfaction.

·♥·♥·♥·♥·♥·

The two men sat side by side at the bar of the W Hotel lingering over coffee as they kept a close eye on the lobby.

'Why isn't she answering my texts? Something's happened to her, I know something's gone wrong.'

'Will you relax already?'

'She doesn't know anybody here. She doesn't have any money. She doesn't even have a credit card. Where the heck did she go?'

Flanagan shifted uncomfortably on the padded bar stool as he stirred his coffee yet again. It was a bit of a puzzle, he had to admit. Diana with no money, last seen at this hotel, now nowhere to be found. They couldn't have lost her, could they?

'I'll text her again. This is really too bad of her to ignore me.'

'Isn't that the woman from the plane?' Flanagan nudged Dan's elbow as the large hat bobbed by headed for the exit, anything to take his mind from worrying about Diana. 'This must be a small city.'

'I think we should go and ask at the desk.' Dan refused to be distracted.

'Ask what? No way she could get a room here, not without any money. Sit down, would you? She'll wander back here when she's ready.'

Another refill later and Dan was about to explode. 'We can't just sit here waiting!'

'Tell you what,' Flanagan sighed. 'I'll bring out my FBI creds and see if the man at the desk knows anything. But don't get your hopes up.' Truth be told, he was worried himself by now. Diana was loud enough not to be overlooked, and the fact that she wasn't visible must mean she simply wasn't here. Flanagan hadn't messed up much in his career with the FBI, but he had a bad feeling this might be the first.

He heaved himself away from the bar and approached the front desk. After five minutes, he returned to where Dan was sitting on the edge of his stool.

'Mark doesn't have a room here,' he told Dan slowly. 'But the guy remembers Diana. Said she met a tall, dark guy here, foreigner he said, and well, they obviously knew each other, if you get my drift. They ordered from room service and went up to his room.'

Dan's jaw dropped. 'But she doesn't know anyone here! Surely she would have told me if she was planning to meet someone ...'

They stared at each other, amazed at Diana's duplicitousness.

'I got him to ring the room, but there's no answer.'

'Right,' said Dan as he jumped off the stool. 'We're going up there. Something's not right, and I need to find her.'

'They may be otherwise occupied,' Flanagan said. 'The guy said they were kissing and groaning right here in the lobby.'

'I don't care, we need to get into that room,' Dan told him. 'Did you catch the room number?'

His companion nodded.

'Then what are we waiting for? Let's go.'

Upstairs, they found the room easily. It was the only door that was swinging ajar.

''Shit, someone's sure done a number on this place,' Flanagan noted.

Dan had made a beeline for Diana's case and when he didn't find what he was looking for, went through the room like a whirlwind, but to no avail.

'The laptop is missing,' he said finally, and sank on the bed. 'And Diana didn't leave here voluntarily, because she would never leave that Louis Vuitton carry-on behind. Something is very wrong here.'

'At least she had time to grab the laptop, and that's more important,' Flanagan said in a comforting voice. He was a man who had never formed an attachment to an inanimate object in his life, so missed the significance of Dan's words.

'The SIM card on her phone!' Dan said. 'Can you trace the SIM card, keep an eye out for it? I'm sure she'll use it at some point, and...

'Let's not be too hasty,' Flanagan cut in, picturing the red tape that request would require at HQ. 'Maybe they went out the back entrance of the hotel, gone out for a drink or something.'

'No,' Dan said with doomed certainty. 'She wore her flats. She was expecting the worst.'

The FBI agent felt an unaccustomed niggling of guilt at the pit of his stomach for it looked like Diana had disappeared into thin air. This was a dangerous city, and anything could have happened to her. Perhaps he shouldn't have tried to mess with her head, because if Dan was right, then it was all Flanagan's fault for letting this loose cannon out of his sight. He would hate to have to admit his mistake to HQ and call for back-up.

He quickly rifled through the black suitcase in the closet. Her companion was definitely a man, but not Mark Quenton unless he'd grown ten inches in height. Flanagan replaced the case exactly as he'd found it, with the exception of a small tracking device now secured in an inner side pocket.

'What are you doing?' Flanagan watched as Dan hurriedly went through the room, rounding up the lacy bits and the silks and shoving them into the carry-on. 'She's going to know we were here if you tidy up after her.'

'Diana did not leave here voluntarily,' Dan stated again as he gave Flanagan a reproachful glare. 'If she does show up again, if she makes it out alive, she's really going to be pissed off that we left her luggage behind, and I don't want to be the one who gets the blame.'

·♥·♥·♥·♥·♥·

Diana was ushered into a spacious room, without Jean-Luc for accompaniment. Maria the maid was a slight, Spanish looking young woman who stood like a statue by the large wardrobe in the corner of the room, hovering over the telephone. She was willing to bet one of the tough guys would be standing guard outside her door to prevent her running away.

Yet this actually wasn't such a bad situation as kidnappings go, Diana realized as she looked around her luxuriant surroundings. A bit over the top in decor, perhaps, but what could you expect from a South American? They tended to err on the side of Baroque over minimalism, and it really wasn't too awful. She peeked into the *en suite* – oh, yes, a gloriously large soaker tub, big enough for two, with gold-plated taps, and a separate shower tiled with what looked like mother-of-pearl. Very glitzy and comfy and it had cost a bundle. Not really her taste, but she appreciated that no expense had been spared.

Perhaps the FBI could hold off a while on storming the castle. No need to rush, for she didn't need to be rescued quite yet, she found herself thinking. Speaking of which...

She smiled at Maria and pointed to the toilet, then locked herself inside. The Spanish woman did not even acknowledge her.

Diana dug the phone out of her pants pocket. It had been turned off, after all, which was a good thing as Dan would no doubt have continued his text haranguing of her all through the capture, alerting the men to its presence.

She hesitated before turning it back on, pausing by the bathroom door to listen. Yes, there was the sound of rustling as Maria moved across the carpet and took up her post outside the bathroom door, probably with her ear to the jamb. She waited until the water was rushing out of the shower heads at a terrific speed before turning the cheap phone on.

Her partner-in-crime had indeed been attempting to reach her. The tone of his texts subsided from anger to beseeching, to worry, but no mention of him contacting the FBI. Did that mean they weren't on the way here after all?

Really? She'd asked him to do one thing, and did he do it? No, not Dan. He was probably scared they would find out he was with her, and afraid he would be charged as an accomplice to enabling her to leave the country. What a wuss. What a suburban ninny he was. No help at all in her plan, and now she would have to find a way to get out of this situation herself.

But perhaps not just yet. She hadn't had a bath like this since.... since the night before Flanagan had arrested her. She needed her luxuries, they were a right, surely. But the tub soak would have to wait. A quick shower in the shell-lined stall with the five jets would suffice for now. She flicked a quick text to Dan before getting in.

It's okay, we're safe. She had to let him know, poor guy, he must be out of his mind with worry over her, and she hit send. Knowing Dan, he'd be calling her back right away and the ringing of the phone would alert the dragon lady who was hovering so closely, so she turned the phone off again and enjoyed the chilled champagne so thoughtfully provided by her host before her massaging shower.

Might as well see what this Hector Vargas had in store for her. At least the man knew what a lady liked.

'Where are my clothes?'

Diana had re-entered the bedroom and was now addressing the petite Maria. She clutched the thick white terry-towel robe around her body, the phone safely tucked away in the pocket.

The woman spoke no English, it seemed, but she opened the large closet, in which a single dress was hanging. Diana's own linen pants and long sleeved top were nowhere in sight.

But that dress, oh that dress. Diana let the fabric flow through her fingers. Pure, good quality silk, and if that wasn't enough, the label itself could initiate spontaneous orgasm. And it fit her perfectly, she soon found as she tried it on with Maria's assistance. Even the Louboutin's might have been made for her pedicured feet.

It was a flowy Grecian number, iridescent shades of champagne and lavender that brought out the blue of her eyes and her lightly tanned creamy complexion and played with the highlights of her blonde hair. She turned and gazed at herself in the three-fold mirror, and liked what she saw. He had even provided a full range of Chanel make-up products. By this point in time, Diana was feeling quite forgiving of Hector's rough invitation to his home, and looking forward to what his dining table would provide.

So she decided to keep the cell phone turned off for a while in order to see what would transpire. There was no pocket in which to slip the cell phone, yet the cleavage produced by the wisps of underwear Hector had provided gave an ample, if uncomfortable, hiding place. It was chilly against her bare flesh, but would warm up soon.

Jean-Luc and Hector had already assembled into the overly lavish drawing room off the entrance hall. Her lover, freshly shaved but still in his own shirt and jeans, scowled at her as she made her entrance. He remained sprawled in his comfy chair like a sulky child as Hector rose to greet her.

'You look entrancing,' Hector breathed as he reached up to kiss her cheek. The fancy sandals made her even taller, but that didn't seem to bother her host any. His hand lingered on her waist, and that didn't bother her one bit, either.

She looked over at Jean-Luc, raising an eyebrow, but he merely simmered at her. Diana flicked her freshly glossed hair and sat by Hector on the huge brocade sofa, then adjusted her hair to fall over her neckline, in order to further hide the phone.

Hector smiled at her as he relaxed into the sofa. Yes, he certainly had the air of Mark, she remembered her first thoughts on meeting the man. That assurance, that confidence, but with a body like a bull-dog, all muscles and strength. He lay his arm along the back of the sofa and she, too, relaxed into it.

Jean-Luc continued to quietly boil across the glass coffee table at the pair.

'Now, Diana... I may call you Diana?' He smiled again, and glanced down at her cleavage before bringing his eyes back up to hers. 'About my yacht.'

CHAPTER TWENTY-FOUR

'I still think you should have left her carry-on in the hotel,' Flanagan remarked as he watched Dan struggle with both his own and Diana's luggage. The men were walking down the streets of Bogota in the soft evening light. 'She's going to know something's up when she gets back and it's disappeared.'

Dan set his mouth grimly. 'Something's gone wrong,' he insisted. 'We've lost her.'

'There's a simple enough solution to that question,' Flanagan remarked. 'Did y'all get a GPS installed on that laptop?'

Dan stopped for a moment and stared at Flanagan. 'I don't know, but I'm going to find out right now. Can I borrow your phone?'

'What's wrong with yours?'

'Are you kidding? Do you know what long distance calls from here would cost?' Dan replied, then he dialled Mrs. Hastings from the FBI issue phone. What luck – she was visiting with Sam and Amelia, enjoying her retirement to the fullest. Flanagan got on to talk the technical side with Sam, explaining a short version of the story so far. He glossed over Diana's disappearance, not wanting to admit any professional malfeasance.

'Uh huh,' he said. 'That's great. So still in Bogota, that's a relief at any rate. So you have this number? Okay, send me the link so we can follow the laptop ourselves.'

Meanwhile Dan was staring at his phone. 'She wrote me back,' he said as Flanagan disconnected his own call. 'I was right, something's happened. She says *they* are safe, but she doesn't say who the other person is, or where she is, or what happened to her...'

And of course Diana didn't answer the call Flanagan put through to her.

·♥·♥·♥·♥·♥·

Hector's smile remained on his face as he looked at her. 'We need to discuss my yacht.'

Diana's eyes grew wide at the thought as she sipped the champagne silently offered to her. This guy would have the queen of all yachts, nothing less than the best for Hector Vargas, she thought as she wiggled her toes in the expensive sandals he had provided for her. Yeah, she could do that.

'I love sailing,' she replied, smiling back at him. Well, it was just a little fib. And not really a lie at all, because the sailing Mark had insisted on back home, physical work in the harsh wind and cold ocean, well, that would be nothing like travelling on Hector's five star yacht. Yes, she was telling the truth. She batted her newly mascaraed eyes at him. 'I can only imagine how glorious it is on the water in these parts.'

He blinked once. Slowly. 'Yes, it truly is. And I miss it.'

She shrugged and a small giggle escaped her as the champagne began to dance in her blood. 'I could be convinced,' she replied. Jean-Luc looked ready to blow a gasket over in his lonely corner. Jealousy, that's all, she thought as she dismissed him and turned back to Hector. Jean-Luc would never provide her with a yacht.

Hector's smile was growing a little strained. 'Convinced?'

'Your invitation to visit was a little... unconventional, I admit,' she said, stretching a little in anticipation, like a cat about to tuck into a lovely bit of fish. 'But I'm starting to warm up to you Hector, you and your unconventional ways do hold a certain charm.'

'Have you ever been on my yacht?'

'Hector, I just met you! That's a little forward, don't you think?'

His smile was definitely growing a touch stony. 'But you rented my yacht,' he informed her. 'And you sank it.'

Diana sputtered into her champagne and sat up. 'What?'

'You rented my yacht, you sank it in order to kill your husband, and now I want my yacht replaced,' Hector replied in his calm voice as he placed his steely arm around her shoulders and drew her back to the sofa. 'It was a very expensive yacht, and I was fond of it.' His black eyes bore into hers. All softness and seduction was gone from them now that he'd brought up the topic of money owed.

'Oh, God, oh God,' Diana said as she tried to think. 'There must be some misunderstanding, Hector.'

'I don't think so,' he said as he shook his head. 'Your name is on the agreement, your signature, your bank account. Which is another matter we need to discuss.'

'Mark must have forged my signature to rent your boat,' she replied, aghast. 'But why?'

'Don't get me wrong, Diana,' Hector said in a more conversational tone. 'I didn't like Mark either, and I applaud your initiative. But...' He shrugged his shoulders and did a latino gesture with his hands, as if to explain that he had no choice.

'I didn't kill my husband!' Diana struggled and broke free from his arm and sat up again. 'No no no. No. You've got it all wrong.'

'Okay, so maybe you didn't,' he said, shrugging again and showing his disbelief. 'But as I said, I need that yacht replaced.'

'Don't you have insurance?' she asked, in a very small voice.

He laughed, a very nasty laugh. 'There is no insurance in my business,' he said. 'Except that which you make for yourself.'

'Hector,' Diana now turned to address him directly. 'Mark killed himself. Or rather, he staged it to make it look like he's dead. He took all the money from the business, leaving me with absolutely nothing.'

He looked at her, with his mouth screwed up a little as he digested what she was saying.

'That's right,' she said, releasing the tension in her shoulders as she decided to come completely clean with the man. He wouldn't like her words, but what else was she to do? 'I can't replace your yacht. I can barely pay rent on the horrible hovel I've been reduced to living in.'

Suspicion was growing in his now small dark eyes.

'I had to steal from the pet trust fund in order to buy my ticket here,' she wailed.

Jean-Luc was now smirking across the room. 'She has nothing,' he told Hector. 'It's true, she is poor.'

Hector ignored the Frenchman. 'Why did you come here, if not to pay me back?' he asked. 'After the accident, I waited. And waited. I understood what you had done, but I assumed you would be honorable and pay me back. But you did not contact me. What was I to think?'

He got up and began pacing the thick carpet.

'I came here because I know Mark is not dead yet,' she called out to his back. 'And I want to get that bastard back for what he did to me.'

Hector stopped short and spun on his heel to face her. His face was unreadable.

A thought came to her, just a whisper of a thought, she could hardly entertain it. But she could see no other way out of this dilemma. If Diana couldn't pay him back for his yacht, he had no further use for her. She didn't know how Hector had amassed his obvious wealth, indeed it was probably a case of the less known, the better off she was. But she was sure he was as hardened a criminal as they come, and no-one would miss Diana Quenton if she didn't return from this illegal trip outside the country. No one, really, except the dogs. She was working to save her life.

'You could help me,' she said quietly and watched his face for a reaction.

He remained stock still.

'If we can find him and get the money back, I can pay you back,' she said. Along with all the neighbor's and whoever else the little shit had stolen from, but she didn't say that aloud. 'What do you say?'

He stared at her a while longer, then a slow smile spread across his face. Diana realized how tense she had been as her body relaxed.

'You and me, eh?' Hector came over and sat on the sofa again, closer this time. 'You and me.'

Diana nodded slowly, her eyes watchful on his face. The idea was not without appeal. Hector had money and muscle and resources behind him, he was a guy who could get the job done. Jean-Luc was.... not these things. Sexy and sophisticated, yes, but he had little to offer other than that.

And Dan... well, say no more. She almost laughed at her former naiveté in thinking the young lawyer was in any way equipped to handle the enormity of this project. Diana found herself looking at Hector with speculation, matching the speculation she saw in his own eyes. There was great promise here.

And the deal was done.

Hector jumped up from beside her and began to pace the room again, this time happily and with a purpose. 'But where do we start?'

'We start with feeding me,' she suggested. 'I'm absolutely starved, and I bet you have a trained chef on call in the kitchens of this palace who can rustle up a five course menu.'

He smiled at her and rubbed his hands. 'I love a woman with appetites,' he said. 'What would be your greatest pleasure?

'Just feed me, Hector,' she said, smiling back at him. 'For now.'

Jean-Luc continued to simmer in his corner, looking quite put out at this turn of events, but neither Diana nor Hector was paying the least bit of attention to him, so entranced were they in their mutual game of seduction.

CHAPTER TWENTY-FIVE

The dining was delightful, of course, and the service as impeccable as expected. The wine for each course had complemented the taste buds to a degree she hadn't experienced since that night in Nice when she and Jean-Luc had first met and began their affair. Diana finally pushed back the last plate with a smear of chocolate still mixed in a swirl of strawberry and cream against the thin gold stripes.

'Oh Hector,' Diana breathed, her voice lowed an octave by the extended pleasure she had experienced. Even the dress she wore had been thoughtfully created for times like this, the flowing folds able to conceal a multitude of sins with nothing to bind her in.

'Ah,' he said. 'Luciano has outdone himself, and for what better cause than the enjoyment of this lovely lady?' He reached and took her hand in his, slowly turning her palm over to kiss the delicate skin of her wrist. His hot breath lingered and sent shivers through her.

'Now, you must excuse me for a moment,' he said to her, and gave her hand a tiny squeeze. He left the room through the door the waiters had used.

Diana glanced up to see her erstwhile lover still scowling over the candle light, having hardly touched his dessert.

'Oh lighten up already, Jean-Luc,' she said. Jesus what a wet noodle he was turning out to be. You never really got to know someone until you went travelling with them, the old saying went, and it sure was turning out to be true in his case.

Her companion exploded across the table. 'Lighten up?' he spat. 'This ... this thug is pawing you and you, you are allowing it? His men were right, you are a *putana*, you... you're enjoying this, *non*?'

'Be quiet,' she hissed at him, and glanced at the door. 'It's all part of the plan, okay? We're going to use Hector to get to Mark – if anyone can find Mark in these parts, it's him.'

'Never mind Mark. Slut!' He crossed his arms and continued to scowl.

She was becoming quite pissed off at him now, he didn't need be such an asshole. Her evening had been so perfect up till this point, so why did Jean-Luc feel the need to ruin it for her? After all she'd been through in the past week, surely she deserved a little pampering and appreciation. He certainly wasn't going to give it to her, sitting there as if someone had stuffed something up his bum, his face all screwed up like that. He needed to trust that she was working on a plan, not end up giving the game away in a fit of childish jealousy.

'You think it's okay for you to carry on like this in front of me?' he demanded, not bothering to keep his voice down. 'You have no regard for my feelings, no?'

'I promised to marry you, didn't I? Just relax and go with the flow, or that will never happen,' she told him, then she lowered her voice again. 'You do realize Hector could just kill us and toss our bodies away? He loved that yacht, and he's very disappointed. I have to work with him... *we* have to work with him, in order to find Mark and retrieve the money. And to save our own lives.'

He gave a sniff. 'You don't care about Mark and the money,' he retorted. 'You don't need Mark's money now, you'll become that drug lord's mistress, and all will be well for you.'

'Drug lord?' Diana squawked, then shut up. But of course Hector Vargas was a drug lord, a ruthless hard-bitten man who had clawed his way to his money through sheer violence. Somehow, this realization made it all more real, and the stakes became higher. Yes, she hadn't really believed it when she'd said those words to Jean-Luc, but yes, Hector Vargas could easily have them killed and not blink an eye.

'What else can we do?' she whispered, bracing herself on the table with her hands as she leaned over. 'Do you have a better plan?'

Jean-Luc lifted a corner of his mouth and sneered. 'I will not let this man dishonor you.'

Seriously? He was worried about her honor when their lives might be at stake. She almost laughed, but pulled a straight face. 'Oh, Jean-Luc,' she began, but was distracted by the sound of footsteps approaching beyond the service door. 'We have to go along with whatever... he wants. Don't worry about me.'

'Diana,' he said to her with perfect seriousness in his tone and in those lovely brown eyes. 'I know you don't want to do this. You could not possibly find that stocky little man as sexy as me.'

He preened just a little, even as the footsteps grew closer, for he was fully confident that his own obvious attractions far outweighed anything that a middle-aged, balding drug lord could offer. A *short* drug lord.

Diana herself was under no illusions about what the night with Hector might entail, and actually she wasn't unexcited by the prospect. The man was ballsy, after all, and he was a solid mass of muscle and knew how to treat a woman. He had taste (in a Baroque, latino kind of way) but that just meant he appreciated a woman's curves, and would never make snide remarks about extra pounds like Jean-Luc was known to do on his crabbier days. But what she didn't need was her lover getting in the way and spoiling the mood for her.

'Look,' she whispered hurriedly. 'It might be best if you left. Hector will understand, and he will let you go, cause you've got nothing for him. He doesn't care about you. So you can find Dan and the FBI, they'll probably be hanging out at the hotel waiting for me to return...'

But before she could reach into her cleavage and pass him her cell phone, the door swung open and Hector himself appeared.

'Perhaps, my sweet, we should retire to the drawing room,' he said, eyes only on Diana.

Now was the time for Diana to prove her acting skills. All those dreams she'd had all those years ago, and all that work she'd put into them – finally coming into fruition.

'Hector,' she said softly as she walked towards him and placed her hand on his tuxedoed arm. 'Perhaps another small... *tiny* portion of that delicious confection you served for dessert...?'

He chuckled and his black eyes shone lustfully at Diana. 'Ah, my sweet,' he replied. His arms encircled her and he threw his head back in a laugh. 'So refreshing to find a woman who embraces life and is not afraid of calories!'

Hector nuzzled her neck. 'One moment dear one,' he whispered. Then he strode purposefully back through the service door.

'We need to get away now, Diana,' Jean-Luc was by her side and whispering. 'Come, let us go. This man will kill you when he has had his way with you, throw you on the scrap-heap like garbage.'

'No,' she whispered back at him in a very firm voice. 'We'll never get past his guards. We need to convince him to let you go. And you can hunt down Dan.'

He shook his head and looked at her with a mixture of sorrow and regret in his eyes. 'You won't get out of here alive. Remember, there's always the insurance money, you have more chance of getting that than escaping from this man's clutches with your life,' he said. 'And I hate the thought of his hands on you, I cannot stand for this.'

Diana started for a moment. The elusive insurance money? She hadn't mentioned that to him, she'd forgotten all about that small detail when telling Jean-Luc her tale. It took her aback for a moment, but there were more pressing matters to address in this short space of time they were allotted.

She took Jean-Luc by the arm. 'Here, take my cell phone,' she said. 'You'll probably have a better chance to use it than me. Dan's number is on it. Keep him informed of what we're doing and where we are.'

'What, so he can alert the FBI? Diana, are you crazy?' He stared at her, refusing to take the phone in hand. 'I told you I can't have them sniffing around.'

'Jean-Luc, don't argue with me,' she hissed. 'If you insist on coming with me on this trip to find Mark, we're going to need back-up. I'm going to need to get away from Hector at some point when all this is over, right? And do you think you're going to be able to save me then? You, without a gun?'

'And besides,' she continued, grabbing the lapels of his pink shirt, pressing her point. 'I need Mark taken alive. Hector would shoot him the moment he sees him. Getting in touch with the FBI means they will take over, take him alive and bring him back home, so eventually I'll get whatever money is left over. For us. Do you see?'

But Hector was back in the room before she could pass on the phone which held Dan's number. He moved lightly for such a solidly built man. He was looking expectantly at Diana. She resumed her place at his side and leaned into him ever so slightly.

'Perhaps, Hector,' she whispered intimately in his ear, and nodded her head towards Jean-Luc. 'Perhaps it might be a good idea to allow Jean-Luc to leave the mansion. It would give us... privacy.'

Hector scowled at the tall Frenchman. 'I don't think that's wise,' he said decisively.

'But,' she continued in her low voice. 'We need to discuss Mark. You *are* going to help me find him, aren't you?'

Hector shrugged. He had other things on his mind at this moment, and finding the husband of this woman was not high on the evening's priorities. 'Time enough to think about that tomorrow.'

Diana drew on everything she'd learned in the few acting classes she'd bothered to go to. Her eyes welled with tears. 'Mark has left me bereft,' she said. 'Without a *sou* to my name. I will never be able to pay you back for the loss of your beloved yacht. We need a plan...'

'There is always my yacht,' Hector agreed, a fond look in his eye as he remembered, then he smiled up at her. 'Good enough.'

'You'll let Jean-Luc go then?' She fluttered her eyes at him. 'It's alright, he'll find his own way back to the city. You don't need to drive him.'

Hector barked with laughter. 'Diana, I am not such a bad host, to turn my guest out into the night,' he said. He turned to Jean-Luc. 'You, you can go to bed. Give me some time with the lovely Diana, eh?'

He made shooing motions with his hands. 'Go on, go to bed like a good little boy. Go now. Leave the adults to their activities.'

With the appearance of one of the afternoon's gunmen, now dressed in tails and ties for evening duties, Jean-Luc had no choice but to leave the room, his eyes flashing warning at Diana, and knives at Hector.

·♥·♥·♥·♥·♥·

Not much hatching of plans happened that evening and night, nor did Diana have a chance to check the cell phone for Dan's reply. However Hector did prove that short middle-aged balding drug lords can have their more positive aspects, and his *latino* tongue was particularly gifted.

She had managed to slip the cell phone out of her cleavage and into the folds of her discarded dress before he dived in. He had looked askance at the red lines between her breasts from the phone having been nestled so tightly all evening, but she placed the blame on the tightness of the upsweeping caused by her sexy underwear. 'Ah,' Hector had said lasciviously. 'Too much woman for that silly piece of lace.'

Afterwards, they lay together spent on Diana's bed, far into the night, watching each other in the mirror above, giggling like school kids.

She turned on to her side and played with the heavy gold medallion around his neck.

'So,' she said. 'My husband.'

'Hmm,' Hector said lazily. 'Yes, your husband. He's dead, no?'

She shook her head. 'No, he's not. I told you. I'm sure he's still alive, somewhere.'

'Yes,' replied Hector. 'Then I must find him.'

She nodded into his chest.

'And kill him,' Hector added.

Diana's fingers paused. 'Ah, that's a little extreme, don't you think, Hector? We could just, find him and bring him back to the States, and turn him over to the FBI.'

'FBI?' Hector gave a shudder. 'I will play no part in that. No, I will kill him like a man should die.'

'Hector...' Diana searched for the words. 'I can't let you have blood on your hands. He's not worth it.'

'No my sweet Diana,' he said, turning toward her and kissing the top of her head. 'My men will do it, you silly thing, worrying about me. You think I will bother getting dirty when I have others to do my work for me?'

He gave her a squeeze. 'Let us make our plans then, for afterwards,' he said.

'Afterwards?' Her plan was to have Mark turned over to the FBI, the money returned, and what little was left over would be hers. Hector didn't figure into the afterwards, not at all.

'When he has been helped to pass through this life,' Hector said. 'Then we will be free. You will live here with me.'

'Wait now, Hector,' she said, sitting up. 'Live here? In the middle of God knows where?' No, despite the comforts of the palace, she had no intention of staying here. Her life was in Baserville, and she would be resuming her position there tout suite. She was really looking forward to giving the jobs back to Mrs. Hastings and Sam, to being reunited with her pets, to flaunting her innocence in Rose LaBlanche's face. Especially that.

Though perhaps Hector could put a hit out on Rose. But this was just an idle thought, and she pulled herself together.

His face fell. 'But the house in Bogota...' He thought further, then shrugged. 'I will buy you another house in the city.'

'What are you suggesting, Hector? That I live as your mistress?' She drew away from him slightly. This would not do, not at all. She had to disabuse him of these notions immediately. Fun as he was, talented as he was, she hadn't signed up for a long term commitment to the man. Think how the tongues would wag back in Baserville if they found out she was the kept woman of a drug lord in Colombia, she'd never be able to hold her head up there again.

'Oh, my Diana,' Hector exclaimed as he hugged her again. His muscular body was now cool and clammy with the drying sweat. 'You drive a hard bargain, but what can I say? You want the present Mrs. Vargas to meet with an unfortunate accident so that we can be wed.'

'You can't kill your wife!'

'Eh, she is a nag,' he said, shrugging it off. 'And she may be sleeping with her bodyguard. A tidy little accident in the hills as they drive to their tryst, simple to arrange. It is easily done.'

'No, I mean, yes you can kill your wife, or have her killed, but not on my account,' she scolded him. 'I can't let you do that.'

'But what other way is there?' he asked, perplexed. 'I am Catholic, we don't divorce. My mother would never allow me to do this thing. I could not bring such shame onto my family, and besides that bitch of a wife would take me for everything.'

Diana stared at him. He wasn't getting it, and she wasn't entirely sure that it was her place to explain it to him. She had no intention of becoming his wife or his mistress, but to bring that point up right at this moment was a sure fire invitation to end up dead in the jungle. This was a tangly situation, to be sure.

She watched as a dried snot whistled from the hairs of his nose. Even in this dim light she could see that his pores were huge from this angle, and his cologne was becoming sickly sweet. He scratched his balls and farted with a grunt, then reached over to light a cigarette.

Suddenly, Hector Vargas was not so attractive anymore. And he was a murderer. Life was cheap at this end of the world. She may have gotten in over her head.

She forced herself to relax and sink back into his arms, suppressing the shiver of distaste that ran through her body. 'So,' she said. 'When we're married – I like the sound of that. And you do know I want a honeymoon this time round?'

'That bastard never gave you a honeymoon to celebrate his luck in marrying the most beautiful woman in the world?'

She shook her head, hiding her face into his chest. She could be excused for lying under the circumstances, for doing a Scheherazade and trying to prolong her life. For with Mark and Diana there had only been that little beach in the Caribbean, the isolated, tourist free stretch of sand, the two of them alone with their dreams of the future.

And their promises to each other. Mark's loose, off-the-cuff boasting of where they would be, what he would do. The island he would buy.

Yes, the island. It made sense, for this would be coming full circle for her husband. She knew this like she had known Mrs. Hastings had lied about the laptop. Mark was on that island.

Now her only problem lay in figuring out how to use Hector to her best advantage without getting herself married to him or worse.

CHAPTER TWENTY-SIX

Diana sighed as she let herself down into the hot water. The bubbles came up and tickled her chin. The sigh turned into a groan as the hot water surrounded her and expunged the tension in her shoulders that not even the sex could dissipate. This was the life, this was what she was born for.

The biggest problem she could foresee, as she lay in the luxurious bubble bath early that morning, her biggest stumbling block was Hector and his enthusiasm, along with his total lack of love and respect for the FBI and other policing agencies. Diana needed to be able to hand over Mark unscathed to the FBI, in order to prove her innocence and to get the money back.

The second-best scenario was to provide them with Mark's body. That would at least ensure she received the five million dollar settlement, and she could probably eke by on that. Could she? Her understanding of finances was still pretty shaky.

So Hector was both the solution to her plan, yet at the same time he was the fly in the ointment. Only through Hector could she somehow make it to that Caribbean idyll, the lonely island they had gazed at from the beach all those years ago. The problem was that Hector would insist on being present and killing Mark and throwing his body into the water to cover up his misdeeds. In which case Diana would be stuck with the drug lord forever, and wouldn't even get the insurance settlement without proof of her husband's death.

Another person, Dan perhaps, or the dour Mrs. Hastings, might point out that Diana did have another option, which was to return to the States after Mark's death (without his body as proof) and just suck it up and live like any other normal person, surviving from money earned through work. But that didn't factor into her line of thinking at all. Work was for idiots, not for Diana, and it looked like she might be stuck with Hector as the only means of supporting her habit of luxurious living. There was no other way about it.

She finally came up with something. It was a loosely formed plan fraught with many pitfalls, but it was her only lifeline. The time had come to get back in contact with Dan. She would have to send a very conciliatory text. Hector was still asleep, she could tell by the grunts and whistles coming from the room.

But her hands were wet, and when she took the phone in her hand it slipped, about to fall to the tiled floor with a clatter and a smash. Quickly she grabbed at it, but in so doing only changed the trajectory of the phone's fall. It landed among the bubbles without a splash, sinking down to the bottom of the deep tub.

'Dammit,' she cried aloud, reaching her hands below the water in an effort to save it before the water got in to it. But feel as she might, she could not find it, and the thick bubbles obscured any sight of it. When at last she found the phone, it was irretrievably dead, no matter how hard she towelled it dry.

'Oh, no,' she said. This phone had been her only link, for it held Dan's number. And of course she hadn't written it down separately on paper – who would bother to do that?

A change of plans was needed, and fast.

Drying herself off, she listened carefully at the bathroom door. Hector's snores had ceased, and there were sounds of his movements.

She wrapped the fluffy robe tight around her and slipped the defunct cell phone deep within its pocket.

'Oh, Hector,' she called out. The smoky glass of the bathroom door slid into the wall.

'Yes, my sweet?'

'I've been thinking,' she confided as she leant in to kiss him, holding her breath as she did so. 'Let's forget about that messy business of killing your wife, huh?'

He paused and cocked his head to one side as he thought, then frowned. 'No, I like the idea. She is a bitch, and she is dishonoring me.'

'But she's the mother of your children,' Diana pointed out. 'They need her. Do you know what a rotten mother I am? I could never be as good as she is.'

He shrugged. 'I have help hired for that.'

'And your mother,' Diana continued, ignoring his words. 'She wouldn't like it if you did that, killed your wife, I mean. Would she? Doesn't she think motherhood is sacred?'

He pursed his lips and nodded in agreement. 'That's right,' he said slowly. 'That would upset Mama.'

'So... let's let your wife live, huh?'

'But you want marriage, Diana,' he replied. 'As a man of honor, I must provide this.'

'What we have, Hector,' Diana began in a saintly voice. 'What we have goes beyond mere human rules. Marriage? Pah! I think it's enough that we can be together.'

'That would be easier,' Hector admitted. He scratched his chest. 'Ah, I have seduced the great Diana, she wants only my love and cares not about conventions, eh?'

She nodded. Sure, whatever.

'But your husband,' he continued. 'You will still let me kill him.'

'We'll discuss that later,' she told him firmly. 'But right now, I have certain needs.'

His eyes sparkled, as much as a hardened criminal's eyes can be said to sparkle and he reached towards her.

'No, not that,' she said shortly, slapping his hand away. 'Breakfast. And clothing, I'm going to need to do a ton of shopping. Because...'

Her eyes slid towards him playfully. 'Because even though we're not going to get married, I demand a honeymoon to celebrate us.'

'Where would you most like to go, my darling?' Hector's face was alight with greedy pleasure. He huffed out his chest all hairy and gold medallions and smelling of last night's sweat. 'Anything for you.'

Really, Diana thought, men were so predictable. One night in the sack and he thought she was in love with him. She batted her eyes and tried not to breathe in too deeply the smell of his stale cologne.

'I want a cruise,' she said.

His face darkened at the memory. 'But my yacht is...'

'Oh, come off it, Hector,' she said, her tone brusque. 'Surely to God you, of all people, can find another yacht to take me cruising.' She stuck out her bottom lip petulantly, just like she'd seen Jean-Luc do. And it worked.

'I have another, but it is not nearly so grand,' he said reluctantly, looking down at the bed covers petulantly.

She chucked him under the chin, forcing him to look up at her clear blue eyes, and she smiled at him. 'It's okay,' she said. 'As long as you and I are together, who cares?'

·♥·♥·♥·♥·♥·

She mentally ticked off her list as she dressed in her travelling clothes of yesterday, the linen pants now freshly laundered and pressed. New clothes were the next thing, as soon as she'd availed of the no doubt sumptuous breakfast to be provided downstairs. Hector's credit card was good for it.

Diana thought for a moment of the clothes left behind in the hotel room. She should really send Hector's goons for her stuff, for she wanted to hold that laptop close to her. Okay. But that didn't mean she couldn't still get Hector to go shopping with her, right?

He was on board with providing her the means to cruise around the Caribbean looking for Mark. She'd tell him the reason later. Or not. She hadn't quite worked that bit of the plan out yet, but the important thing was to get over to that island where Mark was no doubt hiding. She had a rough idea of the location.

Now, for Jean-Luc. The whole plan had hinged on her lover (or ex-lover, whatever the case might be) being persuaded to take her cell phone and contacting Dan, in order for Dan to get the FBI to meet them at Mark's island. But that was no longer to be, for the phone was dead. And since Jean-Luc was refusing to leave her to the mercy of Hector or get caught up with the FBI, she would make use of him another way.

He could get on the internet and lookup Mrs. Hastings' number, and somehow contact her, explain the situation they were in and ask her to tell Dan.

The FBI team would swoop down on the island (Mark had to be there) and snatch him up, then somehow save her from the clutches of this drug lord.

But, she realized, not too soon. Shit. If Mrs. Hastings called Dan and he contacted the FBI and told them where Mark was hiding, where she was pretty sure he was hiding, then they would rush in and take all the glory for themselves. That would never do, it just didn't go along with Diana's daydreams of denouncing Mark herself, of letting him know he hadn't outwitted her. Her revenge fantasy would have all the air taken out of it, as flat as a ten day old balloon.

No, she would have to time it exactly.

She got her chance over the breakfast table, while Hector was off seeing to his business, whatever that might be. Jean-Luc's early night had not improved his mood, surprisingly enough, for she knew he dearly loved his sleep. He was lurking over barely buttered toast and black coffee, even though a full spread was laid out on the sideboard awaiting their pleasure.

'*Non*,' he said definitively as he waggled his index finger in the air and munched on his toast. 'No, Diana, I will not do this.'

'Jean-Luc – surely to God there must be a phone or a computer here in the house so you can look up her number,' she said. 'Pretend you want to check your email or something. I can't do it, I can't risk Hector suspecting anything. But you – he doesn't care about you. I need you to contact Mrs. H. and get her to call Dan or Flanagan, and... and just think – you can be the one to save me.'

But even an appeal to his chivalrous side did no good. He shook his head firmly. 'No,' he replied. 'He will not let me use his WiFi. This I know. And to contact the FBI? Are you mad?'

He munched some more. 'Who is this 'Dan' anyway? Another boyfriend I suppose,' he said with suspicion.

'Eeugh,' she said. 'No, he's my lawyer.' In answer to Jean-Luc's broody stare, she elaborated. 'He's short and pudgy, and can't dress for beans.'

'Short and dumpy like him?' Jean-Luc jerked his head toward the door to indicate their host.

'Believe me, Hector is not dumpy. There's not an ounce of spare fat on that body,' she replied, digging the serving utensil into the bacon and eggs left in warmers on the sideboard. 'And besides,

Dan is the one who can get in contact with the FBI, as I told you. He's brilliant. He'll know what to do.'

'I thought you were a vegetarian,' he said, eying her plate with disgust. 'Anyway, no, I cannot risk this,' he added firmly.

She stared at him in exasperation. 'What the hell, Jean-Luc? This is our only chance. You know, we may not make it out of here alive without help.'

'*You* may not make it out alive,' he conceded, his dark eyes hooded. 'But sometimes the winds of chance change direction, *non*? And we must take our opportunities where we can.'

Her mind racing, she searched for the meaning behind this cryptic message from her lover. 'What are you saying, Jean-Luc? What has happened? You're acting... different.'

He said nothing, just looked down at his half-eaten toast.

'Look, you know that me and Hector... I can't avoid that, no matter how much I don't want to... do it with him,' she said. And truly, she was beginning to regret her haste in jumping into the bed of the South American drug lord. Who knew such a hardened criminal would fall for her so quickly? And after finding out that the depths of his appreciation for her included cold-heartedly killing his wife... she shivered. No way she would become Mrs. Vargas Number Two or Three or Four or whatever the number was. She suspected his wives didn't have long life expectancies, and she loved hers far too much to sign it away so cheaply.

'What are you proposing to do, then,' she asked him. 'It's going to seem sort of weird if we go on a 'honeymoon' with you tagging along, isn't it? I don't think Hector will go for that.'

He looked down into his coffee cup. Was he still in a jealous sulk? She could think of no other reason for that cryptic comment.

'Oh, Jean-Luc,' she said, coming over to him and whispering into his ear. 'You know you are the only one for me, don't you?'

He said nothing in reply, but held her hand hard and looked at her with genuine sorrow in his eyes.

CHAPTER TWENTY-SEVEN

S o it was that Diana and her two lovers made the long trip back to the city. An uncomfortable trip it was, too, despite the luxury vehicle they travelled in, perfectly air-conditioned while the tinted windows protected them from the sun's harshness, and every refreshment imaginable was at their fingertips. Yet the company lacked a certain *joie de vivre* despite Hector's infatuation with the new love of his life. There was a definite feeling that three was a crowd emanating from the men on both sides of her.

Her mind was racing, trying to find a way out of this situation she'd found herself in. Jean-Luc's phone was at the hotel. She would make him look up Mrs. Hastings' home number and call her. The dour Scottish housekeeper would have Dan's contact number, of that she was sure.

She tensed and gasped as a realization hit her. She didn't need Jean-Luc's reluctant help. The laptop which waited at the hotel, she could use that to hunt down Mrs. H herself. Too bad she hadn't thought of securing Flanagan's email beforehand. Or Dan's, for that matter.

They reached the city and as they drove the streets Diana looked half-heartedly for a hint of Dan's red hair, not that she really expecting to find him. She was more concerned with searching the streets for familiar landmarks which would indicate they were nearing W Hotel.

'Hector,' she purred, once she saw they were in the neighborhood. 'There's the hotel! We need to stop here. I want to get my suitcase.'

'You don't need those rags,' Hector said. 'I will buy much better for you, the clothing you deserve as my lover.'

She could feel Jean-Luc tensing beside her.

'Now Hector,' she said, a playful note in her voice. 'I have some of my favorite lingerie up there. And besides...' She whispered a little something to him, for his ears only.

'I'll send a man in,' he replied with a flick of his wrist.

'I don't want one of your men with their hands in my underwear,' she said, forcing shock into her voice. 'And actually, I also need to pee,' she said into his ear. 'Really bad.' She held her legs together. She wasn't lying about that.

'Can't you wait?' he asked with a frown. 'We'll be at the airport in half an hour.'

'No,' she said. 'It's really urgent. You rushed us out of the house so quickly this morning...'

He sighed and spoke sharply to the driver, who pulled in when the W came into view.

Diana opened the door and jumped down, quickly making her way into the hotel. She could have made a break for it at this point, but why bother? Hector was the only one with the means to find Mark and she intended to use him to the fullest.

She came out of the marble and gilt ladies' room to find that Jean-Luc had been dispatched to get the luggage. He stood by the concierge's desk, a single suitcase by his side.

'That was fast,' she said to him. 'You've been up and packed them already?'

He shrugged. 'Mine was waiting behind the desk for me,' he said. 'The hotel maids packed it as the room was cancelled.'

'Where's mine?'

Jean-Luc gave a shrug. 'Who knows? Reception said it wasn't there.'

An alarm bell went off in her head at these words. Had Hector cancelled the room? He had been of the opinion that she didn't need these clothes, that anything from her life before would never be good enough for the love of his life, so he may have had the foresight to do this. However, it didn't sound like something her new lover would bother to do.

And if Hector wasn't responsible, who was? Most likely the person who had booked the room and arranged for Jean-Luc to be flown over. This could only mean the FBI, which in turn had to mean that Dan and Flanagan had everything under control. They had the laptop and her Louis Vuitton, and everything would work out well. At least she fervently hoped so.

She was going to have to rely on Jean-Luc's help after all.

'You have your phone? Have you thought about what I asked you to do?' she whispered, her hand on his arm.

Jean-Luc looked intently at her and said nothing, as if he was weighing his options and making a decision. 'Perhaps I should tell you...' But they were interrupted.

'My darling, what is keeping you?' Hector had entered the lobby. There was a hard glint in his eye as he looked at the two.

Diana turned the full beam of her smile to him. 'We were just saying,' she said. 'That Jean-Luc will stay here. He doesn't need to come with us. Darling.'

'No.'

'*Non.*'

Both men spoke at once, sharing unreadable glances as they did so.

"I will accompany you. I too would like a cruise on the Caribbean,' Jean-Luc said.

'I think it is better that he remains with us,' Hector agreed. He narrowed his eyes at Diana.

She poked the Frenchman in the ribs with her elbow, on the side away from Hector. What was the man playing at?

They returned to the people carrier, the two men sticking firmly at her sides. Something had drastically shifted in this situation, and it didn't feel like it was in her favor. This uncomfortable feeling also took most of the fun out of the shopping expedition.

·♥·♥·♥·♥·♥·

Hector's private jet flew them to the north of the country, to the little tip of Colombia that stretched into the Caribbean Sea north of Venezuela. She watched the screen charting their progress. Aruba was marked, but the little islands around it remained nameless. No matter, they were quite close to the port where Hector's Number Two Yacht waited.

Her feeling of unease grew when, returning from the washroom, she surprised the men in a close conference. They didn't even bother to look guilty as they both looked up at her. It was the smugness she saw on Hector's face which scared her most.

As they prepared to land, she could see the vista of the Gulf spread out blue before them.

Hector's manner changed as he ushered them on board, becoming the perfect host yet again, except for a couple of digs he made about the smallness of the yacht. But he was far more cheerful now than he'd been.

This was his wife's yacht, he informed them. Diana could tell he was fully aware that, despite his assumed humbleness at being forced to offer her the Number Two yacht, it was a far superior craft than anything the pair had travelled on before. Mark was wealthy, but only in comparison to Baserville - his wealth was only counted in millions. Hector had informed them his was counted in hundreds of millions.

'There is only one bedroom,' he confided, in mock despair. 'Diana, you'll have to share with me.'

'How about Jean-Luc?'

Hector sniffed. 'He will bunk down with the crew.'

She giggled and held his hand as they walked into a room that was almost all windows, the vista open on three sides. It held comfortable sofas and a bar, a dining table and was carpeted, of all things. Who'd ever heard of carpeting on a boat? It would get all salty, surely, and start to stink pretty soon. It was on a par with having carpet in a kitchen, say, or a bathroom, to Diana's mind.

Although, it certainly made walking in stilettoes easier.

Still, it held a lovely chandelier, and the windows were open wide to let the fresh salt air in, and the air was warm still holding a touch of jungle greenery in its moisture. Diana smiled at Hector's man who, laden down with parcels and bags from her shopping spree struggled up the gangway.

It wouldn't be such a bad life, really, if it wasn't for the uncertainty of Hector's fickleness in his affections. She could get used to this.

CHAPTER TWENTY-EIGHT

The first chance she got, Diana wandered in a seemingly aimless fashion into the room at the top of the boat, where a man was steering the yacht. Mark would have known all the right terminology. She smiled at the dark man, who stood at attention. Not a bad looker with his slim dark body and so handsome in his captain's hat. He appeared ill at ease in her presence.

She gave him her sweetest smile, and her eye caught the large map spread out under glass. Yes!

'Oh, a map! I love maps,' she said to him, but it was a weird sort of map, nothing like anything she had seen before. The land mass was yellow, and not a single city name, country or highway marked on it. She squinted at it, but it didn't make any more sense that way.

'Where are we? On this map, I mean,' she said as she pointed to the chart.

The captain silently pointed their location, the long white finger of his glove showing a point to the northern tip of Colombia.

'Oh, okay, good.' She scanned her eye around the other landmasses, looking for the island that would be Mark's. She let her long fingernail trail along the glass. No country names were written in.

'That's Aruba?'

Again without a word, he pointed to the island to the right. Aruba was an island which stood off away from the mainland, and there were other smaller islands scattered to the north of it. She felt a thrill of recognition. Yes, it would be... this one there. She could feel it, could almost smell how close Mark was. Justice was coming.

'Hmm,' she said. 'Yes, that's where I want to go.' She nodded and jabbed her finger at it. 'Aruba. So close. We can travel like this.' She pressed her finger along the coast, travelling to the east.

The captain looked at her with horror in his eyes. A fine white cloth appeared from his pocket and he wiped the glass where she had smudged her fingerprint. 'No, we do not travel there,' he told her in heavily accented English.

'But that's where I want to go,' she said, speaking slowly and clearly, keeping the smile pasted on her face.

'No, impossible to go there. Mr. Vargas will not allow this.'

She stared at him, frustration beginning to rankle. To have come this far, and to have done all she had done... She could feel Mark was there, could almost smell him from here, only to have a hired hand tell her it wasn't possible?

'It's my honeymoon, and I said we're going there,' she told him, staring him down and daring him to go against her will. They were about the same height with her newly bought high heels on.

The captain picked up the phone and spoke sharp words of Spanish into it. Hector came hurrying up the steps a moment afterwards.

'Diana,' he said, placing his arm around her waist. 'What is this? You are interested in sailing the yacht? I think we'll leave that to the man in charge.' He laughed and pulled her away.

'Hector darling,' she said as she kissed him on the cheek. 'I want to go to Aruba, and your man said no.' She trilled her fake little laugh, confident of getting her way now the boss was here.

'Ah, about that,' Hector said. 'Have you met Don Juan Francisco de la Quadra, the fine captain of our ship?'

'Charmed, I'm sure,' she said, her smile tight on her face.

Don Juan de Whatnot did not acknowledge her, instead he let loose a spate of Spanish to his boss. She could have sworn she heard Mark's name mentioned. Hector nodded with agreement with him, then spoke a bit back at him. It looked, to her incredulous eyes, as if they were discussing the matter, as if the servant was calling the shots and winning the argument.

Hector nodded, saying '*Si, si*', and then turned to her.

''Ah, my enchanting one,' he said to soften the blow, but gently shaking his head. '*El Capitan* says no.'

But *El Capitan* was not the one sleeping with Hector Vargas, and perhaps he didn't yet realize his position on the totem pole. 'You don't understand, my darling,' she said. '*I* want to go to Aruba.' She looked at him expectantly.

Hector continued to shake his head and try to pull her towards the door. 'Let us talk about it over dinner, eh? The chef has something special prepared just for you.'

She dug in her heels and repeated her desire in a more forceful voice. 'And why can't we go there?'

The captain let loose another volley of Spanish syllables.

'He can speak English, can't he?' Diana was by now pretty pissed herself.

He looked at Hector. 'And this is the woman of the man who wrecked your yacht,' he continued, or at least that's what Diana thought he was saying. It was difficult to make out through his accent. Don Juan spit on the floor in disgust. 'I would kill him with my bare hands, and you also,' he said turning back to Diana. 'You hired the yacht and then ruined it. You should be shot for your actions.'

'Hey, it was nothing to do with me,' she replied, placing her hands on her hips. 'That was all Mark's actions. I'm trying to get the money back for Hector.'

'You!' Don Juan spit again. 'Money cannot replace such a watercraft.'

Hector drew Diana aside. 'He feels very strongly about his vessels, they are like family to him,' he told her. 'He's still in mourning. Please forgive him.'

'We cannot head northeast,' Don Juan turned to her again and addressed her. 'There is a storm brewing. We should not even be out on the water at all this evening, but *Senor* Vargas insisted.'

She looked out the window onto the calm blue sea ahead of them where the sun was lowering in the sky in a blaze of gold and orange and pink. They were headed west into the sunset.

'What storm?' she scoffed. 'Look at it out there. It's gorgeous, not a white-cap in sight.'

She turned to her new lover.

'Hector,' she said. 'We're headed in the wrong direction. I don't want to go to ... to Panama! I didn't come all this way just to...' Diana crossed her arms and drew herself up to her fullest height and stamped her stiletto on the polished wooden floor, which action set off another barrage from the captain.

'Ah, your shoes, my darling,' Hector said, wiping the sweat from his forehead with his hand. 'Not the best footwear for in here. Perhaps we could discuss this over dinner?'

She had no choice, Hector had to be let in on her plan. 'Mark may be on that island. I'll explain later,' she whispered in his ear.

He paused, then gave a single nod. Tugging her out the door, he call back something to Don Juan, who gave a loud humph in reply. As the two headed down the iron steps to the deck below, the yacht gave a sharp swerve as it changed direction, almost knocking Diana off her heels except that Hector had a good grip around her waist.

·♥·♥·♥·♥·♥·

Flanagan lay on his beachside lounger, icy rum drink in hand, and sighed deeply.

'This is the life,' he said as he soaked up the heat and sun. His eyes scanned the beach idly. It was a scene of paradise, the palms leaves ruffled in the gentle breeze, the sun shone off the turquoise waters, the women dressed in their sexiest bikinis.

'Looks like they need a bit of assistance,' Flanagan noted, pointing his drink at a bevy of women in their thirties who were attempting to erect a sun-shade tent on the beach. They'd been taking advantage of the resort's all-inclusive alcohol, by the looks of things.

Dan looked over to where he indicated. 'So go help them.'

'Nah, they're too far away. By the time we get there, they'll have it all sorted,' he replied. 'Not my type anyway. Too skinny, looks like they starve themselves.'

'What is your type?' Not that Dan was really interested, but he needed something to take his mind from his worries about Diana.

'My type is better built, a bit of meat on her bones, a woman with an appetite for life,' Flanagan answered. 'A bit like.... Hell, more like our Lady Di. Now she is fine-looking woman, wouldn't you say?'

Dan screwed up his face. He'd never thought of her as being a desirable woman, quite frankly, besides the fact she was so much older than himself. Diana terrified him, when she wasn't frustrating the hell out of him. Like when she disappeared in an unknown country and made them chase her all around southern parts of the Gulf of Mexico. He was deeply regretting the agreements he had made with both her and Flanagan.

'I still think we should be doing something more active. It doesn't feel right to be lying around on a beach while she might be in danger.'

'That's the army for you, hurry up and wait.'

'I thought you were FBI.'

Flanagan sat up a little, and watched as Dan carefully lathered on the 60 SPF, smoothing it into every cranny where the sun's rays might creep. It got a little messy around the beard line. His belly glared in the sunshine, causing the FBI agent to readjust his sunglasses. He looked down at his own dusky skin in satisfaction, admiring the dark hairs on his solid legs and compared the skin tones against that of his companion.

'You know something? You must be the whitest white man I've ever seen.'

'And I intend to stay that way, thank you very much,' Dan replied. 'My skin is very sensitive.'

Five minutes passed.

'You're *sure* she's over there on that island?'

'That's what the GPS says,' the FBI agent said for the tenth time. 'She's got the laptop, right? The signal says she's straight across the water there, on that little island sticking up by itself. GPS doesn't lie.'

'I'm still not sure that she has the laptop,' Dan said. 'Why would she leave her Louis Vuitton behind? And why would she wear her flat sandals?'

'Give up about the luggage and her footwear already, will you?' Flanagan lifted his glass to the bikini clad women who had given up the attempt to shade themselves and were headed back to the bar to top up their drinks.

'We should be over there,' Dan worried.

'Time enough for that tomorrow,' Flanagan said. 'We've got all the gear packed in the dinghy, just a matter of hopping over after breakfast and scouting out the island. It's not that big.'

'But you think Mark is there with her?'

'I am about 100 percent sure of that,' Flanagan replied, relaxing back on the lounger and closing his eyes. The tracking device had showed him that the suitcase of Diana's companion was presently sailing over the seas from Colombia towards them at this very moment, and Flanagan was sure it was headed for the island where the laptop lay. He had everything in hand.

'Did you ever think,' he began as he looked over his sunglasses to Dan in the lounger next to him, wondering how to break it to the idealistic young man. 'Did it not occur to you that Diana knew what she was doing all along? Her and Mark, the pair of them had the whole scheme cooked up between them.'

'No, that's not how it is.' Dan shook his head firmly. 'No way.'

'Speaking as someone who is older and wiser than you,' Flanagan remarked. 'It's a nasty fact of life, but I'm afraid you're going to have to accept it. Diana was stringing you along the whole time.'

But Dan refused to accept this.

'She might be dead already! She's in danger if Mark is there,' Dan fretted. 'How can you just sit here, knowing she may need help? Tomorrow may be too late.'

'Trust me. My instincts are never wrong. That's why I'm so successful at what I do.'

Dan picked at the seam of his surfer shorts for lack of anything better to do. 'I heard there might be a storm tomorrow. If we went over there this afternoon, we'd be in place.'

'I am *not* sleeping out on the island, not when we have a perfectly good hotel suite by the pool. Diana can look after herself for one night. Now excuse me, I think some ladies over there need a hand with their loungers.'

CHAPTER TWENTY-NINE

'I hope you're happy now,' Hector said to her over the white linen tablecloth. He shot her a glance which told her the gloss was quickly wearing off their newfound love and that she had some damage control to do. Quickly. 'You know that the captain is the boss on the yacht, yes? Any decisions he makes are for a good reason. He did not want to head east, and I have lost a lot of credibility with him for forcing his hand through insisting he take the yacht out in this weather. He may even quit when we reach the nearest port.'

Dinner was quite dull, what with Hector's sulking. But really, if he was going to allow a hired hand to call the shots, perhaps he was better off without the arrogant man. Diana consoled herself with the food which was gorgeously presented and perhaps even better than last night's fare. Being on the high seas sure could work up an appetite.

Jean-Luc was squirrelled away in his room, pleading a head-ache, although she could have sworn she heard his voice through the thin door when she passed his room. Good – he had his phone with him now and must have found an opportunity to phone Dan, although she wouldn't have thought there was much cell reception out here on the water.

She looked up to see Hector sneering at the large slice of cake on her plate. She stared back him as she added an extra huge dollop of cream and placed a huge forkful into her mouth without dropping her eyes.

She chewed slowly, letting the confection melt on her palate, but her mind was working quickly. She was going to have to get Hector back on board, and that meant including him in on the plan.

'I do have a good reason for insisting on Aruba. Like I told you, I think Mark is on that island,' she said to him, finally laying down her fork. She reached across the table to lay her hand over his. He hadn't touched his dessert. She rose from the table and led him to the most sumptuous sofa where they sat together, and she proceeded to tell him the story of that long-ago vacation on Aruba, and Mark's promise to buy an island.

'That's why I think I might know where to find him,' she said softly. 'I need to travel to that island, see if he's there. I ... I didn't want to tell you that.' She looked down at her feet.

Hector was all smiles and cuddles once again. He drew his arm across the midnight blue silk on her shoulders, and breathed in the fragrance of her hair. 'Ah, my darling,' he whispered. 'You did right to tell me. I will send the boat in with my men, and they will kill him for you.'

'No!' Diana gave a small laugh and regrouped. ''Darling, that's exactly why I didn't want to tell you,' she said, giving him a little poke in the ribs. 'I knew you'd get all macho on me and want to wipe Mark out.'

She nestled her head against his chest, then lifted up to speak softly into his ear a sentiment he would understand. 'This is *my* revenge. All mine.'

His chuckle rumbled through his ribcage, and he played with her hair, brushing the long strands with his fingertips.

'You need a gun?'

She thought for a moment. If she came clean about her plan to have the FBI waiting to nab her husband, that might scare Hector off and he'd definitely want to revert to his own plan of blowing Mark's head off in a very messy fashion. She would be able to come up with the death certificate then, but that would only leave her with the measly five million in insurance money. No, she wanted him alive, and she wanted to clear her name. Death was too easy for Mark.

'Yeah, a gun,' she said casually, as if it was the most natural thing in the world. 'That would be a good idea. You got one for me?' Diana had never shot off a firearm in her life, but Hector didn't need to know that. After all, she wasn't actually planning to use it.

Hector barked out a command to the steward who lurked in the shadows, and a choice of revolvers laid out on black velvet was soon brought out for their perusal. His fingers danced over them, until he finally chose the one that had caught Diana's eye, a small, delicate firearm, inlaid with mother of pearl. 'This is the one for the ladies,' he murmured, stroking the muzzle lovingly with his fingertip.

'That's perfect, Hector,' she whispered. 'Just what I need to get the job done.' She felt a thrill right in her very heart at the danger that this little jewel in her hand spoke of. It was a bit of a turn-on, she surprised herself as the realization, and she reached the gun up and drew it along the line of his cheek. His black eyes darkened more and he sat still, the lust visibly growing, till with a groan, he took her hand and forced the gun to fall to the floor. With that, he slipped the midnight blue silk off her shoulder then reached down to the long slit of her skirt, his eyes never leaving hers.

·♥· ·♥· ♥·♥·♥·

They had moved to the state room eventually. Long after Hector had worn himself out and lay beside her snoring, Diana was still wakeful and her mind was working overtime. Funny how soon lust spent itself – she was not having nearly as much fun with Hector now. His little quirks were quickly becoming tiresome, like how he had to have all the attention in the room, and the way he had of stroking his own furry chest. The macho act was all very good but it didn't make up for good conversation, and the man didn't cuddle. She and Mark used to talk and cuddle all the time, back in the day.

Diana wondered what Jean-Luc was up to, alone in the servants' quarters of the yacht. Perhaps she could drop by and cheer him up. She could do with some cuddling right now. Or a decent coffee, whichever came first.

She didn't need to be quiet about leaving the room – Hector slept like a bull.

The storm still hadn't arisen, Diana noted with satisfaction. The ocean lay flat and calm. Captain Don Juan was just being pissy and hard to get along with, blaming her for Mark's misdeeds. As she passed by the iron stairs leading up to the wheelhouse (that's what it was called, Hector told her), she noticed a slight movement. Was there someone up there steering the boat? Made sense to have someone at the helm, after all, they were still moving through the water.

And where there were night workers, there was coffee. She made her way up the narrow steps. Her head was just about level to the instruments when she peered in the door. Well, there was Jean-Luc, anyway, but it didn't appear she would be the lucky one in his bed tonight.

She watched as the two bodies drew apart from their embrace. The dirty little bastard, he was kissing the captain!

Diana quickly withdrew, shocked, but not really. Perhaps he was getting back at her for Hector in a jealous fit, or maybe it was simple human loneliness which motivated him.

She laughed in her mind at the thought. Possible, but extremely doubtful for Jean-Luc was, after all, first and foremost an opportunist, she'd always known that. But Jean-Luc did not give his favors away lightly, so what, she wondered, did Don Juan de Whatsit have that her lover wanted?

CHAPTER THIRTY

The storm was in full swing by the next morning, so Captain Don Juan had been right in his prediction.

Jean-Luc was bleary-eyed, pouring up a coffee in the lounge with his hair was standing on end, the way it always did first thing in the morning after a heavy night of sex. Vain as he was, he would still insist on coffee before his shower.

'You don't look like *you* slept much,' she said to him as she held out a mug for him to fill up, unable to stop the needles in her voice. She was nauseated by the rolling of the yacht and the knowledge that she was so close to finding Mark, yet she needed something in her stomach. With Hector snoring beside her all night, she hadn't slept much either.

A grunt was the only response she received from him.

'Did you manage to make the call?' She leaned into him, keeping her voice low although they were quite alone in the lounge.

'What call?' He wasn't really paying attention to her, being more concerned with watching the roiling gray waves outside the salt-encrusted glass.

Diana turned her back on the heaving ocean outside and looked at him with narrowed eyes. What was he playing at? Her whole plan hinged on Jean-Luc making contact with Dan through Mrs. Hastings and together with whatever FBI had been lurking outside her hotel, and he knew it. They were running out of time. She searched his eyes for a sign he was joking, but there was no humor there.

'What the fuck, Jean-Luc? The call to Dan, remember? So he can get the FBI and meet us there on the island,' she said. 'I heard you talking in your room last night, before...'

He let out a very French puff of air through his lips. 'No cell reception here in the middle of the Gulf, Diana,' he replied. 'What a stupid plan. You probably heard me talking to one of the crew, Don Juan, maybe. Not on the phone.' He turned away, slurping his black coffee between his lips.

Okay. So Jean-Luc was not part of her team anymore. And without the outside help she had been relying on, her team had suddenly shrunk to one. Not for the first time, she mentally cursed the fragility of the male ego, that tender flower so vulnerable to shrinking within itself when exposed to the cold waters of practicality. She'd *had* to sleep with Hector, what didn't he understand about that? Had he been forced to canoodle with Don Juan? She didn't think so.

She sipped the coffee, waiting for an idea to kick in. The seas were high and the wind relentless, yet the yacht persevered north-east. The gray waves splashed against the window, reaching upwards as the boat rocked against them. It looked cold, and she knew the water hereabouts was full of sharks. Only the thin hull of the boat separated her from the depths of the hungry Gulf.

What had she gotten herself into? Her Plan was as dead as her cell phone and they were fast approaching Mark's island. Where she thought he might be, anyway, she was no longer sure of anything. She was stuck on a boat with no hope of escape, and the deep water all around terrified her.

How to switch things around at the last moment? Hector was expecting to storm the island and... what? He would want to kill Mark in retaliation for scuppering his yacht. She could live with that, she thought, but brushed aside the actual horror of the potential bloodshed. And then what? She would be a witness to the crime, no escaping that. And that spark between her and Hector, it was already diminishing, so what was her value to the drug lord? She suspected the worst. Even if he didn't do away with her also, she would be stuck with him and his whims. Her life with Hector would be about as secure as one of King Henry the Eighth's wives and she would be a modern-day Anne Boleyn, waiting for the axe to fall across her neck.

Unless... Diana was nothing if not a survivor, and she had a glimmer of an idea. Perhaps she could convince Hector to let her go alone to the island, and she could throw herself at Mark's mercy, remind him of the good times they'd once shared and how they'd been a team. She could tell him she forgave him for leaving her with his mess and for using Amaryllis's name as his password.

The only problem with that plan was that she was leading Hector right to him, and Mark would not be at all happy about that turn of events. Yet, he was always good in an emergency, could think on his feet and he probably had an escape route planned out already, he was good like that. Yeah, she could trust Mark to get her out of this pickle, especially if it meant saving his own hide.

'Ah my sweet lady, there you are.' Hector strolled in wearing only a pair of jeans and his heavy gold medallions. The hairs on his chest bristled though her silk blouse as he kissed her cheek. He appeared untouched by the rough waves. Indeed, they seemed to refresh him in direct contrast to Jean-Luc. At least he was in a good mood towards her.

'Hello darling,' she said, a bright smile on her face. Good Lord, how would she keep this up for any length of time? The rolling sea was making her stomach leap.

'We are approaching the island you say is Mark's,' he noted, staring out the window the Gulf, although Diana could see nothing out there except the endless waves.

'Yes....' she replied, her hand on his shoulder.

'I will take the launch,' he continued. 'And take care of my affairs, eh?' He gave a chuckle. He was actually looking forward to killing Mark. Oh God, what a brute. How on earth could she have... she pushed aside the memory of last night.

'About that, my love,' she said, then took a deep breath. 'Remember, this is my revenge too, and I've been thinking.'

'That's my job, as the man,' he told her genially. 'You don't need to think, just be the beautiful Diana.'

The tight smile on her face didn't reach her eyes, but he wasn't looking her way. 'Why not let me go to the island? I can convince him to give me the money. You agreed last night, remember, when you gave me the gun.'

He thought for a moment, then shook his head. 'That won't work. He will not have cash enough with him.' he said. 'Nah, I'll just kill him.'

'But where's the joy in that? I mean,' she said. 'Sure, you'll kill him. That'll make you feel satisfied, I understand that. However, who's going to know?'

'Huh?'

'You're killing him to set an example to others not to screw you around, right? That's important, isn't it, that other people learn not to mess with you, that people give you the respect you deserve?'

'Yes, of course. How is a man to have honor if he is not respected by other men of business?'

'Then, killing Mark on a secluded island accomplishes ... what? Wouldn't you be better off letting me persuade him to come back to the yacht with me, and then you can make a public example of him?'

He began to laugh, deep belly laughs that went on and on. This was too evil a laugh for her liking. Had he seen through her thin idea of escape, was he laughing at *her*? She held her breath.

Hector wiped his eyes. 'Oh, Diana,' he said. 'You are my equal. Shall we plan together a devious punishment for Mark, a nice public execution, perhaps?' He chuckled some more.

She relaxed and drank more coffee, her eyes on Hector at all times. 'Yes,' she breathed. 'Yes, I find that a delightful idea.'

A stream of staccato Spanish sounded from the entrance. Don Juan was his usual unhappy self, gesturing towards Diana and telling his boss off by the sounds of it. Hector replied, and there was some back and forth of rapid fired Spanish. By the end of it, all three men were looking at Diana.

Was that a spark of suspicion in Hector's eye?

'*El Capitan* says he must go with you to the island. He will pilot the launch.'

Diana laughed breezily. 'Oh, Hector,' she said, forcing a relaxed teasing note into her voice. 'Nonsense, I wouldn't drag Don Juan away from his precious yacht. I can drive a little motor boat, for God's sake, do you take me for an idiot? How hard can it be?'

They all looked out the window to the rolling gray Gulf and the white-caps and the spray.

She swallowed down the bile which came up with every lurch of the yacht. 'Or Jean-Luc. He can take me.' She grimaced at her ex-lover, who screwed up his face. He was definitely green around the gills.

'I am not going out on that,' he said flatly, shaking his head vehemently. 'In an even smaller boat? No. Don Juan needs to go.'

'Do not argue, my sweet,' Hector said. 'I can only trust Don Juan with your precious life.' He narrowed his eyes as he said this.

Diana caught the smirk from Jean-Luc as he slid his eyes towards the captain, and the small nod he received in return. She had the uncomfortable feeling there were plans afoot between the two, but what they were, she couldn't begin to figure out.

Unless... this was a love triangle of the most horrific sort? Jean-Luc, upset and jealous that she had seemingly thrown him over for Hector, had turned to Don Juan for solace, and the two planned to do away with her for revenge? If so, she would be a sitting duck in that little launch, alone with the captain.

And she had no way out of this, for she was caught between the devil and the deep gray sea. The launch was her only means of escape, and she had no protection except for the little gun Hector had so thoughtfully provided her with.

CHAPTER THIRTY-ONE

The weather cleared up after lunch, or the time Diana would have eaten lunch if her stomach could settle. Between the rolling of the waves and the fear deep within the pit of her stomach, her appetite, usually so lusty, had completely disappeared.

The rain and the wind had stopped, but the waters of the Gulf continued to roil all around them. However, now that the drizzle and spray were no longer disfiguring the view, she could see a small dot of land ahead of them in the distance, a smudge of purple on the blue gray sea, almost lost in the whitecaps. To the far right, other islands appeared, and equally as far away. It was a lonely vista for Diana.

She was scared. Terrified. Not only would she have to go out on those terrible waters in a tiny boat, but she had an uncomfortable feeling that the three men were now working together against her and she had no idea what the threat was. She only knew the situation was fast getting out of her control.

'That is Mark's island, Diana,' Hector said, placing his arm around her as she held tight to the rails of the deck. She tried not to shrink away from his touch. He stared off into the distance, his legs firmly planted. 'You think he's there, eh?'

She shrugged. And if he wasn't? She dreaded to think of that outcome. The yacht drew slowly closer to the smudge until it became a definable land mass, and the other islands, the inhabited islands, drifted further away.

'And you will bring him back?'

She nodded. She would have to, with Don Juan at her side monitoring every move. She wildly thought of using the small gun on the captain. Could she do it? She hoped she would if she had to.

The yacht came to a standstill quite a distance away from their destination. Don Juan came down from his lofty wheelhouse and the two men spoke back and forth in Spanish. The captain was doing it on purpose, Diana knew, in order to exclude her.

'Don Juan is getting the launch ready now,' Hector told her, his arm still around her waist and holding tight. 'You need to prepare. Get changed. You look lovely but it will be cold on the water.'

Cold and wet, Diana thought, but she was glad of the excuse to get away from Hector. She went to the yacht's single stateroom and looked through the closet at her new clothes. There was little inside that looked sensible enough for the open water, the dresses and bathing suits of the shopping trip were gorgeous, but bought for poolside lounging and dining, not a deep sea excursion. She quickly rummaged through Hector's clothes and found a waterproof jacket which she slipped over her cotton blouse, then hauled on a pair of Hector's jeans. They were tight, and only came to her calves, but this would have to do.

Dan. Where was he? Still in Bogota, patiently waiting for her to re-emerge from her amorous adventures? Had he ever found Flanagan or, the more likely scenario, had he given up bothering with the thankless Diana and turned his back on her forever, heading for the safety of his parent's basement? She hadn't turned out to be much of a friend to him, in the end, tossing him aside for a glitzier partner in crime. And after all he'd done for her.

Flanagan must have known she was in Bogota, somehow. He'd arranged for Jean-Luc to be flown in. How he knew, she couldn't comprehend, but the only other person who could have the resources for this action was Mark, and as far as he was concerned she was busy chasing down the carrot of his measly five million dollar insurance settlement. Mark would have had no way of knowing she'd end up in Colombia on his trail, if indeed he was on that tiny little island off Aruba.

A sharp rap on the stateroom door followed by a short bark in Spanish urged her back on deck, and she went to the back of the yacht where Hector was waiting.

He gave a short whistle as he eyed her up and down. 'Very... elegant.'

She pulled her hair into a ponytail and placed her sunglasses on her face. 'A side of me you haven't met yet, Hector,' she said, sounding much braver than she felt at the moment. She looked down at the launch where Don Juan waited. Way down, down amongst the white caps which were still roiling. The fragile little boat was tossing dangerously on the waves.

Hector nodded his chin. 'Your chariot awaits, my darling.' His words sounded sarcastic, and she quickly glanced at him to judge, but his face was a closed book behind his shades.

Diana grasped the ladder's rail and looked below her, and froze. The launch was bobbing about like a cork on that deep water, up and down, and making her dizzy just looking at it. Her stomach was rising and falling too, but in direct opposition to the waves.

Don Juan said something, impatiently.

'Go on,' Hector ordered.

She tried to swing her leg down to the first rung of the ladder, she really did. At least she told it to move, but the necessary communication wasn't reaching her appendages. She only succeeded in making a small, shuffling motion. The launch was too tiny, and the sea was too large.

She felt Hector's hand over her own and grateful, she looked away from the hell below and up at him, but there was no salvation in the set of his mouth as she felt her fingers being pried loose from the iron rail.

'Hector, no!' She started to say but the words were lost as she was pushed off the yacht. She fell, but grabbed the rungs with her flailing hands as did so, and was left hanging there precariously, legs kicking.

'Just put your feet on the launch,' Don Juan told her in a bored voice, sounding very close at hand. 'You're not actually hanging in mid-air.'

And it was surprisingly easy to do, she found, even though the launch was still rocking up and down in the waves. She looked up at Hector, his head just a couple of feet above her own as her feet found purchase. It hadn't been as long a drop as it had seemed. She watched as Jean-Luc drew him away, speaking into his ear.

She sniffed and grabbed for the nearest seat, walking crab-legged and crouched until she reached safety, unwilling to trust herself to stand upright without falling overboard.

Don Juan was already seated at the wheel, behind the protective glass of the windshield. He turned around to glare at her.

'You're really not used to the water, are you?' He sneered in his heavily accented English as he pulled a lever or two and the small launch started away from the yacht.

She sat stiffly, feeling the pull of the powerful engine holding her in place as the boat cut through the Gulf waters, and she held tight to the seat as, with a quick smirk at her, Don Juan began to aim directly at the waves, forcing the small boat to bounce along the top of the waves.

Diana bent over her knees, willing her stomach to stay down, when she spied the life jacket tucked under her seat. She had it on in a trice, but still had little faith in this tiny scrap of orange to save her life should Don Juan manage to throw her over board. And it offered no protection from sharks.

She felt deep with the pocket of Hector's wind-proof jacket, and breathed a sigh of relief. The tiny pearl-handled pistol was still there.

Don Juan quit his high jinks with the waves after she had thrown up over the side a couple of times, but she remained clutching the side of the boat until her arms were quite achy.

The island was drawing inexorably closer. It was the first time she'd seen it so close up, shaped like a triangle and much taller than she'd thought, larger than it had appeared from the shore of Aruba all those years ago because of this height, and much further away from the resort than she'd thought. No way she would be able to dog paddle back to the main island from here, if worse came to worst.

What if she got it wrong and Mark wasn't here? The prospect of a return to Hector and his thinning passion made her heart sink even further down. Of course, Captain Don Juan de Whosit might prefer to leave her here marooned on this tiny island so far from civilization.

And even Jean-Luc didn't seem to be on her side anymore, and she wasn't quite sure where she'd lost that connection.

Seriously, Dan must have given up on her by now. As far as he knew, Dana was handling the situation and would get back to him, and didn't need his help. It was all she deserved. Tears mixed with the salty spray on her cheeks.

Diana clung to the side of the launch as it slowed. The steep rocky slopes ran straight down into the sea. But then there it was, as if the island was magically unfolding for them, an inlet opening between two cliffs. There were no houses visible, not even a straw hut, when they turned the corner and slid in through the narrow inlet surrounded on three sides by the lush jungled hills.

However, in the middle of this protected harbor there sat a yacht, and even Diana with her small knowledge of boats could tell it was a beauty. Sleek and white and shiny, it was bigger than the one they had just left, where Hector impatiently awaited her return. It had gizmos and whirligigs on top, tinted windows all around the sides, and even at rest looked like it was thrusting forward in the water, all glass and light and foam. It was a true beauty, set between the green of the island and the turquoise of the sea like a jewel.

The whole scene looked like a vision of paradise, a movie set for a James Bond movie, complete with the fins gliding in the water close by. Sharks, Diana could tell from the films she had watched, and she let go of the railing she'd been clutching so tightly and scooted to the center of the small launch.

Don Juan slowed the launch further, to approach this vision with reverence.

'*La Princesse 55E*,' he breathed.

They paused about fifty feet away. There was no sign of life aboard this modern-day vision, this angel of the ocean. Don Juan inched the launch closer and around the back to the swim deck. As they pulled up, Mark walked out of the shadowed overhang to greet them.

'About time, Diana,' he said. 'Getting a little slow with age, are you?'

CHAPTER
THIRTY-TWO

It was Mark, looking decidedly undead. In fact, he looked better than he'd appeared for years, as if he'd found the fountain of youth on this hidden island. Freshly tanned and the pudge around his middle melted away, the muscles on his wiry body stood out, defined, as if the last twenty-five years had never happened.

The launch now bobbed against the swim deck of the gleaming yacht. Don Juan looked back at her and jerked his head towards Mark, indicating she should get on board.

Diana scrambled over the side and through the break in the railing, hauling herself up shakily. Of all the ways she had expected to confront her husband, it wasn't like this, on a luxury yacht with him calm and collected, relaxed even. She was supposed to be the one in control, not dressed in Hector's clothing, seasick and scared shitless of her coming fate. He had been expecting her? No, this wasn't how the story had unfolded in her head.

'You seem surprised,' he said, leaning against the wall with a slow grin on his face. The bastard had always been able to read her like a spreadsheet.

In her day dreams, she had walked in on him in tiki hut, alone, surrounded by the piles of his ill-gotten gains. In her heels and designer miniskirt and hair softly floating, she had strong-armed him to the waiting boat full of FBI agents, or at least people who were grateful that she had done their jobs for them, and then she scooped up the money which was rightfully hers (and her neighbors). She saved the day and was the star of the show.

Instead, here she was bedraggled and looking like a nobody with salt tracks on her cheeks and vomit down her front, and a drug lord of a lover who was quickly losing interest. He had done this to her, it was all Mark's fault.

And no FBI in sight.

Right, it was all up to her. Kill the little shit, and at least she'd get the paltry insurance settlement. She fumbled in her pocket for the tiny revolver.

A woman spoke out of the shadows. 'Put your hands where I can see you.'

Diana looked up and squinted into the overhang. Amaryllis walked out, coolly elegant in her long barely-there dress and sunhat. She recognized that hat. Mark's mistress had followed her down here, even being bold enough to get on the same airplane. Her eyes were unreadable behind the large designer shades, but the gun in her hand said it all.

'What the fuck, Amaryllis? You followed me down here?'

'You didn't notice even notice me. And, Diana, you left the information about this island on the laptop,' she said. 'A little careless of you, don't you think, just leaving it under your bed?'

Mark grinned and placed his arm around the younger woman's waist.

'You? You stole my laptop from the hotel?' Crap, she was totally sunk now. Her last vestige of hope had been blown away like the sultry breeze of the island. There were no saviours waiting to rescue Diana Quenton. Not even the useless Dan.

'A bonus for me,' he said. 'This woman was so determined to find me. The sign of true love.' Amaryllis bent down so he could kiss her cheek.

'Mark didn't want you following him, or he would have taken you with him instead of sending you off to the spa the day he disappeared. Don't you see that?' Diana was determined to throw a wrench between the two, show that bitch the real face of Mark.

'As the man said, Diana, it's true love.' Amaryllis renewed her grip on the pistol. 'It is now anyway.'

'You know I would have sent word once the heat was off,' he told her, giving her ass a quick slap.

Don Juan had tied the launch to the swim deck rails and was now lithely climbing on board.

'*Capitan*, I owe you an apology,' Mark greeted him cheerfully, not sounding the least bit embarrassed or remorseful for wrecking the man's beloved charge.

Don Juan looked around at the gleaming new yacht and whistled in appreciation. 'The Princess 55E,' he said again.

'You like?' Mark grinned. 'Go on through, inspect her. You'll find the phone in the wheelhouse. I believe Hector is awaiting your call.'

A grunt of appreciation was his answer as Don Juan disappeared under the overhang, making himself quite at home.

'Don Juan?' Diana called, her voice weak. 'Aren't you going to... to wreak Hector's revenge or something?'

Mark laughed. 'Revenge? Hector will get over his snit when he sees this replacement. It's a step up from the yacht I had to, unfortunately, wreck. I'm sure all has been forgiven even as we speak.'

A low rumbling began beneath their feet, a sound so quiet it was felt rather than heard. Don Juan had found the cockpit and started the engines.

'But... but what's going on?' Diana turned back to Mark where he still stood with his arm around his mistress. 'Don Juan hates you for what you did to Hector and his yacht. He loved that boat like a baby! He wanted to kill you.'

'And now he'll love this boat,' Mark said, shrugging. 'Hector's honor has been restored, and Don Juan has a prettier yacht to oversee. Hector no longer needs to seek revenge on me, so everyone's a winner.'

Everyone except Diana, she realized as she stared at Mark and the tumblers began to click in her mind. Things were beginning to make a little more sense.

'Jean-Luc...'

'Yeah, I have to thank your boyfriend,' Mark agreed. 'Couldn't have done it without him. You sure do pick'em, Di. He's not cheap, but he sure is easy!' He and Amaryllis laughed.

'Wait now, how did you know he was here, that he'd be with me?'

'Who do you think arranged for his ticket over? Jesus Diana, have a clue,' Mark said, that impatient note in his voice again, the note which had been growing over the years. 'The insurance policy was only to buy me a little time to get the final details in place. I knew you'd hunt down the laptop eventually. Thought you'd get to it sooner though, I must say.'

'But you wanted Mrs. Hastings to get rid of it,' she said, still trying to get her head round what was unfolding.

'Like she'd throw out a perfectly good piece of electronics?'

Diana nodded. 'You're right... But,' she said as she seized on an idea. 'Amaryllis – you had no intention of bringing her on board with it, did you?' She turned to the willowy brunette to judge her reaction, expecting rage, but was sadly disappointed as the woman simpered and hugged Mark closer.

'Amaryllis knows I would have come back for her,' he said. 'I didn't want to get this sweetheart mixed up in the messy bits. But she's one smart cookie, she figured it out all by herself.' He looked admiringly at his mistress. 'She couldn't live without me.'

'You had no idea I was following you, did you?' Amaryllis sneered as she said this, and tossed her head proudly. 'Don't feel so clever now, do you?'

Dan had suspected, Diana remembered, and felt a twinge of guilt when she thought of how she had pooh-poohed his worries. She shook the nasty feeling off.

'Let me get this straight, Mark,' she said as she attempted to wrest control of the situation. 'You faked your death, wrecking Hector's yacht.'

'Not without having a brand new one to replace it,' Mark pointed out, smugness apparent in his voice. 'You have to order these babies a year in advance, you don't just buy them off the shelf.'

'Okay,' said Diana. 'So you've been planning this a while. A long while. Meanwhile, you left a trail on your laptop, knowing I would track you down to Colombia.'

He nodded.

'And this island...' Her heart was wrenching, even though the love between them had died years ago. She was grieving for what they had had, all those years ago.

'You have a mind like a steel trap, Di,' he told her. 'You never forget anything. I knew you'd put the clues together.'

'So Jean-Luc is in cahoots with you,' she said slowly. 'How did you know about him?'

He chortled. 'When did I not know about him? Who do you think pays your bills? And that Cartier watch...' He shook his head.

All those years of thinking she was so clever, that she had a secret from Mark. She remembered the scene in the wheelhouse of Hector's yacht last night, her boyfriend and Don Juan together in an embrace. He had no doubt been explaining the plan to the captain, who would have been happy to go along with it. Rage was beginning to set in at the knowledge of this betrayal, but Diana fought it. She needed a clear head.

'But why, Mark?' The question burst out of her. 'Why go to all this trouble with getting me down here? Why not just leave me back in Baserville holding the mess you left behind, wasn't that enough for you?'

'No,' he said, shaking his head as he smiled, showing gleaming white teeth. 'It wasn't enough. I knew there would still be suspicion about me if my body wasn't found. But I figured if your body surfaced, then the FBI would believe you were in on the scam, and it would throw them off the scent.'

'And...,' Amaryllis gave him a teasing poke, and he laughed.

'And yes, I would finally get my own back on you,' he continued, exchanging a smile with the woman by his side, yet his tone was bitter. 'Pay back for all the years of bitching and controlling you've sub-jected me to, making me perform like a friggin' monkey to impress all your small society friends, always demanding more and more and more...' He nuzzled against Amaryllis's neck.

Diana could say nothing as she stood on the deck, white-faced in the hot sun beating down on her. Sure, they had lost touch with each other over the years, but he could have said something. He had been free to leave at any time.

'And no, a divorce was out of the question.' Amaryllis said as if she could read her mind, watching Diana over Mark's head. 'He knew you'd bleed him dry, and it was his money, he'd earned it and created it. All of it.'

This was the last straw. 'It's not your money! It belongs to everyone back home, all those people who trusted you.'

The two merely laughed like that was the biggest joke of all, then Amaryllis stepped forward from the comfort of Mark's arm and the awning. She stood in the sunlight, eyes hidden behind her shades, the backdrop of the lush green hills behind her.

'What's it going to be, Mark?'

'I'd rather not leave a bullet in her,' he said. He put his head to one side as he pretended to consider the options, then smiled as a fin silently cut through the water to the left.

'What do you think, Di?' he asked. 'Think you can make it to shore before our friends catch you?'

She stared at the shark's wake as the reality of her life hit her. Mark hated her, and had done so for years. She had thought for all those years that the anger was only on her side, that he had just stopped caring, but he must have been nursing the old grudges as carefully as she herself had done.

Her husband was the one person in her life who knew of her fear of water and her total lack of buoyancy. He knew she could no more swim to the shore and outrace the sharks than she could sprout wings and fly to safety. She turned to him and removed her sunglasses in order to look him in the eye.

'Mark,' she began, intending to plea for her life when the triumphant scowl she saw on his face stopped her. The sun was beating down on her, but the sweat which drip down her back and collected in the folds beneath her heavy clothes was pure stress.

'I don't think that life jacket will be much help to you,' Amaryllis said, and she giggled, the sun catching the highlights on her silky hair.

'And that windbreaker will only weigh you down ...' Mark murmured.

An impatient yell sounded from the wheelhouse. The captain was ordering him to get the business over with so he could get on his way.

He moved closer to Diana. 'Time to say *au revoir*, baby,' he said, reaching out both hands towards her.

She had no choice, it was now or never. The tiny revolver in her pocket was the only chance she had. Diana had never shot a gun before, hadn't a clue how to aim it, but she was going to learn right now. It was that or die, and Diana had no intention of being shark bait. She was supposed to be at the top of the food chain.

The engines thrummed louder and the yacht gave the slightest lurch, as if the boat was impatient to leave the secluded spot and test its prowess in the large ocean outside. Amaryllis tottered for a moment on her high heels and Diana seized the moment.

The tiny gun was out of her pocket and she held it in both hands, aimed in Amaryllis's general direction as she pulled the trigger.

It fired, to her great surprise, but the recoil caused her to fall against the brass railing of the deck. She had a momentary sight of her husband's mistress staring at her, unhurt, mouth wide open and her handgun brought to half-mast before Mark's full weight fell against her.

'Jesus Christ, what was that?' Mark was screaming in her ear, and she had the vaguest impression of blood, and a lot of it, against his white pants. How had she managed to shoot him instead of his mistress? But then she was tumbling over the rail and into the deep blue water, clutching on to Mark the whole time.

And then there was silence, except for the roar of the ocean against her ears. It went on forever, and she could feel herself sinking ever further into the darkness. Her eyes opened as she sought purchase, limbs flailing as the realization struck her that she was immersed in the dreaded waters. She was dimly aware that she ought not to be kicking and making movement for that, combined with whoever's blood was pouring so freely, would attract the sharks, but her conscious brain had no hold over the body's panic.

Her arm connected with something solid, but it was large and smooth and rounded. She grasped a hand hold on the top of this barrel and without thinking clambered aboard. And then there was air! She'd broken through the wall of water and could breathe, if just for a moment. Until she looked down and recognized the creature who was carrying her. The dorsal fin undeniably belonged to a shark. Panic reigned, instinct took over and she pushed herself away from the dreaded creature.

And she was submerged again, down into the water but it was cloudy this time, with swirls of red and there was Mark in front of her, screaming soundlessly as he was carried away by the very same shark who had saved her life.

CHAPTER THIRTY-THREE

Her brain must have cut out at that point, for the next thing she knew she was bobbing along in the wake of the yacht as it ran full speed toward the narrow inlet toward the open water with the launch trailing behind it. The little life jacket was keeping her head above the swells, but just barely, and she had by now lost Hector's water-proof jacket and one of her sandals.

'Diana!' A voice from shore was calling her name. She turned toward the source and there was a familiar short figure waving his arms, red hair glinting in the sun.

Dan. However had he found her? And more to the point, why the hell was he not coming out to rescue her? She flailed her arms and kicked her legs, and slowly, slowly made her way to the shore. And she found she could do it, as long as she didn't think about what lurked below her.

He grabbed her hand and helped pull her up onto the rocks just as Flanagan appeared from an opening in the trees, a sharp shooting rifle slung across his back.

'You guys,' Diana gasped as she lay back on the boulders and pebbles that made up the beach. 'Oh, my God. You found me.'

'Never lost sight of you for a moment,' Flanagan assured her, telling a barefaced lie, but she was not to know that. He removed his sunglasses and she could see his crinkled brown eyes regarding her warmly. There was relief in that gaze.

She sat up. 'What do you mean?'

'We'll talk later,' he said. 'Right now, we have to make sure you're alright.'

'I think I'm okay,' she said as she mentally checked her body for pain. There was none, despite all the blood that had swirled around in the water. Then she remembered who had been hurt. 'Mark... I think I killed him. I shot the gun Hector gave me, but I was aiming at Amaryllis. I don't know how I did that.'

'No, I shot Mark,' Flanagan assured her. 'In the leg, just a flesh wound to stop him throwing you overboard. We shot at the same time. You missed your target.'

'But the shark got Mark, in the water,' she said, strangely glad that she wasn't responsible for her husband's death. 'I saw it attacking him, and he was screaming, and there was all this blood everywhere, the water was turning cloudy with it...'

Flanagan and Dan were both silent as they looked towards the water. Off in the distance, the shark fins were now swimming away from the spot where she and Mark had fallen into the water, but the men's attention was held by an object being brought to shore by the incoming tide.

'I don't think he made it,' the FBI officer said softly.

'Eurghh...,' said Dan, as his face turned green and he ran into the bushes lining the shore from where noisy sounds of retching were subsequently heard.

'What?' Diana turned her head sharply to look. There, floating on to shore like a child's sailboat in the quietly lapping waves, was a sandal, the really expensive bespoke kind with the super strong velcro, the ones which were made for hiking in the Himalayas and surfing in Hawaii – the ones which would never fail you. And in that single sandal sat a tanned foot and ankle. The velcro had held true, and Mark had got his money's worth right to the end.

'Oh Jesus,' Diana breathed. ''Is that...' She knew it was.

'Mark is dead,' she said carefully, as if trying the words on for size. Yes, she had fantasized this moment, had longed for it, and this possibility had been the impetus for her whole journey down to the south. But this was reality, and it somehow didn't have the same tang and sweetness of her dreams. She had won, but he was no longer around for her to rub his face into her success, and that caused the headiness of the moment to be as flat as two-day old champagne left open by the poolside in the summer sun.

She tried her tongue around the words again. 'Mark is dead?' It came out as a question and she looked to Flanagan for confirmation, despite the evidence before her own eyes.

The FBI officer shrugged. 'Hard to survive an attack like that,' he replied. He sighed as he heaved the heavy knapsack off his back and started to root around inside it. He withdrew a clear plastic bag and strode over to the sandaled foot.

'What are you doing?' Diana asked him, appalled as he waded into the water and leaned over, trying to catch Mark's foot in his hands. It bobbed around like an apple in a rocking barrel, dancing out of his reach until he finally snagged it.

Flanagan straightened up as he triumphantly held the foot aloft. 'Evidence, ma'am,' he said. 'Now I can close the case.' He placed it into the clear bag and sealed it.

'Wait now,' Diana said, alarmed. 'That's not the end. You still have to find the money he stole from everyone. We have to return it, or I'll never be able to go back home. I'll still have lost everything!'

'With all due respect, that's not my business, ma'am,' he replied as he replaced his mirrored shades. 'This case no longer belongs to Special Projects. It'll be signed over to the Financial Investigations, they're the experts in that field.'

She let that sink in.

'So, nothing has changed,' Diana said with sadness as her shoulders drooped. 'I'm back to being Diana Quenton, pariah of Baserville County. I'll be poor forever. And I'll never be able to move back into my home, or... or... or pay the Animals Trust Fund back. I've failed the pets!'

With this realization, more than the perceived death of her husband, she sat heavily back down on the sharply sloping beach and the tears began to run quietly down her face. Everything was in those tears, Mark's death, the tension of the past few weeks, the betrayal of Jean-Luc. It was all too much to bear.

He put his head to one side as he watched uncomfortably at first, then impatiently.

'Ah, shucks, ma'am,' he said. Flanagan was a hardened agent of the FBI, but he still hated to see women cry. 'Diana, you're not poor. You may not be as wealthy as you once were, but you're way richer than most people are, or ever hope to be.'

She sniffed and glared at him, tossing her still damp ponytail out of the way. 'Don't give me a line about being rich in character or wealthy in friends. That shit doesn't buy the Louboutins or pay vet bills or put me back at the top of the heap where I belong.'

Flanagan threw back his head and laughed right from his belly. 'You could probably count on the fingers of one hand how many real friends you have, and still have fingers left over to tell the world where to go.'

'It's a good thing you like your own jokes,' she said as coldly as she could muster as she wiped her face dry. 'Because I am *really* not amused.'

He removed his shades to wipe the tears from his eyes, but continued to chuckle.

'Seriously, Diana,' he said. 'Have you forgotten the insurance Mark took out on his own life, with you as beneficiary?'

She had. She'd been so hellbent on getting revenge, on unmasking her husband and bringing him to justice, that the carrot of the insurance had slipped her mind.

'Five million dollars,' she said.

He held up the plastic bag. 'With this evidence, and my eyewitness account, our medics will sign the death certificate. This is proof of his death, and you'll get the money now, or at least, in a few months down the road.'

'And the FBI won't try to scratch it back from me?'

'Nah, we have discretion over this disbursement. I can cite your willingness to go over and above to help us. There'll be taxes, and a good accountant will help you through that. Maybe there aren't too many pairs of fancy shoes in your future, but if you're sensible, you can live on that. It's more money than most people will ever see in their lifetimes.'

·♥·♥·♥·♥·♥·

They had to hike up the jungled hill and back down again to the other side of the island where Flanagan had hidden the rubber dinghy. Diana, with only one sandal, had to hop most of the way, complaining loudly as she went. Her feet had been pampered for too many years and had never built up a good callous to ease the route. The men did not offer her their own footwear.

And Flanagan would not hear of a rest stop in one of the many luxury hotels in Aruba, no matter how much she whined, even when they stopped at the beachside resort the men had enjoyed while tracking the laptop GPS.

The return of the Louis Vuitton hardly made a dent in her litany of complaints.

'I nearly died,' she grumbled as she slipped her familiar heels on over the blisters, wincing just a bit. 'I came that close to being drowned and eaten by sharks and shot by that vicious bitch Amaryllis. The least I deserve is a cocktail and a manicure. Look at my fingers!'

Admittedly, the polish on her nails was badly scratched with one nail broken down to the quick which had occurred during her scrabble back to dry land after her near-death experience, but her companions remained unsympathetic.

'There's a flight leaving in two hours back to New York,' Dan observed as they stood in front of the Departures Board at the airport. 'Do you think you can use your connections to get us on board that one?' This was of course said to Flanagan, as Diana no longer had connections left anywhere in the world.

And the FBI Officer was able to get them on out of Aruba quickly, using his own expense account and Dan's remaining credit limit.

The three huddled in the back of the plane as it flew over the Gulf and the southern states, attempting to talk quietly amongst themselves amid the still-drunk passengers who had availed themselves to the last possible moment of the all-inclusive bar on the resorts of Aruba.

Flanagan took out his note pad and pen and demanded a full accounting for Diana's time during the trip.

'I have to write up the report,' he told her sternly after she informed him it was none of his business. 'So I need to know exactly what happened in the hotel room, Hector's mansion and his boat.'

'What I want to know is exactly how you ended up on that island,' Diana quickly parried, for she had no desire to examine or explain her actions with Hector. She'd had her reasons for doing what she'd done at the time, but she had an uncomfortable feeling that held up to scrutiny, those driving forces might appear in a bad light.

'Alright then.' Flanagan put down his pen and turned to her, a smug expression on his face. 'Dan's been working with me all along.'

Dan gave a guilty nod as she turned to face him, outraged.

'No, Dan, you were working with me!'

'Your ideas were a little crazy,' he mumbled. 'Flanagan wanted me to ... keep an eye on you.'

'Yep, right from the beginning,' the agent pressed. 'As soon as he was no longer your official lawyer.'

'You traitor,' she said to the younger man.

'Although,' Flanagan interrupted. 'You weren't that hard to follow. That time I brought you the coffee? I knew something was up. You were acting mighty suspicious.'

Diana recalled that day and her struggle to hide Mark's laptop from him. If she had only gotten him on board at the time, if she had come clean like Dan wanted her to, this whole misadventure could have been avoided. No being ripped off by the taxi driver, no evidence of Jean-Luc's betrayal, no hopping into bed with one of Colombia's most dangerous drug lords... That bit hadn't been all bad, though, not the first night anyway.

'You were phoning him on the train, weren't you?'

'He told me what you were up to. He was worried about you, and it did sound like a crazy scheme.'

She turned to Dan, affront in her voice. 'You betrayed me.'

'It was a stupid idea to go to Bogota behind Flanagan's back,' Dan retorted in his own defense. 'It's a dangerous world down there, Diana, you didn't have a clue what you were getting into. And it's a good thing I did, otherwise you'd still be stuck on that island with Mark's foot as your only company.'

'So you knew? You followed us all the way down to Colombia?' Diana was justifiably outraged. She was also a little hurt that her grand scheming had been uncovered so quickly. 'I told you I was going to New York for the week-end, and you didn't trust my word!'

Flanagan opened his mouth to reply, then caught Dan's eye and shook his head with a grin. Why state the obvious?

"I was on the same plane with you,' he told her. 'When Dan got moved up to first class? That was me. I needed to speak with him in private.'

'I remember that well,' she said. She attempted to make her voice drip ice in order to show her displeasure, but she just ended up sounding sour.

'But – you didn't know Amaryllis was on the plane, did you?'

He paused. 'Not... not at the time, no,' he said, reluctant to admit his failure to recognize Mark's mistress. It was another professional oversight which would not make it into the official report.

'So, did you follow her to the island?' Diana was pressing the point.

'In a fashion,' Flanagan replied vaguely.

'When we realized the laptop was missing from your hotel room, we got in contact with Sam, and traced the GPS signal,' Dan interjected. 'We thought you must have had it, and we thought we were following you.'

The FBI agent shot a dark look at him.

So she had Amaryllis to thank for being saved. Somehow that didn't sit well, and definitely left a bad taste in her mouth. 'I had to leave the laptop in the hotel when Hector's men abducted us,' she said. 'Yes, Amaryllis stole the laptop from the hotel. She told me that, before she tried to kill me.'

'You mean you wrote everything down in the laptop?'

'Yeah, all my notes, that's how she knew where to find Mark,' Diana said, a little pride creeping into her voice. 'Otherwise, there's no way she could have tracked him down. Despite what he told her, he had *no* intention of taking her along. I know Mark, and he likes to travel light. True love, indeed! That man has no heart.'

'Had.'

'Huh?'

'*Had* no heart,' Flanagan reminded her. 'He's dead now.'

Diana was silent. Perhaps Mark was dead, perhaps he wasn't. She'd been trying to accept that since his sandal washed ashore, but somehow, she was beginning to have her doubts for Mark couldn't be that easy to kill. On the other hand, if the insurance company wanted to give her five million dollars for his presumed death, she wasn't going to air these doubts.

'The island,' she said, just to change the subject. 'Did Mark buy that island, like he promised all those years ago? Is that something the Feds can grab to help pay back his debt?'

'No, that's a UNESCO World Site,' Flanagan informed her. 'Has been for twenty years. It's one of the last spawning grounds of your friend, the shark who ate Mark. They get pretty crabby when they're disturbed. You're lucky Mark was taking all their attention, with all the flapping you were doing in that water.'

The two men couldn't help but smile at each other across Diana, and when their eyes met, the smiles turned to chuckles, which soon turned into outright belly laughs.

'Woman, you can't swim for shit! You should have seen yourself, it was like you were trying to turn into a helicopter and lift yourself out of the water!'

'Or like Wile E. Coyote running off a cliff!'

Flanagan and Dan howled at the memory.

Diana drew herself up. 'So I'm not a swimmer,' she said, her harsh voice cutting through their laughter. 'Maybe I never had the money for swimming lessons when I was a kid. Maybe I didn't grow up in a rich suburb with pools in every second yard. But I managed it, didn't I? I saved myself in that water. If I was having such obvious difficulties, perhaps one of you two gentlemen could have thought to come in and rescue me. No, you were too busy laughing at me.'

Flanagan wiped his eye. 'You were okay.'

'Besides, there were sharks in the water,' Dan added.

An uncomfortable pause grew between the three.

'You're not taking many notes for your file,' Diana pointed out as she sat back and crossed her arms.

'Right, right, the paperwork's not going to do it-self,' Flanagan said as he took pen in hand again. 'Where were we?'

He glanced at his notes. 'Right, the hotel.' He gave her a hard look.

'I admit you had me thrown at the hotel,' he said. 'I couldn't figure out how you suddenly got the money to stay there.'

She explained the duplicitousness of Jean-Luc, and how he had been in Mark's pay. Her husband had flown her boyfriend over to Bogota and put him up in the hotel she'd found during the web history search.

'But why?' asked Dan. 'I mean, it doesn't really make sense to involve Jean-Luc. In fact, the whole set-up seems a little... over the top, don't you think? Too complicated. Surely Mark could have just left you holding the bag, and then he could make a clean get-away.'

Diana was silent for a moment. These guy didn't know her husband the way she did, and couldn't understand the depths of his rage towards her. 'Mark had a twisted sort of mind,' she began. 'He could play scenarios out in his head for years in advance, and automatically calculate the odds of events happening. That's how he was so successful with investment banking.

'And...' Here was the hard part to admit. She swallowed back the lump in her throat. 'He hated me, and wanted to see me ruined totally. By leaving my body on the island, it would have looked like I was involved in his scam up to my eyeballs. Am I right?' She turned to Flanagan.

He nodded slowly. 'Yep. That's the conclusion we would have drawn.'

'It wasn't enough that he would kill me.' She looked down at her feet, at her pretty purple nails freed from her shoes for the flight. It was hard to take in the depths of her husband's spite.

'It would have been a lot easier for us all if you'd stayed in touch with Dan,' Flanagan remarked after a short silence.

'Yeah, why didn't you answer my texts?' Dan was now remembering his grievances. 'I thought we were a team, but poof! You threw me over and went off on your own.'

'But I thought the FBI were the ones who'd booked the hotel and brought over Jean-Luc,' Diana told them. 'I didn't think Mark knew about him. I guess I underestimated him and his scheming, and I had no reason to believe Jean-Luc was not on my side. That slut. I wanted him to contact you, because I was.... busy with Hector. But then I dropped the phone in the tub and I couldn't answer your texts when I most needed to when I found out he wasn't on my side anymore. Instead, that brat was keeping Mark informed of every step. And later, on the yacht, he told the captain what was going on, and Hector. They didn't care about me by then, because they were getting a replacement yacht from Mark.'

'It was rather dangerous,' Flanagan said, after listening to Diana's explanation of the events that had led to her being on Hector's boat, minus the more lascivious details. Neither of the men needed to know about that side of things. 'A very dangerous game to play. And you put us all in danger, you know,' he added.

He paused to as the announcement sounded to buckle their seatbelts to prepare for landing.

'But,' he continued, a smile on his face again and a look of admiration in his eyes. 'Ma'am, you got balls, that's for sure. If you're ever in the city and at a loose end...'

He took out a business card and scribbled on the back. 'That's my personal cell number,' he said in a low voice as he handed it to her.

Diana could have sworn there was a flirtatious note in his warm brown eyes, but she'd had enough of men to last her a life time. She shoved it deep into her purse.

CHAPTER THIRTY-FOUR

It was a bit of a let-down being back home. Of course, it was good to be re-united with the animals, and Mrs. Hastings too. The welcome from the dogs more than made up the cool reception from her former housekeeper, who merely expressed her opinion that it was about time she stopped gallivanting around foreign parts and took her responsibilities seriously. Sam stated he had enjoyed the dog-sitting, and indeed, Outhros and Cerberus were glowing and well-exercised with much better manners than before she left. The cats, as was their wont, merely bickered amongst themselves and demanded more food before claiming the best spots before the fireplace.

But that dreary old house with no central heating - there was no joy in Diana in returning to that, and there was no denying that life had become flat. Long runs on the beach were few due to the inclement winter weather on the coast, and frankly, she had no friends.

Mrs. Hastings quickly took herself off to Florida shortly after Diana's return for an undisclosed length of time, stating as she did that it was the first time she'd been able to take a decent vacation and that she was making the most of her retirement. Before Diana had the chance to inquire, Mrs. Hasting informed her there would be no extra room in her cousin's apartment for additional guests. She did reluctantly agree to lend Diana her car, at least until the insurance money came through.

Dan was all tied up establishing his own business, trying to help out the poor and down-trodden, bla bla bla. He had no time for idle chitchat either.

Sam was delighted to see the dogs when Diana took them for visits, but it didn't take very long for Diana to tell him the expurgated version of her adventure down south to use for his book if he should choose. The details of her exploits with Jean-Luc and Hector would have made for more interesting reading, perhaps, but Sam didn't write to the erotica audience.

She did get the phone numbers of the twins from Mrs. Hastings before the good lady left, and contacted them, but Theresa and Giles both spent the entire calls complaining that their trust funds were running low, did she know how expensive it was to live in California / Thailand? They weren't very interested in either her woes or the renewal of her maternal instincts, and seemed to blame the whole fiasco of Mark and his death and their subsequent lack of money on her.

At Diana's lowest point during that harsh winter, she even played with the idea of tracking down her immediate relatives, her siblings and mother. Was the old lady still alive, perhaps living out the rest of her life in a comfortable, warm state-sponsored old age home? Her brothers and sisters were no doubt still dwelling in the trailer park, unable or unwilling to move themselves out of their accustomed poverty and bleak lives. She shivered. No, she hadn't quite stooped that low.

The only bright spot came when the insurance money was finally coughed up, thanks to Flanagan's people signing off on the death certificate. Dan handled the transfer, being the only lawyer still talking to her, and he made sure to repay the animal trust before signing the cash over to her in order to get the charges of embezzlement against her dropped. That had been Rose's doing of course, Suzie would never have had the nerve to actually press charges when her misdeed was discovered.

At last, she could resume some semblance of a real life, but therein lay another problem. She had no life to go back to.

With almost five million dollars in her pocket, she could have bought back her house in Baserville, or a cheaper one in the same neighborhood, at any rate. But every time she visited that small town, she found herself unwelcomed and ignored, even at the Animal Sanctuary, which by this time had whittled its operations down to a minimum and changed its name, removing any mention of Quenton and the graphic of her on its signage. There was talk of the city taking it over as the local pound.

No, Baserville was too depressing for Diana to spend any amount of time in these days. She did, however, find herself scouring the local paper at the coffee shop on Main Street, just to see what news she could get, drawn to any mention of the Women's League. It was sort of like the irresistible lure of picking a scab off an old wound.

Of course Rose LeBlanche had gotten herself elected as president, Diana thought sourly when she read the news, and was instituting 'much needed' changes to the organization, making it more democratic and do-goody. The animal fund was hardly mentioned at all, except in the list of causes the group was cutting off their support for. That was okay, nothing less than she had expected. Diana would get her own back on that woman. Some day.

'Just you wait, Rose,' she said aloud. 'I'm not dead yet.'

Since Baserville had turned its back on her and her name, Diana would likewise not have anything to do with the place, she decided. She would not be gracing the town with her presence or contributing to its economy in any way through buying real estate or even another cappuccino. She was hatching a new plan that involved a bigger pond for her to swim in. Metaphorically speaking, of course.

Despite other people's opinion of her, Diana had always prided herself on being a woman of her word. And once she had made up her mind what the next stage of her life would be, she got on the phone.

'Morry? Yeah, Maurice, okay. You still have an extra bed? Well, clear the room out, I'm coming to stay. No, don't worry, just for a couple of days till I get an apartment in Manhattan. Just you wait, have I got a story for you...'

So this wasn't the new beginning she'd dreamt of, but it was something at least. She would figure it all out, no doubt about that, for she was Diana Quenton after all, survivor extraordinaire.

The end

·♥·♥·♥·♥·♥·

Dear reader, I hope you enjoyed reading about Diana as much as I enjoyed uncovering her story.

The good news is, her story continues in *The Auction*, (#1 of *The Unlikely Shorts*, a short story which happens right after the present book). All her seized possessions are up for sale at a public auction. Her furniture, her clothes, even her shoes.

This short story is for sale at your favorite retailer and through my shop. Please sign up for my (very rare) newsletters which will keep you abreast of all the latest news with Diana and the other worlds I inhabit, at LizGraham.ca

Thank you!

Thank you for purchasing this book. If you would like a personally signed book plate, feel visit LizGraham.ca to order!

MORE BOOKS BY LIZ (E M) GRAHAM:

WITCH KIN CHRONICLES (E M Graham)
·An Ignorant Witch, Book 1
·An Arrogant Witch, Book 2
·An Errant Witch, Book 3
·An Obstinate Witch, Book 4
·An Enigmatic Witch, Book 5
·An Embittered Witch, Book 6

CARMEL MCALISTAIR MYSTERIES (Liz Graham)
·The Cut Throat
·The Garrote
·The Iron Dog
·St. Jude Undone

OTHERS (Liz Graham)
·An Imperfect Death (The Unlikely Heroine)
·The Auction (An Unlikely Short Story)
·A Northern Romance
·Man from La Manche

All books are available in Ebook, PaperBack, Large Print and Audio formats from LizGraham.ca or through your favorite retailer.

ACKNOWLEDGEMENTS

It takes a village to publish a book. First of all, I want to thank the Writers Alliance of Newfoundland and Labrador for their assistance, and of course for introducing me to the wonderful editor and fellow-writer Joanne Soper-Cook. Your encouragement over the years has set me on the writing path!

Huge thanks also to my Beta readers Sylvia, Bev and Victoria – your input has been invaluable and I hope to work with you again.

And of course, thanks to my readers over the years!